No One's Time

M. von Lindenberg

Dedicated to waning mental health and the monotony of everyday life. To REvL for existing and breaking down walls; to CMvL for flooding the plains and leveling the real estate; to FS and DJI for unending support; to JEH for endless platitudes; and for JDM for strange conversations that spark runaway ideas.

Part One:

No One Has Time For That

Prologue

I know they know. They have to know, right?

Eighteen thousand, three hundred, ninety-seven days. Fifty years and change.

If I would've known… if anyone would have sounded the alarm when he first showed up, I wouldn't be here at all. Wrong place, wrong time. Fitting really, since it's how I got into this whole mess in the first place.

The guards have all changed hands -- retired, even, and left this life for something better, more wholesome. Any familiarity with my cellmates has slipped away with the days.

The months.

Years.

I have to escape, somehow. I have to get out of here before, well, I just have to get out of here.

I tried once, long ago, and it just landed me in solitary. Three hundred days longer than legally allowed. I think they knew then. There has to be a file somewhere with the wardens, the state, country, hell, the CIA probably has a room slated for me somewhere just for kicks.

If I were to escape, I'd be the world's most wanted criminal. Or… history's most-forgotten man.

Chapter 1

Grady Sachs was an unassuming man. Mild-mannered, long-tempered, and utterly, fatefully forgettable. His tousled brown hair, muddy brown eyes, five-foot-ten-taco-bell-and-pizza with a mildly rigorous, albeit inconsistent, workout regimen stature were nothing anyone would glance at twice. Grady was completely average. He was everyone, but also no one in particular.

Grady knew this. Grady wasn't always the biggest fan of this, but sometimes it was an obliging truth. Sometimes Grady even preferred it. It allowed him solace in restaurants, although the wait staff would often forget to refill his Diet Coke. He could walk around car lots any day of the week without being bothered even if he was really wanting to test drive a new Honda Civic.

In another life, perhaps, this would have gifted Grady with a certain skill set befitting a man working for the United States Government as an undercover operative for criminal embezzlement and insider trading. Grady would assume alternate identities, breach stringent security protocols, and infiltrate lucrative, albeit nefarious, businesses throughout the continental United States and sometimes Canada. Uncovering huge international scandals like in Wall Street, Bad Education, or Weekend At Bernie's.

Grady would daydream about a life of espionage, threat analysis, and turn-on-a-dime tactics that would have him pitted against the likes of Bond, Bourne, and Powers. A life of grandeur and mystique. A life hidden from the world, shielded from casual conversation, and a small smile stowed away in the corners of his mouth. Grady's own, personal little secret.

Bland had always been Grady's forte, though. His life had always been kind of... beige. Taupe, maybe? The color of the walls throughout a doctor's office so as to not solicit a feeling of ease, or unease. His forgettable goldendoodle, Marv, his silver 2003 Chevrolet Cavalier; the cream carpet in the modest seven hundred sixty square foot apartment, with the painfully typical high rent and crappy management.

Entirely, completely, and quite comfortably ordinary.

Chapter 2

Westin, Howard and Schultz was a less-than prestigious business law firm that was looking for some fresh blood. Someone with vigor, vision, and a hairline that would make them all look at least a little bit more approachable. Their billboard stood high above I-86 east out of town with "Westin, Howard and Schultz: Business is our Business" scrawled across it. The fine print should have read "Another law firm you won't call because you have no clue what in the world three *more* white men with degrees could possibly be doing with their time that was possibly worth a second of yours".

Grady found an ad for the firm in the paper every few days. The ad shared the same faces as the billboard, reminiscent of Manny, Moe and Jack. "Position to be filled: Help Wanted", read the header. If there was one thing that *wasn't* bland about Grady: he interviewed very, *very* well. He also had an entirely unimpressive collection of Haggar off-the-rack suits for just such an occasion.

He dialed the number on his cell, was greeted with a stock voicemail greeting making it impossible to know whether or not Grady dialed the *correct* number, and not just the correct ten digits. He left a message inquiring about the position in the West Elm Whistler. He'd left his details and a polite note that he was excited to hear back from them -- he'd hoped he hadn't come on too strong.

A few days passed and Grady had all but forgotten about the potential job. That is until Grady was startled to have gotten a call on a Thursday afternoon. His goldendoodle, Marv, raised an ear at the unfamiliar sound -- an odd thing to hear since Grady was on top of his quarterly 'do not call' registry and the phone rarely rang as a result. Before resting his head on the couch, Marv huffed and nudged at Grady's leg to stop the interruption then turned and continued watching reruns of Three's Company. Grady answered the call and the voice on the other end of the line informed him he'd have an interview the following Monday.

The weekend came and went, completely without incident, just how Grady liked it. His normal Friday treat of pizza, wings, and diet root beer left at the no-contact card table he'd set outside of his doorway. He'd enjoyed his usual movie-laden Sunday afternoon -- Indiana Jones this weekend. A typical Sunday night shave, Waterpik-ing, and facial exfoliation, then off to bed by nine-thirty with Steve Harvey hosting Family Feud in his ears on a twenty minute sleep timer.

Monday arrived, Grady ate his plain cornflakes at his Ikea bistro table while Marv scarfed at this water and kibble. He went on a mid-morning run which was something he liked to think was habitual, but truthfully only happened when he'd gotten up early and had nothing else to do with his weekday mornings. After a quick rinse in the shower, he'd grabbed his muted yellow tie hoping the color didn't make him look desperate. His brown twill suit really made the tie pop and then he was off to speak with his prospective new employers.

Grady answered their poorly-prepared interview questions well enough. He looked the part with his half-windsor-knotted tie and ketchup stain on his breast pocket from his fast food lunch. Westin, Howard and Schultz, of whom Grady had no clue which was which, all nodded in blithe agreement and offered him the position on the spot. A paid internship -- mostly due to the fact the trio still wasn't sure what exactly they were hiring for.

Chapter 3

On Grady's first day, he brought his brown-bagged lunch and a set of highlighters just in case. He also carried his red Swingline stapler just like Milton's from Office Space which he'd bought years ago after seeing the movie. It made him laugh to himself while he window shopped at the local mall and he just had to have it. He chuckled to himself when he'd packed it up that morning too. The irony that he was going to have an office job tickled him pink.

Grady arrived and was shown to his folding table and his garage sale appropriated "file cabinet" on three casters -- the fourth was broken and made a horrible noise when he tried to move it from the left to the right and back to the left side of his new "desk".

Westin -- or possibly it as Howard -- greeted him while he fumbled for his keys to unlock the pane glass door of the end unit in the West Elm Shopping Plaza.

"The security alarm subscription has lapsed", Schultz, or maybe Westin explained, "and we can't afford tubes for all of the lights just yet, but it's the trench we've dug to start making a difference".

Howard, quite possibly Schultz, uttered these very practiced words with such conviction, Grady hardly noticed the rodent traps in the corners, the stale cigarette smell, and the incessant beeping of the smoke detector long overdue for batteries.

He proudly took his seat on a stack of two milk crates from the mom and pop convenience store on the other end of the plaza. He sat tall at his desk, displayed his stapler and organized his highlighters alphabetically by color, just to be different.

The other two men -- his new mentors in the enterprise of the Business of Business -- came slogging in some two hours later, both trying to wipe the tired out of their eyes. Grady took the opportunity to hop up from his crates as unenthusiastically as he could, and offer a handshake and his sincerest gratitude for the opportunity to work in such a great, impactful, and meaningful field with such a remarkable group of men.

His eagerness was met with mild recoil and squinting from both men and Grady mewled silently to his desk and rearranged his highlighters by actual color. It was rather strange that pink was before yellow, the more he thought about it.

Chapter 4

Months passed and Grady spent his time at Westin, Howard and Schultz looking over business documents for the convenience store at the other end of the plaza, tax records for Wang's Wings and Taekwondo, and the other neighboring establishments in their suburban wannabe strip mall.

He'd get Howard, or perhaps Westin, his decaf flat white -- basically just bitter milk without the real espresso. He'd grab Schultz's -- or potentially Westin's -- morning paper. He'd get Westin -- he really had no idea who was who and determined it didn't matter after a week -- his daily bearclaw and diet Dr. Bob every morning. He'd click and clack away at his company-funded laptop, which he suspected was also from a garage sale and which he still couldn't change the background picture of a gap-toothed kid holding up an unremarkable fish. He'd occasionally take Howard-Westin-or-maybe-Schultz' newspaper from their wastebasket and skim the business section and stock exchange looking for something that he'd "just know" when he'd seen it.

Then, he'd seen it.

Wait, this can't be right. This stock was in the toilet last week, and now it's up something like six-hundred percent!

Sure he'd found something of prospect, Grady took the paper to Westin-Howard-or-maybe-Schultz to point out the oddity. The men all conferred privately in the "conference room" which consisted of two privacy dividers, like the kind you'd undress behind in a studio apartment, clearly also from a garage sale. They decided that it was a good idea for Grady to investigate the find. They told him to take some time out of the office working on his own if he needed to.

Grady hopped to it and started browsing the internet with their shoddy connection for anything that might point him in any direction at all. Stocks, trade papers, and OpEds about the would-be tech start-up, when suddenly he found it. This was this thread that would unravel the entire thing.

Months of litigation ensued; court fees and legal battles toe-to-toe with big shot lawyers on both sides of the case. Westin, Howard and Schultz couldn't keep pace with the rigors of a trial as big as this one. A much larger firm requested full disclosure of Westin, Howard and Schultz' evidence, witnesses and files. Once they were handed over, there wasn't much they would be able to provide as a partnering firm. As a result, they lost their shirts and everything they'd invested in their operation. Grady had started to suspect it was only twenty bucks at yard sales and a few day-old bagels, so he wasn't sure how much of a loss it really was. To Grady, however, it was a total loss and found himself unemployed and without prospects.

The big shot lawyers assumed the case, got the government involved, and turned it into a breaking news phenomenon that got the attention of the world's stage. Small town West Elm would have been thrown into obscurity had it not already been there as the case overshadowed the small firm that had dug up the keystones and toppled the structure in the first place. Grady had boxed up his red Swingline Stapler and the sole orange highlighter still left from the pack. He'd then realized a box may have been a bit audacious for the task.

Attempting to start his silver 2003 Cavalier in the parking lot at three fifteen in the afternoon there was a light tap on his window. Attached to the offending appendage was a man in a navy blue suit with a face only a mother could love. Holding out an obscure identification card and a business card with a phone number on it, the man did not speak a word. There was no other information at all, which Grady thought was very *out* of the ordinary than what he was otherwise used to.

Chapter 5

Grady sat at his Ikea bistro table eating his corn flakes every morning for nearly two weeks looking at the ambiguous business card. He spent his afternoons looking over the newspaper for new job prospects with the business card constantly in his peripheral. He spent his evenings over a Hungry Man TV dinner watching reruns of Curb Your Enthusiasm on his ninety day trial streaming subscription thinking about the phone number on the business card. A phone number he most definitely wasn't going to call at one thirty-nine in the morning on a Tuesday.

He called the number at one thirty-nine in the morning on a Tuesday.

The line rang twice. On the other end, a long, low boop sound caused Grady to hang up fearing he'd dialed a wrong number and interrupted someone's sleep.

He called the number back at two-oh-six that same Tuesday morning.

The line rang twice. On the other end, the same tone sounded once again. Grady looked anxiously at his nineties GE alarm clock that he'd appropriated from Howard-or-Westin-or-maybe-Schultz desk. He didn't ask for it, and he knew it was *definitely* stolen from a hotel by one of them, but he figured he was owed some sort of severance. The line was silent as the tone ceased and the chipper voice of a woman sprang to life

"This is us, is this you?" the voice inquired.

"This is me, is this you?" Grady returned the serve.

"This is definitely us, Mr. Sachs. Who else would it be?" The voice chirped in the cadence of a life insurance salesman cold-calling the elderly. *How do they know my name?* Grady thought.

"How do we know your name, Mr. Sachs?" the voice chortled.

Yes, exactly that, Grady's face turned up as his mind raced.

"Well, we followed your case with the Innovexacon Corporation closely when you were working for Westin, Howard and Schultz. It was very impressive work you did", said the customer-service trained woman, "and we'd like to have you in to discuss a unique opportunity with us".

Who's us, Grady said in his mind before realizing he should probably be using his outside voice instead of his inside voice.

"Who's us?" he corrected aloud, almost yelling into the receiver as he overcompensated.

"How about we send a car for you in the morning and we'll cover all of the bases over brunch? Say, eleven thirty?" the songbird chirped.

"I have an appointment at noon", Grady lied, trying to sound important, or at least like he wasn't an unemployed deadbeat.

"You don't. We'll be there at half-past eleven Mr. Sachs."

Just like that, the line disconnected and Grady was left wondering how he, of all people, had wound up in such a strange and atypical position.

Grady laid out his best blue Haggar, his favorite green tie, and his musty brown Hush Puppies and laid back down in his Costco bed until the sun crept into the bought-in-bulk miniblinds. He got up, showered, ate his corn flakes, read his newspaper, and sat by the door until eleven thirty when he was shaken from his dissociated state.

The knocking at the door startled him. His goldendoodle groaned, then sighed, having been disturbed from his peaceful, pre-afternoon nap. He answered the door, the same mediocrity he saw in the mirror was on the other side of the frame, with an extended hand and an entirely forgettable smile.

Grady shook his hand, limp like a wet noodle, and found himself hoping that there was hand sanitizer in the vehicle he'd be soon entering.

Chapter 6

The champagne colored Mercury Marauder drove cautiously through the streets. Twenty minutes moved along in silence until the car pulled up to a gray, concrete building with standard windows, standard doors and way too many floors. Grady was ushered out and to the entrance of the entirely unassuming building. He'd felt considerably more comfortable being back in his beige-toned life as he walked inside and was surrounded by beige-toned walls.

An elevator, fifty-six stories, one burnt Folgers coffee too hot to hold and a walk down a boring hallway later, Grady and his escort arrived at a door. Behind that door was a conference room with a real table, real chairs and a light blue paint that was calming to Grady's heightened nervousness.

He sat down and thought how the plush of the seats felt *so* much better than the milk crates from which he still had a nearly-permanent crosshatched impression on his butt. The table was nice and shiny, but he had noticed some of the veneer pulling from the underside. Grady took comfort in the cosmetic flaw. It was nice knowing that, even here, things were just as they were anywhere else. The door cracked and a woman entered. Brunette hair, mauve nails, and a tweed business casual outfit that was forgotten as soon as she'd left a pitcher of water and turned to exit.

Grady took the Dixie cup from the stack in the center of the table and poured himself a drink. He slowly sipped on the cool water, sniffled, and promptly choked on the liquid before he could swallow completely. He sputtered and coughed. The door opened once more just as Grady ejected his drink down the front of himself, covering his lap with folded hands.

The man at the door held out a hand for a hearty shake. As Grady stood he'd realized how much it looked like he'd wet himself -- because of course he had looked like that in a strange room, with a strange man, on a strange Tuesday in his otherwise boring life.

The man revoked his offer of a handshake, looked at Grady with the hint of a grimace and sat across from him at the table before unfolding an accordion case of files in front of them both.

Chapter 7

There was a long, drawn out explanation about the case that Grady had worked on which, evidently, these people had been following. They'd followed it so closely, it seemed, that they completely redacted the fact that Grady had worked on it at all. In fact, it was entirely possible that they thought he was Schultz or Howard, and they were headhunting for a new lawyer. A lawyer being something Grady, most certainly, was not.

The man walked him through the ins and outs of the court proceedings, all for which Grady had been there; the dissolution of the firm he had worked at for which Grady only had a cheap alarm clock and butt scars to show. He covered the eventual verdict of life in prison, no chance of parole, for the CEO, CFO, and CIO of Innovexacon for the embezzlement of some three-point-eight *billion* dollars in federal assets and another nearly five billion in liquid finances from various shareholders -- details which Grady read about in the newspaper he skimmed for jobs over his Ikea bistro table and bowl of corn flakes.

Without much more said, the man slid a plain manila folder across the table with "Grady Sachs" hastily written across its label tab. Maybe they did know who he was after all. Within the folder were three pages of paper. The first was an outline of what looked to be an offer of employment, but the more Grady read it, the more it was very clearly not an offer so much as a set of instructions proceeding from that day forward. The second was a financial table with insurance quotes, technology allowances, and a bottom-line salary he was to expect for his contributions to the organization of which he still hadn't learned the name.

The third was...

Whoa, hold on; is that a monthly Hulu reimbursal?!, he thought, thumbing over the second page again to see if he'd missed any other perks.

The third page was a landscape oriented sheet of paper with drop-shadowed Comic Sans writing that said "**Welcome Aboard**" in a royal blue color with clipart confetti, balloons and a cupcake. Grady smirked, but it was cut short by the grumbling of his stomach wanting the paper-cupcake. It had been four hours and just as brisk as his entrance had been, he was rushed back to the Marauder and whisked away to be deposited back at his West Elm apartment with orders to report for duty at seven o'clock sharp the next day.

Chapter 8

Thursday is a very strange day to start a new job, Grady thought as he listened to soft rock radio one-oh-three-four, Breezy Listening.

The reality is, Grady didn't have any clue whether it was a strange day to start a job. Grady had only ever had one job since he'd lived in West Elm and he was unceremoniously laid off on a Wednesday, so there couldn't be that much of a difference. Grady decided Thursday was a perfectly normal day to start a new job.

Grady parked in the garage, on the green level, and took the elevator up to the fifty-sixth story. He carried his red Swingline stapler, a brand new pack of highlighters and a fancy Pilot rollerball pen he'd treated himself to for getting his new position and salary increase. Proudly, he walked through the glass double doors at the front of the office area, pulled them, and was greeted with a sore shoulder from the recoil as the door stammered a bit, but ultimately remained closed.

Grady sat in the lobby holding his office supplies, deflated but still excited to learn what he would be doing in his new role. Five people walked by him and toward different ends of the building. Down webs of halls and labyrinths of doorways, worker bees in banal attire coursed to and fro, here and there, thither and yon.

A tap on Grady's shoulder startled him back to attention.

"New guy?" a gruff voice choked up from a throat still full of sleep and morning cigarettes.

"Grady Sachs, sir. It's a pleasure to meet you", Grady exclaimed a bit too exuberantly to which the man winced and scratched his chin.

"Yeah... sure, whatever you say, kid", he muttered before he pinned numbers into the keypad adjacent to the glass obstacle that had, until now, been Grady's bane for the day.

Grady followed the clearly un-caffeinated man down the cozy, eggshell colored hallway. Three right turns, two lefts, and another right through the myriad of endless nothings filled with doors, they finally arrived at a small-ish room with a clean, gray, faux-marble-topped cubicle. On top of the desk sat a quaint name placard that read "G. Sachs -- Business Investigation Unit".

Grady chuffed at the sight, looked at the man for a signal or some validation of his tiny triumph and realized the man had slipped away entirely unnoticed. Grady paid no mind and settled into the maroon office chair, sat his prized Swingline down on the right corner of the veneered marble top and sat back twiddling his thumbs in his lap.

As he sat staring a hole through the wall beyond his opened, gray-framed door, he thought about the words "Business Investigation Unit".

Unit, huh? That has to mean I'm on a team, right? Wow, a real team. People to work with, collaborate. Talk about lives and aspirations. Maybe they have families? Oh, or pets?! Hobbies involving topiaries or ant farms. Man, this is the best day ever.

Grady's phantasmagoric thoughts were interrupted by a knock at the door frame.

The man from the interview stood in the doorway, his rimless glasses pulled down to the tip of his nose as he looked over a stack of loose papers. The man licked his fingers and turned through the pages. Over and over, until nearly at the end, and then he finally looked up to address Grady.

"Mister...Sachs, is it?", the upturn of his voice indicating he had no recollection of their meeting two days prior in his doorway, or yesterday in this very same building.

"Sir", Grady responded, like a soldier to a drill Sergeant.

"Naylor. Frank Naylor, that'll do instead of all of that 'sir' stuff", Frank replied in just as nonchalant a manner as he'd arrived in the doorway.

"Pleasure to meet you, Frank. Grady Sachs. We met the oth-"

"Since this is our first meeting, we'll have to just skip the pleasantries for the time being. We have a big case, I'm talking *big*, that we'd like you to look at."

Handing the dossier to Grady, the man turned to exit the broom closet of an office before looking over his shoulder.

"We really think you're gonna like it here. We've got great plans for you, Mister Sachs. Great, great plans." Frank enigmatically declared his approval as his voice trailed with him down the hallway, bearing a smile on the last syllables.

Grady sat back in his chair, looked at the dossier and pulled out the stack of loose papers. He smiled a small, content, smile and grabbed his coveted red Swingline and christened his new vocation with a resounding *clunk* as the stapler compressed the papers neatly.

The stapler jammed.

Chapter 9

As he combed through the stack of papers, Grady studied every word. Unsure what he was supposed to be doing, and only having the notion that he was hired for his work with Westin, Howard and Schultz, he looked for something to jump off the page at him.

Newspaper clippings -- scanned and poorly faxed, nearly unreadable due to the low toner warnings that are constantly ignored in big business -- OpEds, social media posts, and countless tax records and stock readouts of a company, not entirely dissimilar to Innovexacon, were spread across the faux-marble desktop.

Inventaratus Technologies, the child company to a much larger conglomerate, was one of the largest, albeit youngest, technology research and engineering corporations in the country. Only in business for seven years, they'd built themselves up from a meager bedroom-to-basement-to-garage hardware development company to the massive power they'd become.

Waylan Scott, owner and CEO of the massive Guided Technologies Fabrication Operative, began building small bug-like drones for fun to spy on his neighbors' dog that kept pooping on his lawn. The neighbor in question worked for one of the three-letter agencies and after stepping on, and incidentally impaling his foot upon the small titanium-legged roach, he spoke to Waylan about the mechanical creature. Waylan explained that his dog's constant greensward defecation was causing herbological distress to his Kentucky Blue. The neighbor pointed out the bug -- and his bloodied heel -- and the rest was history. GTFO was born.

Now a head government contractor and a commercial superpower in research and development for all sorts of military, intelligence, economic, and recreational technologies, the dough was rolling in and the stocks were higher than any other company of its kind. Inventaratus was created, like many other of Waylan Scott's endeavors, to specialize in certain products and services.

An article from a paper local to Waylan's hometown had called out *Enron* by name as a direct comparison to Inventaratus Technologies in its posture for growth and renown.

Enron… wait a minute. When was this written?

Wasn't Enron that company that Martha Stewart met Snoop Dogg over?

Wait, no… she was redecorating cellblock D somewhere because of Enron, right?

Grady's mind reeled, marking mental push-pins and strings tying things together.

Enron had fallen from business-class piety due to an accounting "error" that was later found to be a purposeful scheme to keep the business in constant profit. Multiple counts of fraud, money laundering, insider trading, and conspiracy were pled guilty to, and courts sentenced the various parties to jail time respective to their part in the crimes.

Am I reading into this, or does this rinky-dink paper have something here?

Grady excitedly began hand-writing notes on a fresh steno pad he'd found in the desk drawer. After he'd composed his magnum opus, he'd stood up to find his superiors when it occurred to him he had no clue who they were, nor where they would be.

He wandered the halls playing Marco-Polo, or in this case, Frank-Grady, and eventually ran across the disgruntled gentlemen from the early morning that let him in. When he asked whether or not he knew where Frank Naylor sat, the man scoffed, pointed, and turned back to his desk where he was watching a YouTube video of epic gym fails and cracking walnuts in his palm.

Grady wandered the hallways a bit more, stopped to get a cuppa Folgers and then he smelled the Clubman aftershave Frank had wafted into his office. It wasn't long before he turned into the right doorway and met Frank, asleep, sitting behind his desk -- a desk exactly like the grumpy door-man's desk, like Grady's, and exactly like everyone else's on his floor. Politely, Grady knocked at the half-opened door.

“Mr. Naylor, sir? Uh... Frank?” he stammered.

Frank’s eyes shot open like lightning had struck him, he sputtered and coughed, choking on the drool that was teetering on the corner of his mouth before inhaling deeply and blinking a few times to adjust to the light and the figure in his doorway.

“Oh, mister...?”

“Grady. I was looking through the papers you’d giv--”

“Yes, yes, you can hand them off to Grady, the new guy, he’ll be taking the case”, Naylor interrupted.

“Well, yes. I...” Grady began, “I was looking through them and I thi--”

“Grady. Yes, he’s down the hall on the left. Or was it to the right?” Naylor pinched the bridge of his nose.

“Three rights, two lefts, past the coffee mess, another right and the third door on the left”, Grady sighed.

“Oh, you know him! Good, good. Big things for that one, big things. Big, big things”, Frank yawned as he nudged his door shut in Grady’s face like he was never there in the first place.

Grady took it upon himself to dig into Inventaratus. As he walked down the hallway, back to his eggshell office with his gray marbled desktop, he began plotting his investigation.

Business Investigation Unit. Grady Sachs, Business Investigator.

Well, Grady, let’s go ahead and get to investigating.

Chapter 10

Over the next few days, Grady pulled information on Inventaratus and started his casual perusal of the corporation. Within a few weeks, he'd found a job board advertising for a mail clerk at the company. He'd applied and set something up for an in-person interview for the position.

The morning of the interview Grady ate his corn flakes at his Ikea bistro table just like every other morning. He'd laid out his gray tweed sports coat with the substitute teacher elbows, his black slacks, and his favorite skinny black tie. He'd gotten into his 2003 Chevrolet Cavalier and driven to Inventaratus's auspicious high-rise some three hours away.

Don Johnson's "Heartbeat" was playing on the radio when he pulled into the elaborate parking structure attached by a massive skybridge walkway to the building of the Inventaratus Technologies corporate headquarters. Parking in the visitors only spots closest to the doors, Grady pressed the button on the touch screen panel and the elevator took him to the eighty-fifth floor. A warm smile from a well-dressed woman named Elenor came to the lobby area to greet Grady. He was welcomed with a freshly brewed cup of coffee and a choice of blueberry-lemon or butterscotch scones of which he took both.

Elenor asked him about his morning, how his drive was, and what he thought of the new elevator cars they'd just upgraded to.

"The touch panels are Bluetooth compatible! So, if you wind up stuck, you can play your music or watch movies endlessly on the free Wi-Fi until someone arrives! Isn't that just the coolest?" Elenor lilted cheerfully as Grady sipped his gourmet brew.

Grady felt a stirring of appreciation as he walked alongside the delightful Stepford receptionist. Maybe he'd actually take *this* job if it all goes well today. He smiled at the thought of warm coffee pastries every morning as he followed Elenor closely to a large glass conference room.

Seated there were six men in high-dollar suits, clearly bespoke, and perfectly coiffed hair. Grady couldn't help but be reminded of the business card scene in American Psycho and briefly wondered which of these indistinguishable men the homicidal psychopath was. The men stood, shook his hand, and addressed him by name one at a time, failing to introduce themselves at all. They welcomed him to take a seat, folded their hands in unison on the table and the man seated directly before Grady spoke.

"If you worked in the medical field, mister Sachs, say as a doctor, would you be a general practitioner, a specialist, or would you work in emergency medicine in the ER?", he'd posited with calm sincerity.

That's an odd way to start an interview.

After pondering his response, the meaning of the question holistically, Grady folded his hands in kind to the other men at the table and spoke as eloquently as possible.

"I think I would like to be a specialist", he'd started, thinking of his current position with his organization, one that he still didn't know the name of -- he'd have to work on getting that from someone. "But I know that I would fall into the role of general practice. At least I think that's how it would go".

It occurred to Grady that this was a horrible answer to a rather interesting question. He sat across from the six imposing men, suddenly seeming to loom over him as his nerves took over his racing mind. Grady felt cold sweat run down his spine and he resisted the urge to shiver.

Why am I so nervous? I'm here to infiltrate them, to learn about them. It's a mail clerk job. Who cares what kind of doctor I'd be? What are they even talking about?

Grady felt his face flush with irritation and just as he was about to speak, the gentleman in front of him placidly replied, "Good. Honest. That's the kind of thing we like here at Inventaratus".

The interview continued for a tedious amount of time. Questions about his formal education -- a time Grady barely remembers at all. They asked about his upbringing and where he was from -- details Grady thought it best to fabricate. They made inquiries of similar banalities until all stood, shook his hand once more, and escorted him to the gigantic glass doors where Elenor's warmth met him.

As they walked through the organized offices and various sitting areas, Elenor chirped about the company's perks package and healthcare. She detoured them through the adult play area full of arcades, ping-pong and air hockey tables, and even some quarter machines for little tchotchkes and trinkets.

Pausing at her desk, Elenor grabbed an envelope, handing it to Grady as she ushered the elevator to their high-rise suite overlooking the busy, bustling city.

"Now don't peek until you get back to your car", she playfully sang as the doors closed behind him.

Grady tore open the envelope in the elevator. Enclosed was a letter of acceptance, a DataWatch keycard for the facility, and an ID badge that he'd had no recollection of having his picture taken for. He'd make a mental note that they have cameras hidden in places, good ones too.

Gonna have to be careful about this place, Grady. They've got eyes everywhere, and you've got to have eyes on their eyes if you want their eyes turned away so your eyes can look at what their eyes are seeing. Wait... what?

Grady exited the elevator, sat in his lackluster car and smiled to himself. He'd done it. He can go back to his as-yet named employer and tell them he was on track to uncovering what could be the biggest financial scandal in decades. Then Grady recalled that no one even remembered he worked there so he celebrated on the way home with a Big Mac, Diet Coke, and a warm apple pie as a treat.

Life was good. Life was normal. All was as it should be.

Chapter 11

Grady awoke the next morning and got his shower, ate his corn flakes at his Ikea bistro table, and opted to dress down in a pair of khaki chinos and a white polo shirt. He laced up his New Balance and drove himself to start his new cover job of mail clerk at Inventaratus Technologies.

The three hour drive was something that Grady didn't mind in the least. Radio one-oh-three-four, Breezy Listening, played all of the yacht rock hits of the decades. He hummed along and tapped his fingers as his hands held the steering wheel at ten-and-two.

Pulling up to the building, he'd noted a few construction crews along the street that he didn't recall from the day before.

Must be some sort of outage or pipe break or something.

He thought nothing more of the laborers lining the cross streets and alleys flanking the massive concrete-and-glass marvel as he walked in the front door opting to park on the street today instead of in the garage.

The elevator rose impossibly high to the floor he'd been so warmly welcomed on the day prior, and like a syndicated sitcom, Elenor greeted him with a quaint, friendly smile, a cuppa coffee and a selection of danish. She floated along the hallway, beaming and waving at the other employees, and showed Grady to the freight elevator towards the west-facing corner of the building. Pressing the call button, Elenor's musical voice addressed Grady directly.

"Once you get to the sublevel, please exit the elevator promptly as the gates will close after sounding ten consecutive beeps. Once you've exited, please follow the green hallway to the mailroom. There, you will meet a lovely older fellow named Oscar. Oscar will be your liaison to the facility and a mentor to the ever-important job of Clerical Dispatch and Logistics Department", she cooed like a dove on a cool spring morning.

Grady did as he was instructed. Counted the beeps and watched the door close. Walked through the green hallway. Found the marquise for the "Clerical Dispatch and Logistics Department" and found a firm handshake on the end of an arm belonging to one Oscar Peterson, Head Dispatch Clerk and Clerical Administration Engineer.

Man, I hope I get a nametag like that someday.

Grady nearly forgot this wasn't his *real* job and the nametag would only cause someone to remember him. The point was to be covert. Incognito. Business Investigation Unit, Grady Sachs.

Engineer sounds so much cooler. Maybe I'll talk to Frank about getting my unit's name changed.

Grady spent the rest of the day shadowing Oscar as he regaled him with tales of his thirty-some years with GTFO working as a mail clerk. Grady met dozens, maybe even hundreds of people that day. Filing envelopes, packages and parcels of all shapes and sizes into various crates, slots, boxes, and trucks. After a long, fulfilling and completely unremarkable day, Grady got in his silver 2003 Cavalier and drove the three hour drive back to his normal apartment in his normal suburban neighborhood.

He sat on his couch, the TV muted, giving off a glow just bright enough to see the coffee table, and he started drawing up the plans for his snooping. His goldendoodle nuzzled his elbow every time he tried to move something before he finally laid on the opposite end of the couch and sighed himself asleep as Grady worked through the night.

Chapter 12

It had been weeks since Grady started his cover job at Inventaratus Technologies and he was rather ashamed of how little progress he'd made uncovering the pitfalls he just knew were hiding in the high-rise offices and C-suites throughout.

The construction crews had grown in size outside of the building, at this point making it impossible to park on the street. Grady swore he recognized one of the hard-hatted men standing next to the utility pump truck, but he couldn't be sure past the Pit Viper sunglasses and patchy beard. He thought little of it after that one day, only noting that the streets were more and more crowded and parking was a hassle in the sixteen story garage with countless spaces, always filled with executives and visitors, would-be consultants, and business partners.

Greeting Oscar, just like any other day, he began his Thursday routine -- his favorite day by far. He was treated to a visit with Elenor Thursday mornings and reveled in the arbitrary small talk and delicious culinary treats she always seemed to have on hand. Beyond this, Thursday was the only day of the week he was granted access to the top floor: the executive C-suites of Inventaratus. These were the playgrounds Grady needed to focus on for his investigation for the Business Investigation Operative Corporation -- Grady decided he liked that name the best out of all of the ones he'd tossed around for the company he was *actually* working for.

He'd been poking around the building for nearly three months now and he noted that only these suites were without surveillance. He thought that was a bit odd, but realized that would probably be the best move when talking to hot shot brokers and business consultants. It only made sense they'd want privacy and that's what led Grady to think it was the perfect place to do his digging. As he dropped his packages and letters off, he came across the executive suite of one Waylan Scott. As it happened, he also had a package for him.

Grady pinned numbers into the door's keypad for which he was granted temporary access, but only on Thursdays, and he walked into the opulent quarters of Mister Scott. He sat the package on the empty bar cart next to the immaculate oak desk. It was real wood, Grady noted, not something printed on plywood from Home Depot. He strolled around the massive office and started fingering pictures, books, and shelves looking for something. What? He did not know.

As he pulled on books in the floor-to-ceiling bookcase, really hoping there was a secret doorway, there was a clamor from the other side of the enormous wooden doors to Mister Waylan's suite. Grady thought nothing of it until the clamor sounded more like a bulldozer.

The bulldozer sounded more like a stampede.

The stampede had voices shouting in accompaniment.

The door burst open and a figure appeared with a black helmet, black vest, black cargo pants, black boots, and more importantly a black rifle trained on Grady. Grady raised his hands as silence fell back over the room, save for only the demanding voice of the man standing in front of him -- a man wearing Pit Viper sunglasses, of all things, under his helmet's browline.

Grady had trouble understanding what the man was saying through the balaclava, or maybe because of the bewilderment of what was happening. He's just the mail guy, what were they scared of him for? Wait, no, he was just the Business Investigator who'd infiltrated the Inventaratus Technologies paradigm. The man kept speaking and realized he wasn't being understood, perhaps from the look on Grady's face that was like the one his goldendoodle would give him when he didn't understand what he was saying. The man lifted the helmet from his head, pulled the sunglasses up like a headband and yanked the balaclava down.

"Frank!" Grady shouted, a smile from ear to ear. "Man, am I happy to see you. I just knew this place was some--"

"Mister Scott, you should do well to keep your hands above your head and your mouth shut. We're here because we've uncovered a huge corporate embezzlement scheme you've been implementing for over almost a decade here", Frank nudged his gun towards Grady syllabically as he walked towards him.

"Frank, I... It's me, it's Gra--", his words fumbled from his mouth.

"Apparently shut up doesn't mean much to you, does it, you piece of corporate scum?" Frank pressed. "Beyond the *trillions* of dollars we've uncovered you stealing and laundering from multiple government and foreign agencies, we're also got enough dirt on the hits, trafficking, and midget tossing parties to put you away for a long, long time".

What is he talking about? Does he seriously not recognize me?

"We have our own Grady Sachs to thank for uncovering these heaps of damning evidence, Mister Scott, if that is even your real name. If we hadn't gotten that guy in here and set him up with remote access to throw all of his daily reports at us, you might have gotten away with this a lot longer. Yup, Grady Sachs will go down in history for this one. He'll be the guy responsible for the fall of the Inventaratus empire", Frank declared, turning his gaze directly toward Grady.

He's got to be up to something. He's messing with me, right?

This is all just a really, completely absurd, over-the-top prank or something. Right?

They have the real Scott in the lobby, or in a transport in cuffs?

They're sweating him in an interview room or something, right?

RIGHT?!

Frank just barely turned one corner of his mouth up. Almost a twitch, something no one else would have noticed. Grady nearly missed it himself and probably would have entirely had he not been looking for every diminutive detail in this building for nearly three months. A glint in his eye, only briefly, and the slightest shutter of a wink.

"We've been waiting for your involvement to rear its ugly head. We had to plan and time everything just right. You're not an easy man to find, Mister Scott. You're not an easy man to identify in the midst of all of the people involved in this machine of yours", Frank spoke directly, pressing his point. "You blend in well with every other corporate trash heap at the top of the food chain".

Grady looked at Frank, puzzled by his choice of ambiguous words, and even more so by the simpering, almost smug look he'd nearly failed to hide.

Seriously, they have to know I'm not the guy they're looking for. They are looking for someone else, someone who looks like…

Grady looked over his shoulder to see a twelve foot tall painting with a name placard below that read "Dr. Waylan Scott, Esq. -- CEO". As he craned his neck, he looked at the portrait of the man: tousled brunette hair, muddy brown eyes, and a suit that wouldn't cause anyone to look twice other than to assume he was shoplifting it from Target before deciding it really, truly, did not matter. An everyman, a nobody. Someone that Grady and just about a third of the population could be easily mistaken for.

He looked like someone who'd accepted a business card from a stranger at their car window the day they were laid off.

He looked like someone who'd sat in the presence of another unremarkable man, one who Grady might have even confused himself for had he been a third party seeing them shake hands.

Like someone with a small footprint, no ties to social media, and no friends or family to speak of, outside of his goldendoodle, Marv.

Like someone who could have been hired by an agency with no name to work undercover, at a Fortune Fifty corporation under the guise of breaking a huge story.

Someone who liked fresh coffee and pastries.

Someone who always found himself in the wrong places, at the wrong times.

Interlude

Retiring. The warden is retiring. Has it been that long?

Have I lost count of how long it's been, how long I've been in here?

No, no. It was eighteen thousand, five hundred, twenty-six days before my last cellmate "hung himself", right?

Eighteen thousand, five hundred twenty-six... Let's see.

Carry the five, plus four hundred twelve in solitary for suspicion of involvement with the untimely suicide. Ninety days in the infirmary for not *being involved and getting the shit kicked out of me for it. Renovating the mess hall for that fire...*

That's sixty-four years now.

I haven't heard anything from the inmates about this new guy heading things up.

I wonder what he knows, if *he knows.*

I don't recognize half of the guards anymore. Maybe no one remembers anything about when I got here.

Maybe no one remembers my face anymore.

Chapter 13

The arraignment was hasty and Grady was still caught up in the confusion of a few days prior.

Everything was going fine. It was a regular day of mail and snooping. What in the hell was Frank doing, and why didn't he recognize me? Smug little prick.

Before he had the chance to contest, an attorney he'd never met claimed he pled 'nolo contendere' -- a very particular two word combination that indicated Grady didn't plan to contest the charges, but was willing to accept all sentencing otherwise. Guilty, just without the word being spoken.

I definitely do *contendere!*

"Your honor, I would like the cha-"

"Order in my court. Your representation has spoken, you'd find it in your best interest to remain silent or you'll be held in contempt. Not a good way to start your proceedings, Mister Scott", the honorable judge Peter Wilkerson boomed into the oddly packed court room.

"Sir, if I could just state my ca-", once again, Grady's voice was silenced, this time with a gavel.

What in the world is going on here? I can't even speak for myself, and who is this schlub saying he's my representative? Why does he look so familiar?

As the thought crossed his mind, Grady noticed the slightest turn of the head from his "attorney", and a glint of a half of a wink.

Is that? No, no way.

"Your honor, we would like to waive proceedings, if possible, and go straight to trial. This man has put these people through enough pain. Have it known that Doctor Waylan Scott would like to show his remorse by standing trial before them all and having his comeuppance publicly broadcast for all peripheral parties to receive a modicum of closure from his actions." The attorney's mouth barely turned up into the slightest, smuggest simper.

Frank?! Just who in the hell is this guy?

Just then, Grady Sachs did something very unique and entirely out of character for himself: he lunged at his turncoat, once-was employer, now the damning voice of his menacing judgment. This everyman, this fraud, this *bastard*.

Is this a set up? Have I really gotten so dim that I trusted all of this cloak and dagger trash? Grady, you idiot. You ignored everything. You wanted some excitement so bad, you forgot all of the rules.

Lost in thought, Grady's assaulting dash towards the enigmatic Frank startled him back to reality just as his shoulder checked the treacherous prick in his jaw. They both clamored to the floor. Grady's hands cuffed, he couldn't do much more than flop around on top pseudo-Frank before the bailiff and armed officers were yanking him off and physically restraining him.

A knee to his back, binding zip-ties cinching around his forearms, elbows, thighs, knees, and ankles. Grady laid on the crowded courtroom floor, humiliated at his own actions. At the order of contempt from a shouting judge and the jeers and booing from the now-inflammable rout behind him, he was hauled to the doorway and out the back of the building shrouded by a dozen or more officers with SWAT gear.

Escorted to an impressively armored vehicle, Grady was thrown inside like the sack of flesh they'd relegated him to. Floundering on the floor of the truck, a half-dozen officers filed in and sat, three to a side, surrounding him. The doors slammed shut, audibly latched and locked, and then two stern strikes to the door signaled for the truck to lurch from its position. All Grady could hear beyond the ringing of his ears from the impact of being slung so violently to the steel floor were the muffled shouts and screams from outside and the blows to the sides of the vehicle.

Even with all of the dirt I dredged up on this Scott slime ball, there's no way all of this is for corporate embezzlement. No way in hell all of these people could even have noticed how much he'd skimmed from paychecks, fraudulent shell companies and raw back-alley deals. He'd been doing it from the second he sold the patent for his spy bugs. What is all of this about?

Raising his head while trying to turn his body so he was at least face up on the floor, his neck was met with the heavy sole of a boot and another's heel thrust directly into his temple.

Grady's entire world fell from view as he sunk into a swelling, enveloping blackness.

Chapter 14

A blast of freezing cold water shocked Grady to life. Laying naked on the concrete floor of somewhere he did not recognize, he backed himself against a wall. The cinder blocks had no intention to allow him to escape the torrent of water blasting his skin raw.

"Welcome to County, you sick fuck", the man behind the firehose grunted.

Grady was ushered through a white room while a man in a white uniform awaited him. He'd handed him a bright white jumpsuit, white sneakers with no laces and a snide side-eye on his way out the door. He was then shoved unceremoniously down the hallways and past the single story of barred cells, of which there were fifteen. He stood before cell seven, the doors buzzed open and Grady was kicked in the small of his back and thrust into the steel cot hung from the sterile-white wall.

How did this happen, Grady, you imbecile? How could you have been so stupid to have gotten put here?

Mistaken identity.

They'll have to figure it out, right?

Someone will go looking for Grady Sachs at work...right?

Laying on the cold, rigid cot, Grady turned from his side to relieve the pressure on his shoulder from using his arm to sleep in lieu of a pillow. The cellblock was deadly quiet, which he thought odd considering all of the movies he'd seen that always seemed to make these places out to be rowdy and raucous. Maybe that was the "big house" though, not this limbo-land of a prison.

Chapter 15

For eighteen weeks, Grady was dragged from his cell, placed in a bulletproof car, and whisked to his trial. Eighteen weeks, that's one hundred twenty-six days of being tossed into a car, yanked out of it -- most times slamming his head into the doorframe which he was beginning to think was intentional -- and chucked into a courtroom full of very pissed off people. People who were there to see to it that justice was served to Doctor Waylan Scott, Esquire.

People were actually there to watch a nobody, Grady Sachs, stand trial for a list of crimes that were heinous under any pretense, the lightest of which was a few trillion dollars in corporate funds being misappropriated like petty cash at a Dollar General.

Laundering, larceny, murder. Government conspiracy, human, specifically child, trafficking and drug charges that would make El Chapo blush. There were a few other things that Grady couldn't decipher but he knew he'd heard the words "judicial jobbery" and made note to find out what that meant if he could.

This guy really was a scumbag. I would have had the biggest break of the century with him. He's still out there though, he's still probably doing all of this.

Grady Sachs, for all intents and purposes, didn't even exist but on paper. Papers which were provided to the courts as evidence of Doctor Scott's involvement with all of these sordid wrongdoings. Papers that identified Grady's involvement with a shadow agency, the name of which was redacted, to uncover corporate corruption. Grady Sachs was offered a handsome severance, relocation services, and was soaking up the Tuscan sun. Grady Sachs was enjoying early retirement.

The *real* Grady Sachs, sitting in an uncomfortable wooden chair that made him long for the milk crates at Westin, Howard and Schultz, realized he had been set up. To the world, Grady Sachs had disappeared. He had become Doctor Waylan Scott overnight by some fateful mishap.

It dawned on him, after hearing the list of charges and barely paying attention to them, that he was utterly and completely screwed. Up to this point, it seemed futile to bother interjecting since he was already in for whatever they had planned as far as a sentencing. He wasn't, once, asked to the stand for questioning either, come to think of it. Even if he were, his public attorney had dropped his services after Grady had assaulted him in the courtroom.

Chapter 16

Three more weeks of deliberation. The news radio blaring in the cellblock that housed cell number seven, belonging to Grady and only Grady, claimed that the jury may have been hung. Grady knew better though. The jury was debating whether or not he'd be sentenced to death, or serve years in prison. Neither of them sounded like a great idea to him, but he had little to do with that decision it seemed.

If they put me away for life, I can make parole in twenty-five years.

If they sentence me to death…

No Grady, can't think about that option right now.

Keep your head down, see what they come up with. We'll cross whichever bridge we have to cross when we get there.

It was evident that either bridge was rickety and spanned shark-infested waters of toxic sludge and human waste.

Day one hundred fifty-six, and the jury finally made their decision. Twenty-two weeks and one day and the trial of the millennium came to a close. Restitution was awarded to the countless families broken, discarded, and defamed by Doctor Waylan Scott, a sum of which was barely a paltry ten percent of his total financial charges. A guilty verdict was unnecessary due to the claimed no-contest plea of faux-Frank, his arraigning attorney.

"Doctor Waylan Phillip Scott, Esquire. You are hereby sentenced to four life sentences, a minimum of twenty-five years each, in federal prison for the financial crimes you've perpetrated to include grand larceny, corporate embezzlement and tax evasion, and defrauding multiple government and judicial agencies", the judge stated aloud. "You have been sentenced to six life sentences, a minimum of twenty-five years each, in federal prison for the convictions of murder in the first degree", the judge continued.

Nineteen counts of second degree murder, each with a life sentence of twenty-five years minimum. Another two counts of drug trafficking charges and adjacent illicit substance enterprising (life-plus-thirty years), nine racketeering charges (twenty years each), and a final two thousand eighty-nine years for the various other felonies and legal besmirchings Doctor Scott was found guilty of.

"All of these sentences will be carried out consecutively, with no eligibility of parole. As a safeguard to yourself, Doctor Scott, and the world at large, we defy your assimilation back into society and it is the wishes of this court, the jury, and those you have wronged that you rot in a cell until your dying days", the honorable judge Wilkerson summarized.

From the corner of his eye, Grady caught the head juror's face. Horn-rimmed glasses, tousled brunette hair not so dissimilar to his own, muddy brown eyes.

Grady wouldn't have caught it at all but for the tailored suit he was wearing, an interesting thing considering the Macy's off-the-rack sale suits he'd worn in the months prior. This caused Grady to pause and look the man up and down. He wore a face of true disgust save for a hint of expression on his lips. The smallest simper turned the corners of the head juror's mouth upward. Staring a hole straight into Grady's eyes. It was Frank, once again, playing another role in this charade. It was Frank all along, somehow.

Why me, Frank? How did you get in the middle of all of this to play such a role here? Why me, Frank?

Grady fumed at the juror, ignorant to the restraints being placed around his wrists and ankles, binding him in a way making him unable to make a break for it. The guards walked him through the side door of the courtroom. The world moved in slow motion as he was shoved past the jurors' box. He and the head juror were nearly side by side, albeit Grady was much lower than the risers.

He walked by in an awkward, truncated gait. Then Grady saw it and suddenly everything made sense. Head juror-Frank's cufflinks, almost invisible under the well-made suit jacket, a monogram embossed in gold, and the periods, diamonds.

Just two letters: W. S.

Chapter 17

Cell number seven in the holding pen for blundered criminals was a thing of the past now. Grady's white jumpsuit was revoked, his shoes with it. He was handed a lengthy file of papers to sort through before they were all removed save for the last marked only with an X where he was to inscribe his signature. The signature block was struck through and yanked from his hands and placed with the others.

Even here. That dirtbag Waylan even has these guys in his pocket.

Exiting through the front of the prison, Grady was greeted with flashes of cameras, clambering of reporters looking for statements, and droves of everyday people with picket signs, megaphones, and an inconceivable volume of cries and angered shouts.

"Kill the bastard!" Grady heard.

"Child fucker!" screamed another.

Signs with the words "Hang Him High! Let Him Swing!" scrawled on them cascaded throughout the crowd -- apparently it had become somewhat of a chant for his trial, unbeknownst to him. Others read "Death Isn't Good Enough", "I Hope They Bury You Under The Prison", and "My Family Would Be Here Too If You Hadn't Killed Them". Waylan Scott, or at least the man that Grady was being framed as, was the truest definition of evil from what Grady could surmise from the roiling masses.

"Doctor Scott, what do you have to say for yourself?" a reporter inquired with a microphone stuffed in his face.

"Waylan Scott, you pled no-contest to all charges prior to even being read the list. Why is it that you'd opted to be punished for all of these allegations?" posited another.

"Hey Scott!" a shout erupted from the front of the barricade. A shot rang out, one of the guards beside Grady fell to the ground holding his arm, the one that had been shielding Grady's torso through the crowd.

For the first time in nearly two years, Grady spoke. His voice boomed from his throat causing a thunder clap in his chest as he turned to the other armed guards in riot gear.

"GET ME THE HELL OUT OF HERE YOU PIECES OF SHIT!"

The guards all looked at him for a second of ringing silence. Staring in awe of him, briefly, but like a person would stare at a car crash as they slip by in a passing lane of traffic. Grady was silenced by a swift and peremptory blow to his gut. The wind being wholly removed from his lungs as he doubled over in agony. He knew that would get their attention and they, indeed, got him the hell out of there.

Chapter 18

As he was hoisted -- or more specifically thrown -- into the back of an armored truck once again, Grady was beaten ruthlessly by the guards on his detail.

To serve--

A resounding thud to his head.

And protect--

A boot to his ribs. A crack bounced off of the metallic walls.

My ass.

A weighted baton to the jaw and a molar ejected from his mouth.

Grady was beaten within an inch of his life. He had no recollection of his commitment, nor being stripped naked and placed on a gurney and admitted to the prison infirmary. There he was treated, albeit unmercifully, for six broken ribs, a dislocated jaw, and a swollen brain. The guards had done well to make him unrecognizable, not that Grady had ever been accused of being recognizable in the first place.

Sixteen days later, he was transferred to a recovery ward from the ICU. He had awakened a few times, only for minutes, over the next few days. Some of these were of his own accord, others were much more forceful, and rousing him simply to remind him of the trash they thought him to be.

Another sixty days and Grady was wheeled, graciously, to his general population home. Bars lined the walls endlessly, arms and faces reaching and peering through. Sneers and gnashing of teeth, mirthless faces and the cacophony of banging and stomping echoed through the enormous liminal space between the countless cells.

His wheelchair was upended and he was poured into cellblock F, cell thirty-six. Bleary-eyed, Grady tried to survey the area. A consolation, finally: Grady was alone.

Two empty bunks. Thank you.

Grady crawled his broken and battered body into the bottom bunk and curled into the fetal position. He drifted to sleep, or more pointedly, blacked out from the pain.

Interlude

W.S.

Waylan Scott's initials on Frank Naylor's cufflinks.

Frank Naylor is *Waylan Scott.*

Waylan Scott profiled you from that internship at Westin, Howard and Schultz. He must have been working with one of the firms that stole the case from us.

Or maybe he was working in the courtroom?

Did he pay off the entire judiciary system in this state? Are the feds in on this too?

Just how far does his billfold reach?

Doesn't much matter now, does it? You're going to be in federal lock-up for the rest of eternity with the hopes of you rotting away into senility, being driven crazy by the time inside.

They'll find out at some point.

There is no way they won't figure it out.

I can't be in there too long before someone, somewhere, sorts all of it and I get transferred out of the place.

Hopefully I can do something about that sooner.

I can't stay in this place forever.

Someone is going to figure it out.

Chapter 19

A violent banging shook Grady awake. Slowly he opened his swollen eyes, bloodshot from lack of sleep and burning as the light broke into them. A guard stood at the gate to his cell, slamming his baton against the bars shouting something incoherent to Grady's ears. He tried to read his lips, and could only make out "motherfucker". Assuming he was speaking to him, Grady tried his best to get off of the bunk. Moving too quickly, Grady's head rushed and he blacked out again, slamming into the floor.

Another piercing crack at the bars. Grady had no idea what day it was, where he was, or how he had wound up on the hard floor covered in his own mess.

Scrambling to get up, finding no purchase with his weakened limbs, he managed to get to all fours and tried to straighten himself up. The pain in his ribs shot through him like electricity, no doubt exacerbated by lying on the concrete floor for god knows how long. Hunching was the best he could do. He stood as upright as he could manage, his legs trembling like a baby deer learning to walk. Shakily, Grady propped himself on the walls as he walked to the gate of his cell.

Prison. You're in prison, Grady. You are in prison because you were set up, and you are going to be here a long, long time.

The guard whistled a piercing tone that rang between Grady's ears and caused his eyes to roll back in his head from the pain. The gate grinded open and he was pulled out by the elbow, his ribs once again searing with pain.

"Chow time, pig", the guard snarled. "You get to meet your housemates. They *all* know why you're here. They *all* know what you've been into. They are all just *dying* to meet you". His words were of no solace and Grady surmised there were not intended to be.

General population was like a zoo. Everyone loitering in corners, tribes of sorts broken up between quads of steel tables. Matching tattoos in some areas, matching skin tones in others; matching facial hair, matching ways coveralls were worn. Grady quickly made note that everyone was wearing a slate gray jumpsuit, while his was bright orange. This came as no shock to him as he was pointed in the direction of the cafeteria line.

Walking through the crowd, a hush fell over the room. The entire place, just seconds ago a wall of sound, was so silent you could hear a gnat fart two states away. Grady's back was suddenly soaked in cold sweat. This wasn't going to be an easy stay.

Every eye on him as he walked through the cleared mess line. The entirety of the inmates ahead of him backing up to the railing like Moses parting the seas. The inmates working behind the line scowled at him as they flung unrecognizable foodstuffs onto his tray. As he turned to walk back to the tables, every gaze followed him as men cracked knuckles, raised eyebrows, nudged neighbors, and nodded their heads upward at him. He meandered the walls of the cafeteria and found a seat at a small, round steel table with two round seats attached. He sat, and like someone had un-paused a film, the warble of the room burst into full volume once again.

He sat, pained by his ribs and jaw, and tried to eat as much of the swill as he could. It all tasted like salted feces and cardboard, but it was all he'd had that wasn't administered intravenously in at least three months. His stomach lurched as he shoveled it into his mouth. He retched, and then vomited all over the table top, his tray, and the floor. It had been long enough that his body wasn't sure what to do with solids, much less how to deal with the deluge from a voracious appetite.

He cradled his aching torso and rubbed his sore jaw. He stood up and walked back to the doorway he was shown on the way in. A guard turned from the wall to face him, nodded his head toward the table he'd left, and slowly padded the palm of his hand with his baton.

Grady returned to his puke-soaked table, sat with his head in his hands and stifled the brief urge to cry to himself, pitying his erroneous fate.

Chapter 20

Weeks passed and Grady had started to finally feel like a whole person again. No longer sore from his welcoming party, finally able to eat without incident. His keenness for detail had come back as well. He studied his surroundings daily and with painstaking scrutiny.

The gangs of the prison became prevalent to him fairly quickly. All of them flew flags of sorts so that there was no mistaking them for another clique, or even another person. The way some walked, the way some talked, almost like foreign languages for their idiosyncrasies. Hair styles, tattoos he'd previously noted, and all kinds of minor details most would miss had they not spent years attuning themselves to their surroundings.

Grady had always been attentive to details. Grady knew, in some way, he'd only survived this long for doing so. Maybe that was paranoia of this place getting the best of him. He had lived a life of observation prior to his fateful misstep of trust that landed him here, though. Events in his life had forced him to be careful, heeding everything around, behind, and ahead of him, both physically, and speculatively.

He'd sit in the corner of the mess hall against the wall gazing over the top of a book he'd feign reading and through the emergency-lit cellblock as everyone slept and did their nightly deals of trade and bartering. He knew who smoked which brand, how they got things in and out of here, and who was whose bitch. Grady felt a sort of sense of peace the more he understood the microcosms of commerce and daily life within those concrete walls.

Everything was starting to feel... ordinary, once again.

Chapter 21

The gate to Grady's cell grated open on its archaic and unoiled mechanism. He snorted himself awake as two men were standing in front of him, silhouetted by the flood lights in his dilated pupils. One man shoved the other into his cell and the door groaned shut and locked. The man stood before Grady with a grimace on his face. Grady couldn't read whether or not this was the face of a friend or a foe. The distorted expression lent no idea as to whether the man was despondent of his situation, or incensed by his bunkmate.

Grady wasted no time figuring out who this man was. In fact, Grady hadn't even made a sound before he launched from his bottom bunk, taking out the man's knees and slamming him to the ground. Wadding his hair in the palm of his hand, Grady heaved his body toward the steel basin of the toilet and proceeded to smash this stranger's skull against it until his feet quivered and his body convulsed, then fell limp.

Grady laid back down in his bunk and waited for the guards to tend to the racket. It would be a little while, them all being used to the din of the animals that shared this concrete and iron jungle. This behavior wouldn't go unpunished, however. This behavior would have Grady noticed by everyone. Grady wanted to avoid this, but there was no way around it, not after everything he'd gone through to get here.

No way am I trusting anyone they put in here. Waylan has this whole place wrapped around his finger too, I'm sure of it.

He'd regretted the abrupt beating of the man lying on the floor, his life oozing into the hallway under the painted iron bars. He would have, at least, had he not landed here through betrayal and ignorance. Never again.

The guards sprinted to his cell after an inmate detailed to mopping the halls hollered that there was a body, clearly deceased, "fucking up his floors". The door slammed open as two guards pushed it against the straining motor and they spilled onto him. Turning him over, cuffing him, and smashing batons into his back and neck, they hauled him up and all but hogtied him. Carrying him like livestock, tied up by his ankles and wrists, they walked him briskly to the freight elevator.

Down three floors, deep underground now, they took him through a dimly lit hallway with riveted doors. Nearly at the end of the hall, they stood Grady up, un-cuffed him, and chucked him into the tiny eight-by-eight room. No windows, not even a porthole to peer through in the door. A slot in the bottom slipped open, a flat pillow was stuffed through and it was smashed shut again.

This must be solitary confinement. Fitting name when you really get to see what the place looks like. Finally, some quiet.

Thirty days, by Grady's count, and he was removed from the hole. When he was taken back into the light, he was escorted to a different wing completely. Cellblock C held criminals of the prison itself. All of the men here had wronged someone inside in some way. Bribery and assault of guards, repeat rapists of inmates and, in special cases like Grady's, murderers of inmates or correctional officers.

The looks he received here were different from those of the folks in the seven floors of cells in his old block. These men, here, were hard boiled. They'd put others through things that most wouldn't dare repeat once inside. Stone faced, all of them. No matter, Grady had spent years being in the background. He'd learned his face was essentially emotionless anymore as a result of his isolated, boring life. He figured he'd fit in just fine here. Blend into the masses once more and remain unseen. This is all he could hope for.

This is what he needed to happen.

The truth would come out in time. He knew it would.

Chapter 22

One thousand four hundred twelve days in. No one has figured it out yet. It hasn't been long enough.

Months moved along and became years. Grady had remained relatively unnoticed, untouched, and left alone for the duration thus far. There was a certain fear among the other inmates in General Population of the men in cellblock C. There was ample respect paid to one another within his cellblock as well. Terse nods of faceless men, unbothered by one another, and unaffected by the need for showboating affiliations to gangs.

Isolation among the backdrop of a crowded room. Alone, yet surrounded by everyone else. Understood that each and every one of these men was a wolf among sheep, when truly they were wolves among wolves. Each and every one was waiting for an opportunity to present itself. To Grady, this was both comforting and unsettling. He knew he had to keep his head on a swivel, but he couldn't look like he was watching anyone. Wandering eyes would, undoubtedly, raise suspicion and suspicion caused paranoia and rash decisions.

I'm not gonna die here. Someone is going to figure it out. Eventually, they'll learn the truth. I can't die here.

Grady reassured himself that he could keep it together. He'd act faster if he needed to. He'd be tougher if it came to that. For now, though, he'd keep his head down and blend in with the rest of the depraved ranks he fell into. One day that came to a crossroads and a choice had to be made -- a choice that would ordinarily be life or death for anyone other than Grady Sachs.

A flash from the corner of Grady's eye while in the showers -- a literal flash as the caged bulb overhead was shattered raining sparks and glass all over the wet tiled floor beneath it. The darkness fell quickly, and slapping feet grew closer. Grady quickly soaped his arms and as much of his head and neck as he could before holding his hands out.

"This is for those little kids you shipped out to Hong Kong, you sick bastard!" the shout gave away the would-be assailant's position.

Grady turned to meet the sharpened point of something going through the palm of his right hand. With his left, he swung his palm upward connecting with a jaw, the teeth clicking together and a muffled groan followed. Another hard swing with his wounded right hand, still embedded with the makeshift blade, and he connected again, only this time his hand stayed stuck. Grabbing the man's throat, he shoved him backwards in the darkness until he felt the flailing body slam into a surface.

A knee into the groin, stomach, or hip caused the man to fold in half. Another knee to the offender's jaw, once more, causes a shower of shattered porcelain to bounce off of the tile. Grady knelt down, wrapped his elbows under the man's armpits, hoisted him upward and threw himself onto him with his full weight into whatever was behind the antagonist's back. A crash of metal on tile, water blasting Grady in the face and showering the area around them, Grady reached for whatever had broken in the forceful fall. Finding the bowl of a sink basin, he brought it over his head and only heard the beginnings of a shriek before he cut it short and the body under him lay entirely still.

It took him long enough. I guess Waylan was hoping I'd get killed sooner than this. He's gonna be pissed when he finds out I took another one of his cronies down.

Grady sat under the cooling fountain of water, perched atop his trophy. As the guards approached he held his hands, half-heartedly, out to his sides.

"I'm guessing saying self-defense isn't going to matter much to you assho--"

The customary blow to the face, knee to the neck, and chrome bracelets followed. Grady was becoming a bit too used to the abuse he'd grown to expect. But, then again, expecting everything was the name of the game here.

Another stint in solitary, no doubt.

Finally, some peace and quiet.

I can get some sleep, rest awhile until they throw me back in with all of these ingrates. The more time away, the better.

Someone's got to know something by now.

Chapter 23

Ninety days this time. That seems excessive, but maybe there's been enough of a change that I can sink into the cut again, lay low awhile.

Grady was taken back to cellblock C, but only to gather his pillow before he was shoved through the door at the end of the hall and into a wing he hadn't seen in his time here before. Wooden doors, this time, and windows at the back of each room. Empty beds, but actual beds.

This is too good to be true. Where the hell are they taking me? What is this place?

Steered to the cracked door at the end of the fluorescent hallway, the guard knocked. The door was opened by an unassuming man, a small smile, kind brown eyes, and a bald head. Holding out his hand, he placed it on Grady's shoulder and simply smiled wider and blinked, slowly, like a cat showing its affection.

"My name is Doctor Winston Curdy. It's a pleasure to meet you, Mister..." his words hung in the air, a question for Grady to answer.

"Grady. Grady Sachs, Doctor Curdy. Likewise, good to meet you", he'd responded.

It was evident almost as soon as the words left his mouth that Grady had made a huge mistake. He was not Grady Sachs here, he was Waylan Scott. It was the first question of being admitted into the psychiatric ward.

It was a test and Grady had failed it miserably.

While the accommodations of the psych ward were considerably better than that of his two previous homes here, it was still very apparent that Grady was still, very much, a prisoner. Not only a prisoner, but a prisoner under heavy watch by multiple people every minute of his day.

This was the opposite of what Grady had wanted. Now he had no way to fade into the scenery. Here, more so than just in the prison, he was unquestionably *someone*. The irony only being that he, in fact, was *not* the someone they thought him to be. A bit of information that he did well not to disclose after the first day of his admittance.

Six hundred eighty-six days. The time is adding up, but at least I've been in a few different places now. Doesn't matter though, Grady.

They'll figure it out.

Soon enough, someone is going to figure it out.

It's been nearly six years since I showed up here, six years may not be long enough for anyone to have dug that far.

Give it time, Grady, they'll figure it out.

Doctor Curdy took a vested interest in Grady. Personally, over the last nearly-two years in the ward, he had tended his casefiles, curated his therapy sessions, and observed the group activities. Every last inmate here was tended, almost exclusively, by a nurse practitioner and reported back to Doctor Curdy. Grady never once saw him personally engage any other patient directly, however.

Why am I so special to this guy? No one's killed two people here before?

Like Samuel Loomis to The Shape in *Halloween*, Grady became the subject of this doctor's studies. Time passed endlessly and painfully slowly at that. There were no amounts of group coloring activities, movie nights, or outings to the garden behind the prison that would overshadow the servitude he was enduring. Small rewards for the feeble-minded crazies Grady had watched day in and day out. He was nothing like the drooling, babbling, erratic members of this ever-devolving tribe. Again, he'd found himself in a unique position which was the exact opposite of his lifelong happenstance. That is, until the second anniversary of this admittance, a time that was even celebrated for all of the smooth-brained idiots in the ward. Grady did something that was increasingly less unique for him the longer he was imprisoned.

Grady grabbed the arm of the woman who had gently undone the restraints around his wrists that were attached to the bed in his room. He grabbed her wrists, flung himself off of the bed, and kicked the door shut. His hand over her mouth, he hissed in her ear.

"My name is Grady Sachs. If you do not get me the hell out of here, I swear this is the last day you will ever see", his curt words pressed against her temple as he leaned against her.

"I am Grady Sachs, *not* Waylan Scott. I have never *been* Waylan Scott. If you do not do your *fucking job* and care for me in the correct manner to the fullest of your ability, I will end you." His words had a finality to them.

The woman trembled as he let his hand off of her mouth slowly. Unfortunately, as he'd anticipated, she immediately began to scream. A hand clamped over her mouth once again, he snarled at her that they wouldn't think twice about a single scream from one of these godforsaken rooms.

> "But if you scream again, they will come. If they come, it will be too late", he warned.

The woman nodded her understanding and Grady helped her up but kept his hand over her mouth until she walked, slowly, to the door. Grady's eyes locked with hers and she nodded once again before pressing her thumb to the fingerprint lock. She walked through the door and Grady let his hand go from her as he followed closely behind.

As they walked through the long hallway, she looked back at Grady and he could see the glint of a tear in her eye. He felt horrible for his actions -- he was turning into a monster that he'd never expected to become. A man that was markedly outstanding from the rest. He looked at her face and shame washed over him.

He didn't want this. He couldn't go through with it. There had to be another way.

"I'm sorry. Please, take me back. Take me to my room and forget everything I said. Please?" He'd hung his head, whispering behind her before he paused his stride.

She turned towards him, reached out a warm hand and touched his arm gently. She escorted him back to his room, her arm wrapped around his like they were on the way to prom. Closing the door behind them, she helped Grady to bed and tightened the restraints as tightly as she could while still allowing them to be somewhat comfortable.

Sitting on the edge of the bed, she stroked a tender hand across his forehead, brushing his disheveled hair from his brow and leaned closely to his face. Her breath slid over her lips and against Grady's cheek as she grazed it with her own.

She cooed in his ear "Mister Scott sends his regards".

Grady attempted to yank himself from the restraints, but she was well practiced at her job. He rattled the bed, horrified at the five words that had seductively breached his defenses. She slammed a syringe into his leg, pushed a plunger, and it was lights out for Grady Sachs.

Chapter 24

Waylan had no idea how long it had been. He'd been in the same hospital for as long as he could remember. He didn't remember any of the people there. He didn't recognize anyone that worked there, any of the doctors or nurses. The only person he recognized was the gentleman that sat with him in his room every other day. The same gentleman that would give him his pills, feed him his meals, and make sure he was wheeled out to the garden for sun for a half hour every day.

Waylan Scott was his name, he was assured when he would question it. Doctor Waylan Scott. He was being treated for dementia. He was told that his brain had kind of holes in it -- lapses of memory and cognition. Waylan was grateful for the pristine care he was being given in this place.

Waylan was very, very grateful for the Jell-O, too.

During one of his routine visits, the gentleman spoke kindly to Waylan. As always he introduced himself.

"Hello mister Scott. I'm Doctor Curtis Winslow. Do you remember who I am?" he asked warmly.

"W-Waylan Scott", Waylan stammered.

"No mister Scott", Doctor Winslow chuckled. "You are Waylan Scott. I am Doctor Curtis Winslow. We've met before. I visited you yesterday evening as a matter of fact".

"Oh, oh. Right, right. Mister, er, Doctor Winslow. Yes, yes I remember you", Waylan feigned.

"Would you care to talk today about yourself, Mister Scott? I'm very interested in what you might have to say." The doctor sat back and let his words fill the space between them.

Unassuming, kind brown eyes, his balding crown framed with a bit of brunette hair around his head, and the smallest smile. A smile that Waylan thought he'd almost recognized.

"I had a dream last night. I think I've had it before. There was a man, Grady Sachs was his name. He had something to do with me… in my past maybe? I was younger then, much younger than I am now. Brunette hair, almost the color of yours, and brown eyes too", Waylan recanted, reminiscent of his youth. "I'm not sure what happened to him, but I think I knew him. I think we were close, connected by some event".

Doctor Winslow jotted something down on his steno pad and nodded, smiling at the senile man before him.

"Of course, Mister Scott. What then?" he inquired.

A feverish thought ran through Waylan's mind, something from his past. Something that suddenly made the world around him explode from view and he felt like he was falling backwards. The room spun around him and he hung his head limp on his neck.

"You. You did this, didn't you?" he growled at the doctor. "This isn't happening. You keep plugging me full of that, that shit. How long have I been here? How long have you been playing this game?"

Waylan raised his head and scowled at the doctor sitting but two feet from him. Simpering toward him, the doctor sniggered to himself.

"You must be building a tolerance to those drugs. I will have to make a note of that for the warden", he scoffed, pinching his nose and inhaling sharply.

"You've been here quite a long time, Mister Scott. It's been nearly forty-five years since you were placed under my care", the doctor spoke softly.

"How… what do you mean forty-five years?"

"I think today, however, today is the day you will be discharged. You see, I am retiring in a few days and I can't pass you along any further. Doctor Curdy was kind enough to mentor me about your condition and I'll be sure the warden gets a full report so he can better tend to your needs out there with the rest of them", Winslow smiled.

Dumbfounded, at a complete loss for words, he stared into the eyes of the doctor in complete shock. Memories formed in blurred recollection, but nothing coherent.

"I'm an old man. How can I go back out there in my condition? How can you put me back out there?"

"Your case however, Mister Scott, has gotten quite a lot of buzz lately. It's the fiftieth anniversary of your indictment. Sorry we didn't bake you a cake", the doctor remarked, sarcasm dripping from each syllable.

"My... my case?"

"It has been appealed! You won't be happy to note that more time has been added for additional uncovered offenses. The *whole* prison is aware of the heinous things you've done." The doctor unlocked his desk drawer as he continued.

"Prison?"

"Every last one of them is eager to meet you! I can't say I blame them either. If I were in here with you, I'd want to make you pay for what you did too."

"What I did? What did I do? I don't understand."

"I'll definitely make a note to the warden that you may need some extra help jogging your memory. Please, do take care."

The discharge papers were in a folder that the doctor produced. Every line was written in and initialed already. The doctor looked over his glasses and fixed his gaze on the demented man before him. He simpered at him, ever so slightly, and signed on the line of patient *Doctor Waylan Scott, Esquire* as if he'd been signing it that way for decades.

"Wait... Just wait!" the man yelled as he was wheeled out of the Doctor's office.

Who is Grady Sachs?

The blurred lines of faded memories started to sharpen into focus.

Grady Sachs...

The puzzle pieces began to fall into place, deliriously.

I think… no…

I am Grady Sachs.

Interlude

Eighteen thousand, three hundred, ninety-seven days. Fifty years and change. Fifty years that prick has been messing with my head. Keeping me in here, keeping me sedated and forcing me to think I'm him! Miserable sociopath.

No, wait. Thank can't be right. His corporation was over thirty years old when I took the fall and it toppled. He had to be in his seventies then. He's dead. Didn't I see on the TV that he'd died?

Jesus, Grady, like you can remember anything from the last, what did he say, forty-five years almost. You barely remembered you're you!

He had money. He paid off the entire legal system to orchestrate this. What's to say he didn't set something up in perpetuity?

That's gotta be it. He needs this to stay buried. His kids would have to do time for it, right? Isn't there something in the law about next of kin, or estate, or something like that? It would ruin their lives if nothing else.

I mean, this guy was as evil as they come. He stood on the backs of so many people, and took advantage of every possible loophole and underworldly avenue he could just to get paid.

Grady, you moron. As far as anyone is concerned, you're him! Even if he is dead, Grady Sachs is the man time forgot.

If what that doctor says is true, there's no way anyone here will remember me. It's been too long.

I can blend in somehow. I can be nobody again.

He said they all knew though.

If they don't, they will soon enough. It's only a matter of time.

It's always only ever been a matter of time.

Chapter 25

Grady was wheeled to his General Population cell. He recognized the walls of this place, but there had been some changes in the last few decades that were disorienting. The cells were slightly larger, allowing for four bunks instead of the typical two. The barring mechanisms had been replaced with sleek belted machinery and three-inch thick, double pane plexiglass.

Bulletproof? Soundproof?

His thoughts were whipped to reality when his transference was seized suddenly. He sat, feeling feeble and old.

Those fifty years have done some damage.

He was let gingerly out of his chair and sat gently onto the bottom bunk of the otherwise empty cell. Grady laid back against the cold steel cot and lifted an atrophied arm to rest his head on. Drifting between groggy, drug-withdrawal-induced sleep and awake, he hardly noticed the door shushing open on the new belted rails.

Three men filed into the cell as Grady's eyes struggled to focus through the haze of his forty-five year forced sedative addiction. With one eye cracked, he noted the clenched fists of two men while the third was pulling the pillow from the bunk above Grady's.

In a flash of bodies, all three were on top of him. Grady had no time to register it was happening at all, he just pulled his arms to his face to try and shield himself from the blows. Hands, feet, elbows, and knees all struck him seemingly at once. These weren't hazing blows -- not your typical "let them know you're in charge" bumps. These men meant to kill him.

It was only a matter of time, Grady.

You knew they would come for you. Just didn't think it would be the second you got dropped back inside this hellhole.

Waylan Scott was guilty of a lot of things that even these degenerates hated.

You knew they'd come.

Grady propped himself on an elbow and rolled himself as quickly as he could so he was facing the corner of the wall and the cot. He pulled his knees to his chest molding himself into a fetal ball, taking blows to the back and kidneys. Gripping his bare toes against the block wall, he inhaled as best he could and shoved off with all of his strength.

To his astonishment, he shot off of the cot and into two of the three assailants, throwing them back into the other two beds attached to the opposite wall. A head connected to the top bunk with a resounding clang and a man fell limp to the floor. The second slid between the two bunks, taken out at the knees from the thrust.

The third man leapt onto Grady and straddled his ribs pressing the pillow into his face firmly. Grady reached for purchase on the man as he pried for anything he could grab. The thug's wrists were sturdy and his elbows just shored his pressure into Grady's face. Grady shoved a flattened hand into the man's armpit and pressed equally as hard into his flesh.

An arm on the pillow buckled and Grady rolled from his grip. Standing beside the man, staring him in the eye, he sprang back into action. In a split second, he raised a fist and threw a heavy haymaker to the bastard's jaw and connected with a crack. As the man regained himself, rubbing his jaw and grinning at Grady menacingly, Grady noticed the thick door was still open.

These men were sent to kill you, they don't belong here.

This is your fight, Grady! You've got to remind everyone in here why your name is still on their tongues!

Grady crouched as he ran at the man and speared his shoulder into him, shoving him towards the gaping opening of the door. The man's wind audibly knocked out, he doubled over and Grady was able to knee him square in the jaw once more, teeth smashing together with the blow.

Teach all three of these pricks a lesson. Teach this whole damned place a lesson, Grady!

Grady reached up with both arms and dead-hung from the thick rubber belt and yanked it down as far as he could. Luckily, the man stood up directly into Grady's intentions. The belt snapped against the hitman's jaw and the tension dragged him upwards just enough to startle his hands toward his neck. Grady reached out the side of the cell and smashed the emergency button with his palm, lacerating himself on the glass encasement.

The door slammed shut, much quicker with the new upgrades and the man's body pinched, gruesomely, between the wall and the door. No safety measures in place, the snap of ribs echoed against the bare walls of the prison. A rattle choked from his throat as crimson red sputtered from his lips.

Grady turned to the other two men in his cell and booted the man between the bunks in the face with his bare heel. His nose crunched, but didn't faze him much, so Grady kicked again, and again, then once more for measure. As the would-be murderer stumbled backward into the bottom bunk holding his face, Grady grabbed the top bunk and flung himself, both feet forward, directly into the man's head smashing it against the block wall.

A seizure, a guttural whimper, and finally silence.

Grady panted, winded from all of the excitement, utterly in awe of the power adrenaline could have on the human body, even after a drug addled forty-five years. He knew what this would mean, but maybe some time in solitary would help him recalibrate and figure out a way out of this place once and for all. Maybe, just maybe, he'd be able to figure out how to put an end to all of this Waylan Scott trash.

He stood up, stretched his aching back, and for the first time caught a glimpse of himself in the chromed mirror bolted to the wall. The drugs that had muddied Grady's mind seemed to have spent from his system with the lives of the three men. His eyes were more focused, his senses felt sharper, like he'd remembered they had been decades ago.

A man considerably younger than Grady's fifty year tenure in this place stared back at him.

Grady remembered what he'd hoped everyone else would not find out.

Chapter 26

Grady Sachs sat in his small, windowless cell in solitary. It had been sixty-six days of blissful silence, save for the occasional sliding of ancient metal doors and the screams of men being tossed into the darkness that Grady had befriended long ago.

No telling how long they'll leave you in here, pal. Good thing is, the more time you have here, the less time you have out there.

Unfortunately, the less time out there, the less chances you'll have to get to know the new guts of this place.

The bones are all the same though, so there can't be that much difference.

Be careful.

Be prepared.

Those three pricks weren't the last people that will come for you.

Grady's door shuttered to life and was yanked open by a sturdy guard detailed to him and him alone. The man waved a hand at Grady and nudged his head outward. It was his time, now, to be set back into the wild amongst the rabid dogs awaiting him in the overworld.

Mess hall, once again.

Well, the food hasn't improved.

Grady swirled a plastic utensil around in the pig swill on his cafeteria tray. Sitting in the corner, he observed, as he'd always done. Watching the same moronic gangland exhibitionism, all attempting to arouse fear and respect in one another. The same idiotic skinheads, the same self-indulgence cholos, the same panthers and all of the lowly plebs looking for a home among them.

Grady smirked over his excuse for food, stood up, and slid his tray to the floor with a loud clang. The entire room went silent. He raised a hand, and held on high, his middle finger.

"Fuck each and every last one of you. You bastards all know where I'll be sleeping. You all know what happened to the last crew that tried to wake sleeping beauty, too", he stoically taunted the crowd. "Try your luck, I've got a long time to go in here. See ya around, shitbirds".

He held the hand high above his head as he walked with his back turned towards the door, nodded to the guards, and walked back to his cell.

If I can't keep my head low here, I might as well run the place.

Chapter 27

Before too long, the bagboys of the larger factions in the prison were running between Grady and their own leadership. Whispers of Waylan Scott hissed among the lowlifes and Grady sat on a pedestal for at least a bit of time.

The attempts against him would come in waves. Leaders of the gangs would send their biggest and most brutal men to Grady to "negotiate" things that he'd had no bearing on in the first place. They were sent, Grady would chisel another tick into the bottom of the bunk he slept beneath as the body count stacked up. He'd take his licks, sure, but once he got out of the infirmary, he'd always come back swinging.

This was life now.

Eventually, he'd bartered with a guard to allow passage to the common area. He used this as a tool to gain a little inside-security from two of the gangs, each of which had their enforcers celled on either side of Grady's.

There had been talks of Waylan Scott forming his own gang in the system. The guards were wary around him as he walked to and from the allowable areas of the building. The bodies parted before him instead of piling at his feet after a beating. He'd have heads of the gangs approach him at all avenues paying respect to him, keeping in his good graces, and trying to join this rumored coterie. Just like the real Waylan Scott had done in his life and time, Grady was doing in prison. A company of nefarious and unscrupulous morality was born.

If it was this easy to do in prison, where everyone is watching, it couldn't have been that difficult on the outside. I can see why Waylan would have leaned into all of this.

Grady, you can't be serious?

Get your head out of your ass -- you aren't the same as this guy!

You're getting a little too cocky here, and that's what led Caesar to his untimely demise at the hands of Brutus.

Watch it, old friend. Dial it back.

Books, reading glasses; fade into the ether once again.

Disappear like a gray ghost into the foggy dusk.

Grady spent the next few months reorganizing his syndicate, negotiating with prisoners and guards alike for his meals to be brought to him, books to be ushered in and out at his beck and call, and any messages to be relayed directly from him, and to him, at his cell from the proverbial horse's mouth.

He'd set himself up in an isolation chamber of his own solitary confinement, but this was at least his doing, and it had a slightly nicer view. There was silence, even amongst the hoard, and he relished in the order of it all.

Chapter 28

The prison teemed around him and time passed.

The guards shifted from old faces to new. Grady's cronies were cycled in and out of positions of power through means of suicide, mutinous infighting and even some successful paroles. Time took a lot of the men he'd acquainted himself to. Grady was happy, peaceful, finally in the shadows enough to be something of a myth -- natural lore, an urban legend of the penal system he'd been shunned to.

Twenty-seven thousand, three hundred fifty-three days. Pushing seventy-five years, old friend.

Security still protected Grady. Or had he truly become Waylan Scott now? Occasional mishaps occurred and cover ups of the bodies staged as suicides so he wouldn't endure any more truly-solitary confinement.

Just as the prisoners and guards, the authorities above likely came and went as well.

How long until everyone has finally forgotten about Doctor Waylan Scott? Surely after seventy-five years, all records would be archived somewhere. The wardens must have changed hands a few times by now.

Grady thought it was a bit odd that he'd never heard much about any of the wardens, but then again, it's not like the wardens typically do speaking tours around the prison. Kissing babies and shaking hands was a mayor's game, not a man in charge of hardened criminals. Still, strange that for the time he'd served in this pit, he'd only heard of a warden in passing twice: once when he was ingested to the system and once more upon his retirement a decade or so ago.

At any rate, Grady had gone relatively unnoticed in the last few decades and that brought him solace. He was able to reacquaint himself with the life he'd led for many years before that shadow-agency "hired" him and ultimately set him up.

The comfort of his empire was unsettling to Grady some days, but it was better than the violence that had wrought the thing in the first place. He'd spent most of his days reading endless pages of books. He'd even started writing his own little tale. A story of a man martyred wrongfully for an outlandish claim that would damn a whole region. A pseudo-faithed nobody, a wool merchant without a footprint, but a mad Celt was eager to cover his tracks and had the unwary man put to death. A retelling of what had brought Grady to this point in his life set against the backdrop of the Black Death in the fourteenth century.

All was well enough in Grady's world once again. Maybe this wouldn't be so bad after all.

I could live out the rest of my life here, the way things are going. Seems luck may be on my side, for once.

But, as Grady had come to learn, luck can always change.

Chapter 29

A hail from, of all people, the warden came down to Grady through the grapevine of prisoner-to-guard-to-prisoner-to-guard. He was summoned, apparently, to mark his seventy-fifth year of incarceration. The warden thought it was such an accomplishment that he'd made an actual lifetime of his life sentence that he'd parody him to his face.

Juvenile. New guy making a name for himself, no doubt. Mock the old man, the safe bet. No chance of a geriatric lunging over the desk to rip you apart then. He's got a lot of nerve.

Grady was given an unexpectedly nice afternoon. He received a fresh haircut, his mundane brunette hair combed over. He was treated to a straight razor shave, something that he'd anxiously endured waiting for the barber to be a mercenary, even after seventy-five years, exacting his duties in Waylan Scott's posthumous wishes.

A meal of his choosing and the gift of an evening of movies. Sci-Fi's like Mr. Nobody, romances The Fountain and Age of Adeline, action thrillers, Old Guard and Hancock. Even cheesy throwbacks: Highlander, The Holy Mountain, Chronos, and She.

Grady spent that night in a real bed, the first he'd felt in nearly eight decades. A foam mattress enveloped him, the feathery down pillow cradled his head. He awakened the next morning and enjoyed a light morning massage and meditation. Real coffee, fresh and aromatic, as if it were roasted that very morning in the smallest batch. And a bowl of his favorite breakfast, one he'd longed for: corn flakes.

Grady sat in bliss, entirely aware of the condescension in all of the pomp and circumstance of the last twenty-four hours. He chose to pay it no mind as he munched his bland breakfast cereal. As he finished spooning the milk from his second bowl, he sat back in his seat and stretched, yawned, and sighed with a cheshire grin.

A guard stood at the door of the room he'd been given for the night and gave a governing nod to Grady. He stood, walked towards the door of the room, and the man asked him to turn around. Customary procedure for a prisoner, even one with so many years in a cell, was to bind their hands behind them to reduce the risk of incident. Grady put his wrists together and was pulled, candidly, onto a Hannibal Lecter dolly to which he was bound to the sides by his wrists, forearms, and upper arms with thick straps. The same were also fastened to his ankles, shins, thighs, and a final two belting his hips and chest to the contraption.

What gives? All of that pampering just to make a show of me along the way. This guy has a lot of gall. Self-righteous little poser.

Whatever, let him have it Grady, it doesn't change anything.
You're still here until you're not.

Chapter 30

As he was wheeled, intentionally no doubt, from the east wing of the prison to the west wing, he was jeered at, cheered for, hissed at and spat on by the inmates. Clearly, fear mongering was the only thing that had earned him his solitude and now that he was shackled like a rabid beast, he was seeing the true colors of all of his cohorts.

Just missing palm leaves and a crown of thorns.

Grady shook his head as he laughed at the image in his mind. His snigger was met with a vicious strike to the side of his head. Stars blocked his line of vision as he groaned and another blow was served to his midsection.

Wincing from the pain in his head, Grady kept an eye closed as the other started to swell, a black eye forming quickly from the bash to the face. He was ushered onto a small, dimly lit elevator. Suspiciously, the elevator lurched and then started to drift downward beneath the prison into sublevels well below his home away from home, solitary confinement.

Christ, they are actually going to bury me under the place, aren't they?

Off the elevator, down a series of corridors with no unique markings, of no unique color, to a door just like all of the rest along the winding hallways, Grady's conveyance was halted. He was stood up in the trolley as the door unlatched. A few ominous thunks and clicks, the door hissed on pistons as it opened. Cinematically slow, the door swung wide and he was shepherded fifteen feet into the room.

Inside sat an enormous oaken desk, leather bound desk blotter and golden pens sitting just so. A high-back leather chair had its back facing Grady. Monitors spanned the wall ahead of him, four-by-three, twelve in total. Each of these monitors had multiple feeds from cameras within the facility. Nothing at all unusual for a warden to keep track of. Except one monitor showed only one feed. A single, solitary camera, panning left and right, in an empty cell that had, until yesterday morning, housed one Doctor Waylan Scott, Esquire, convicted felon of multiple offenses. A man also known as Grady Sachs. A man who was once no one at all.

"Mister Scott, I've been watching you", a low slimy voice slithered through the air. "A long, long time has passed since you entered these walls. A long time, indeed."

"Get to the point. You brought me here to make me an example or something, right?" challenged Grady. "Well I don't have all day, I have books to get back to."

"Au contraire, Mister Scott, you have all the time in the world, it would seem", the man waved a folder off the side of his chair.

"Well, a few thousand consecutive life sentences gives a guy a lot of time to spare, I suppose", Grady replied, feigning cool.

"Oh, Mister Scott, you and I both know you've had plenty of time even before all of that business of conspiracy, trading, and etcetera." The man continued, a smirk hanging on his every word. "I would even go as far as to say you've known hundreds of years before these were handed to you to live out in this dingy building."

He knows.

"Mister Scott, or should I say, Sachs?" the mysterious voice inquired, almost provocatively.

He knows!

"You see, I've been keeping an eye on you for a very, very long time. Before your time here, even, with the agency, and prior to that with your leasing office. So few records of Grady Sachs exist, it was rather hard to track you down, but I've gotten pretty keen after all of these years in my ways." he continued.

"Would you just get to it alrea--"

For the first time in nearly three decades, Grady was cut off mid-sentence.

"It's my turn to talk, Grady Sachs", the voice commanded as the chair slowly spun to meet Grady.

Brunette hair, muddy brown eyes, no discernable features -- a man easily confused for any other man stared at him, simpering slightly with a glint in his eye.

"It's a pleasure to meet you… or should I say meet you again in one of a countless number of times. Though, now I will gladly use my real name, or at least the one that's been adopted over the years", the man placed his hands on his desk and stood.

As he walked around the desk, he stayed his gaze on Grady's and stood mere inches from him, still confined to his transport.

"It's almost like looking into a mirror, isn't it my old friend?"

Getting a closer look than ever before, Grady studied the man in front of him, completely stupefied at what he was seeing.

It can't be. There's no way, after all of this time. No. No!

"Mister Grady Sachs, or should I say Evescha Heller", the unmentionable man sneered.

Son of a bitch!

In a rush of memories, Grady recalled Frank, the doctors from the ward here in prison, his old landlord, and in a flash from many years ago, a face of a man not unlike his own. Distorted through clear Scottish water, simpering at him with ill-intent. His life began anew that day. A life of secrecy and of practiced shadow-walking and blending into the background of the tapestry of time.

"Pleased to meet you, I am Doctor Waylan Scott, Esquire, but you knew that, didn't you? Perhaps you'd recall Frank Naylor better? Doctor Winslow?" he chuckled again. "Or perhaps your mind is still as sharp as your reflexes."

The man that had framed him for larceny nearly seventy-five years ago was the very same man that took Grady's life over seven hundred years prior. The man that, unwittingly, granted Grady eternal life as a thirty-something year old man who looked exactly like everyone else and also like no one at the same time.

The man that had stared into Grady's muddy eyes from above the water as he tried to drown him in the Garbh Uisge. The man that, then at least, was known as Fionnghall Alba. An infamous thief, rapist, and murderer of fourteenth century Scotland. The man whose brother wasn't as careful as he was in his participation in those crimes. The man that framed Grady for everything, including the introduction of the Plague to Scotland, posthumously, and evidently lived to tell the tale another day.

"I've always known we'd meet again, Heller", Alba spoke slowly, concisely. "Something happened that day and you are, now, just like me it would seem."

Alba paused, met Grady's gaze staring under his browline, sneering.

Epilogue

I was never forgotten.

He *always knew.*

Fionnghall Alba, chasing me through time itself, he'd known all along.

How long has he been watching me? How long was he waiting to spring this trap?

Who could hold onto such a vendetta for over seven hundred years? What could I possibly owe him that he hadn't already taken from me so long ago?

I was never anything to him, just a man who had seen the wrong thing at the right time and dealt with it. But this?

I'm just Grady Sachs.

I am Evesha Heller.

I am nothing to him.

I am no one.

I am eternal.

Part 0.5:

No One Lives Forever

A Grady Sachs Origin Story

As Written By Grady Sachs

Prologue

The bastard child of a bastard child of a bastard child. The trend was a family trait, it would seem, and family obviously a term being used rather loosely, all things considered.

A mamzer, more specifically, was the word used within the Jewish community. It would be trite to note that Jewish societies -- although rife with bastardry due to the times and persecutions of religious and cultural systems -- didn't take very kindly to mamzers. Some were more lenient than others, but the more orthodox the sect, the less inclined they were to treat you like a person. Or at the very least, like one of their own.

My mother was the mamzer of a Germanic cocotte, a bastard child of her own rite, who was the daughter of a Jewish refugee from Hungary. She was cast out of her own community for, you guessed it, also being a child out of wedlock. The paramour fell in with other homeless children, and oftentimes traveled with gypsies from town to town.

Displaced through the generations, the perforated bloodline found its way through Europe and had settled across the oceanus britannicus. That bloodline has, thus far, settled in a boy after generations. It was settled in me, Evescha Heller. The proverbial red-headed step child of a faith that has never been mine, and a culture that I had passed down to me in fragments almost as discontinuous as my lineage.

The only thing lost, here, is time.

Chapter 0.0

Obviously, I do not recall my birth. At the time of my writing this, it has also been many, many years so I could have forgotten the details. What I do know of it, I was told by my dearest mother, Marioziota Heller, the most breathtaking woman I had ever seen. To this day, that holds true, even after all of these dreadfully monotonous, harrowingly protracted years.

Marioziota is a foul name for a child. Being that she was a child out of wedlock, to a whore no less, "whelping young dog" seemed apropos I suppose. At a very young age, she was wrapped in a blanket with fifteen garas. Her mother kissed her head and bid her farewell as she was left beside the halted erection of the Kolner Dom in the early thirteen hundreds. She was found by a wool tradesman, Carl Heller, who took her in and raised her as his own.

She was brought up with fractured teachings of a migrant faith from Carl's childhood -- yet another by-blow of a Romanian immigrant -- that had traveled with his own ancestry. As such, she practiced it to the best of her ability under the caretaker's roof. She loved him like a father and knew no better than to think he was just that.

A devotion to ancient texts was instilled in her by her adoptive father, most of which he'd recanted by memory. Her favorites, poems and songs, recited by a fire and sung to her as she fell to sleep each night. These things brought her fathomless comfort in her younger years.

Once a year, Carl would take Mari on an early morning walk, before the sun rose, for her favorite ritual: the planting of a fruit tree by a bank of nearby water. There she would toss a coin, a seed, and an agate into the meer and sing a song to herself three times over -- one that she was taught by Carl, who'd learned it from his own mother as a child.

Când te întorci la mine,

astfel soarta mea va fi anulată.

Such was the rearing and cultivation of learned traditions of my mother's life through the years. She would spend her days shearing sheep and refining wool for clothiers and tapestry weavers alongside her father. She would spend her evenings wrapped in the warmth of the hearth, head in her father's lap. Blanketed in stories of magick and miracles until she was fast asleep, her father softly singing one of many melodies to whisk her away.

In that sleep, one fateful night, there was an ominous knock at the door of Carl's modest home. A bellowing voice was shouting for the master of the residence. Carl awoke, sneaking to Mari's bedside and instructing her to hide beneath the burlap sacks of wool. She did as she was told, leaving a small hole for herself to peek.

Carl opened the door tentatively and with a loud slam it was kicked from his hand, knocking his arm against the wall. He braced himself in the door frame, or tried to at least, but it was no use. Storming into the house, three men shoved passed him and grabbed him under each arm.

"Carl Heller. You've been keeping something here for quite some time and dues are owed for it", the dark haired man's voice sounded like rolling thunder, deep and loud.

"Ulrich, we've been over this time and again, there is no person here other than myself. The girl you see is my apprentice, she comes and goes from the hills. I haven't a clue where she may call home", Carl calmly stated. Clearly this was a very well-rehearsed, and often recited fallacy.

"Carl, you are swine", the man guffawed in Carl's face. "You and I both know she's here, and we're going to find her. Tonight."

Mari heard the threat loud and clear and slid herself further beneath the bags that sheltered her. As she pressed backward, the hole she'd left for herself shrank and the bag sitting on top of her slipped forward and slumped to the ground. Much to Carl's dismay, and Mari's shock, she was given away immediately.

Ulrich lurched forward from his seat and closed the space between Mari and himself, spanning the room with only a few steps. Grabbing a handful of hair, he pulled the girl up and slung her into the corner of the room. Carl was held at bay by the two men in Ulrich's company and was forced to watch as Ulrich's body slithered down to Marioziota's. Not his daughter by blood, but in truth and in his heart, better than any child he would have even been able to bear.

Ulrich commenced to treat Marioziota, my dearest mother, like the discarded ragdoll she had always felt like. The trash that she had been named after, used and tossed aside after she'd served her purpose to Ulrich.

Carl watched, seething and writhing in blind rage. As Ulrich stepped away from Mari, wiping himself with her torn clothing, adjusting his trousers and spitting on the floor. Walking over to Carl, he placed a bloodied hand on his shoulder.

"That's dues. Interest will be collected soon enough", he grunted in Carl's ear.

Carl lunged within the confines of the men's arms holding him down. Ulrich flinched, almost comically, and lunged back, sinking a blade into Carl's abdomen. Pulling the knife from his flesh, Ulrich licked the crimson from the edge before placing it back in its small leather scabbard.

"That's interest, mongrel", Ulrich's voice trailed out the door as Carl was released from the thugs' grasp and slumped to his knees holding his stomach.

Mari's world fell silent as her vision narrowed to a pinhole. She trembled on the muddy floor and watched her father's life ooze from his body until he turned cold and gray. She fell into a deep sleep and awoke the next morning.

Pulling Carl's stiffened body from the house, she exhaustingly traveled up the nearby hill. Digging a shallow grave, she buried her dear father as she sang one of the songs he'd sung to her as he lulled her to sleep so many times.

She tried distracting herself with the labors of her father. Shearing, studying, singing, reciting verses and stories to herself. For months this went on, and for months she did well to stay hidden from the collectors and anyone else of status. She stayed in the shadows away from anyone hungry enough to try and take what she had left.

She tried to go back to the routine she'd learned over the last fourteen years, but she struggled more and more to fend for herself as her belly grew and grew. Nine months passed and silently, over the hillside where Carl was laid to rest, Marioziota gave birth to a small, feeble child. A baby boy.

Atop that hill, Marioziota held her baby as she shushed his cries. In the morning she would take herself to market in the commons. She would shill her wool, collect her coins, and at the end of her day as the sun set behind the buildings, she would return to her child, helpless and starving.

By day she would continue as she always had. By night she would sneak into Carl's home -- her home -- to tend her son in the warmth of a small glowing fire. She would tell him stories she remembered from her father. She would sing him songs of their people, if you can call them that, and he would fall asleep in her arms.

And once a year, she would plant a fruit tree by the rivers' edge and sing a song as she cast tokens to be swept away in the current.

I remember those songs so keenly, like she was still whispering them in the dead of night in my ears. I had nine beautiful years with my mother. Almost an entire decade before she disappeared. One morning she left for the market and that evening she never returned. I was left with my knowledge of wool, some songs and prayers and a few gulden lying about.

Nine years old, three thousand two hundred eighty-five days. That's when my second life began. My life as no one, as nothing. Entirely unremarkable just as all of my kinfolk before me. Alone and without direction.

Without purpose.

Without use to anyone.

Chapter 0.1

I spent the next few years of my life trying to make my way with wool, textiles, and all sorts of other menial things. The unfortunate thing about being a small, brown haired child with muddy brown eyes was that I was completely unnoticeable. This made selling things at a market very difficult, but it did make stealing a bit easier.

I would lift things from the market goers, clerks, and shopkeepers and hole up in the only home I had ever known. At some point, I found myself satisfied with this life. I stole only what I needed and tried to sell what I could. Some days worked out better than others. Some days I'd limp home after having been, quite literally, kicked in the tail out of shops and stalls.

At age twelve, a woman noticed I had been at her shop four times in one day and she caught me red-handed with pockets full of berries. Instead of a reproach or beating, she embraced me, the same way my mother would have on those cold nights as she sang me to sleep. I left the only home I'd ever known that night. With my home, I left my entire miscreant life behind me.

We boarded a small boat on the shores of what is known today as Norden and set sail to Kirkcaldy Scotland. That's where my new roots were set, and that place was what I called home for quite a few years.

The woman, as it turns out, was mute. I never learned her name, but we got along well enough. The widow of a shepherd, wool was also the only life she'd known. She was getting older and the work to keep the livestock healthy, shorn, and cart everything to town had taken its toll on her. The poor woman walked with a hobble, was hard of sight, and a prominence on her back caused her to groan as she sat and stood.

Kismet, it seems, brought us together. It had been nearly four years since my mother had vanished -- four wearily long, lonesome years -- and I was finally starting to feel at home. Home, however, without a mother is no home at all. Whimsical, beautiful, and indelibly etched in my mind were her songs, songs that I began to hum to myself as a comfort throughout the days and nights.

As I had done with my mother and as she'd done with her father before, once a year I began the tradition of planting new life. The old woman and I would venture to the bank of a river, stream, or loch in the highlands, and there I would plant a seed, or carefully press a living twig into the soil. I would cast tokens into the water while trying to recite the song as well as I could remember. I did what I could to keep the company of my mother with me, wherever she may have been.

Chapter 0.2

Years passed, sixteen of them by my count, and the kind, feeble woman passed with the last of them as the winter turned to spring in my twenty-ninth year. She had left me her earthly possessions which consisted of three sheep and one stout ram. They, too, were getting rather long in the tooth, and it would only be a matter of time before my supply of wool and consequent income would dwindle.

As such, I did the best I could with what I had. I would shear the sheep, making only a few pund per sack of wool and that had to stretch unmercifully through summer, autumn, and winter. I had made enough to purchase a new ewe and managed to get she and the old ram close enough that nature took course. One hundred forty-five days later, I welcomed two new lambs to the flock, an ewe and a ram, what luck!

As the cold months approached, and coin ever shorter in supply, I spent the winter tending the sheep as best as I could. Though I was no shepherd, I kept up with them well enough and they didn't seem to mind my methods. I sealed the paddock to insulate the walls from the winter chill.

The season seemed harsher than the years prior, so much so that a fire was lit and fed constantly throughout each day. There was no reprieve from the frigid elements though. Without money and barely any food other than what I could trap or find dead from the bitterness of the winter, I resorted to old habits. I began to steal from the farms, walking acres between each, risking frostbite with sopping boots and trousers.

Firewood, kindling and the occasional egg from a chicken coop sustained me for weeks. I rationed everything carefully to keep myself and the livestock alive and well. Halfway through the season, tragedy struck.

In the dark of midnight, an eruption of sound shook me from sleep. Rumbles of bleating and howling, yelping and snorting reverberated through the frozen twilight. Running to the paddock, I found a feral, emaciated wolf snarling at me over the carcass of three of my sheep. The two youngest and the ram had succumbed to the beast, but he trembled, bloodied from the mothering ewe.

Five against one aren't good odds for anyone, man or beast.

Pitying the animal, I edged towards the remaining ewes and shuttled them towards the house. At least there we would be safe and I had an ax if the poor canine followed. Piling in by the low flame of a dwindling fire, I fed another log to the glow and the sheep and I hunkered into an exhausted sleep.

I awoke the next morning and found one of the ewes had died in the wee hours. Down to a single living companion, I sheared, skinned and butchered the four decedents, premature by three months or so from the season. The harvest of wool was just shy of a single sack and selling it wouldn't happen until the thaw. The meat was paltry and leathery, hardly enough to sustain myself. The third ewe, which I named Margot, was the only survivor of the disparate winter. She and I would keep one another company until the weather began to warm. Spending freezing days, and brutally cold nights in our humble shack.

I found myself humming the same lullabies that my mother had hummed to me so many years ago. A comfort in an otherwise perilous situation.

Chapter 0.3

Early April and finally the thaw had arrived. Shearing the wool from my only friend, we traveled to the commons to sell our wares. Bringing her to the market square with me, the din of people was overwhelming. Every man, woman, and child were haggling and bartering for goods. The winter had been tough on everyone, and it showed in the pallid, vicious faces and hissing, angry voices. I sat in my small corner of the street with Margot.

I was approached by no less than three separate patrons, vehement that I should part with my scant goods for half the price. Insisting on full price, or an ample barter, I was spat on once, kicked twice, and threatened to have my home razed by a passerby just trying to get in on the action.

Late in the evening, while packing up exactly what I'd brought with me, I was approached by a rather dignified looking gentleman. He'd offered three times the price of my wool without allowing negotiation. I wasn't in a position to refuse, so I handed it over to his man-servant in shocked humility, humbly.

"And the ewe", he'd stated in earnest.

Surely I couldn't part with Margot, she was all I had left. I debated pleading my case, but thought of the long months ahead. Sure, I'd gotten a decent dividend, but what would I do next year?

Next year, Evescha? There is no next year, there is one sheep. This is all you have, yes, but it's all *you have.*

"Double", I rebutted curtly.

An eyelash was not batted. The man opened his pouch and spilled the remaining contents of it on the ground in front of me, clearly insulted by my confident reply. The man sneered, yanked the rope around Margot's neck, and stomped away in disdain.

The money he'd poured at my feet was considerably more than double, in fact it was nearly enough to purchase an entire new flock of sheep. Had we all not had the same horrific winter that may have been an option. If I were to have purchased a new flock, surely I wouldn't have made it off of the purveyor's property before I was killed for having this kind of money. Even still, no one would have fared any better than I had, and livestock was surely sparse.

Chapter 0.4

Meandering home, no reason to hurry now, I took long winding roads over the rolling hills of Scotland. Hands full of coins -- I had no place to carry so much money -- I found myself hailing merchants' carriages as they traveled home from selling their own goods. Purchasing a satchel, I filled it with bread, fruit, vegetables, and two portions of salted meat.

A few hours of mindless walking and shopping, it occurred to me that the same distant high blowing of a horse had been trailing behind me for quite some time. Turning my head to look over my shoulder, a man appeared to be following me in the distance.

Surely a coincidence, I thought foolishly.

I took my time winding through the hills and doubling back a few times to see if, perhaps, the man and his stallion would divert from my course.

He did not.

It was clear he had meant to follow me and the hour was getting too late to stay far from home, even with the night being balmy. Circumspectly, I traveled homeward, looking over my shoulder to confirm I was being pointedly, albeit ploddingly, hunted.

Arriving home, I made haste into the door and grabbed my ax, dull from a winter of splitting frozen firewood and chopping trees. I exited the hovel and stood by the doorway leaning on the tool. As the hoofsteps finally approached, the massive animal blew once more -- this man was clearly not kind as even the horse acted as if it was threatened by him.

"I believe you have something that belongs to me", the voice tacitly spoke.

"I believe you have the wrong man, sir, and I'd ask you kindly to leave from this place", terse with my reply.

The stout man moved deftly from his steed and to his feet, inches in front of me.

A finger finding my sternum, "You have something that belongs, kind friend, to me".

This man was not kind, and he certainly was no friend of mine. Raising the ax to my shoulder, he looked at me and smirked and grabbed my wrist, lowering it back down despite my best efforts to hold him back.

"I won't ask you again, shepherd", he hissed.

"You didn't ask in the first place, you cur".

Name calling may have been a mistake.

Chapter 0.5

The sun shone brightly in the sky as my eyes, or rather eye, cracked open. My head felt like it had been trampled by a mule, and it may well have been for all I know. Picking myself up from the ground, I brushed myself off with bloodied hands. I could not tell if it was my blood, or someone else's.

I walked to the stream towards the south end of the fields to clean myself and saw my reflection in the water. I had, very clearly, lost a fight I didn't remember having. A broken nose, an eye swollen shut, a bleeding ear, and a massive purple bruise on my jaw. The man looking back at me in the water's reflection was someone I did not recognize.

Cleaning myself up was a chore. As it turned out something was dislocated in my arm and it felt like my brain had dislodged itself from my skull. Vision obscured, I made my way back to my home tentatively. Opening the door took all I had in me.

Startling awake on the beaten earth floor, my head throbbed and violently I retched forward expelling any contents of a meal I'd had the day prior. I rolled to my side to prop myself up and the pain in my shoulder sent shockwaves through my body. Screaming, vomiting again, and falling from the pain, I smashed my head into the floor and passed out once more.

Wearily, I opened my good eye after some immeasurable time had passed and gingerly propped myself on my unaffected arm. Groaning to get to my knees, I managed to sit against the shoddy wooden door. My head was still screaming, and my eyes wouldn't focus. I slowly stood myself up and walked to the bed and sat on the edge. Very nearly falling over from the spinning of the room, I righted myself and reached for my satchel.

I came to find, as my hand returned empty that it had fallen off sometime between my apparent assault and my concussive return to consciousness. Laying back on the bed, I kept a foot on the floor and slipped in and out of sleep for what felt like days.

After the blackness dissipated my view once more, I no longer felt as though my head would split in two. Propping myself on the wall, I stood to find that my satchel had certainly not fallen off in the house. Trudging to the doorway, I looked outside and saw no trace of it either. Clearly I had been robbed. A point that would have made much more sense to someone with less of a concussion.

Chapter 0.6

I was now sheep-less, without money and with a busted up arm and patched up eye. What a sight to behold, eh? I opted to go to town that morning to see if I might be able to barter my services as a wool refiner, or textile dyer for something to eat, or information about the massive man on his equally ominous horse. Lo and behold, sometime after noonday, the felon himself ambled through the square tossing a bag of coins into the air and catching it. What's more, the rat was carrying my satchel!

I was in no condition to muster any kind of courage, so I watched him instead. Observing from afar as he mocked clerks, spat on beggars, and vandalized carts and stands. Truly, this man was scum.

I paid attention to him and his swaggering actions for an hour or so before he disappeared down an alleyway. *The hunter has become the prey*, I thought to myself with an over-exaggerated sense of confidence.

The man meandered around aimlessly, it seemed, through alleys and side streets of mud and stone. East to west, north to south, then back again. He was walking in circles. It dawned on me, possibly too late, that he'd noticed the shambling man with an eye patch and arm sling doing something that resembled walking after him.

I turned to renegotiate my own bravado, but it was too late. Once again, I was faced with this enormous man's chest. He grunted out a laugh that sounded like a bull ready to gore someone. A hand on my shoulder, a shove to the ground, and a boot to the face once more.

"Didn't learn your lesson the first time, didja?", he snarled.

Evidently I was hard-headed because I started to get up, asking for another strike to the ribs this time.

"You'd do well to stay down, you foul, mewling quim", his voice rumbling in my ears now.

I moved to prop myself against the wall I'd been thrown towards, but that move was too much for his comfort. Another swift kick.

This time I stayed down.

Chapter 0.7

Nursing myself back to health was no small task. To make things even worse was we were in the year thirteen forty-nine -- the year the Black Death had scoured Europe and had made its way to Scotland. Common areas were sequestered and back streets collected the dead. Plague doctors walked the streets with harrowing beaked masks and long leather dusters. Everything in the air smelt of lavender and death when they passed.

There was no work for a shepherd, much less a lame one on the road to recovery. I was able to find myself a bit of work tilling fields. The pittance it paid was enough to, occasionally, eat fresh bread. I had, once again, resorted to petty theft to keep myself alive.

On a nightly excursion to some of the more affluent domiciles in the region, I noticed a massive horse tied to a post outside of a tavern. I walked in, curious, and saw the man that had beaten me half to death sitting in the corner with a woman. I got myself closer to the thug and realized his company was no woman, but a girl, no older than I was when I came here with the kind mute.

His hands slithered over her legs and pried at her dress's hem. Her face twisted in disgust as he leaned towards her and placed his mouth on her neck, sloppily. She pushed him away, but she was so small in comparison to most and assuredly no match for the behemoth of a man. Slapping at his face, kicking her legs to get away from him, he swung a massive hand against her cheek and she immediately fell limp.

He stood and draped her over his shoulder before walking up the stairs to the rooms for rent. I followed him with trepidation, unsure of what I would do once I got to the top of the stairs. I grabbed a wrought iron stoking pole from beside the fireplace and slowly ascended the staircase. As I reached the landing, I heard an earth-shattering shriek from the room down the hall.

Fast as I could, I ran to the door and barreled through it re-injuring my shoulder. The man turned and was attempting to try and close the gap between us but his footing was blundered by his trousers around his ankles. The girl leapt from the bed and passed me out the door and down the stairs as fast as she could fly.

Standing above the man, I raised the iron rod overhead and slammed it into his skull.

"You've stolen something", I gritted my teeth, spitting the words out.

Wiping his brow, he turned to me. "And you've made a grave mistake, pig! All of this over a bag?"

A lunge toward me, and I with another blow from the fire poker. He fell back, eyes lolling in their sockets.

"My satchel isn't the problem, coward. You've stolen something from that little girl, something you'll never be able to return!" I stepped towards him.

Grasping for my ankle, I delivered one more blow with the pole and heard the snapping of his arm resonate after. A yowling scream, panting between his teeth, the man backed himself into the corner like an animal awaiting slaughter.

"Finish me now, whelp, or you'll not see the next spring thaw", he grimaced.

I dropped the poker to the floor, turned and walked out of the door. Down the stairs, and towards the exit, all I could hear behind me was the shouts of a humiliated man. Threats on my life, threats on my home, threats on anything he could anxiously name.

"Threaten all you wish, good man. I know your secret", I taunted him before walking out the door and back to my home. Hands empty, no food to eat, I laid my head down on my hay-stuffed pillow and fell into a satisfying sleep.

Chapter 0.8

Months passed and I was rewarded with balmy weather, which helped with crops and livestock in the area. Soon tilling the land of one farm turned into rotations of three separate plots. I no longer had to resort to theft for my meals. I was able to pay for my food at the market and prepare my meals in the comfort of my home.

By the beginning of autumn, I nearly had enough money stashed to afford three new lambs another shepherd had birthed on his own farm. They were slated for slaughter, but I convinced him they'd be better used to provide wool down the line in case we were in for more harsh winters such as the one that had passed. Three lambs would bear no coats being born so late in the season, but I'd had enough left over to keep us comfortable for the coming cold. I fixed up the paddock, prepped the wood for the impending months, and began preparation on the house to make sure I'd be able to stay warm and fed.

As the daylight hours became less and less, the seasons crawled towards cold -- winter was upon us. The village had recovered from last year, but everyone was wary to indulge in anything superfluous lest they be left with nothing and find an untimely end in another cold snap. Peaceful winds carried snowfall through the hills and valleys.

Among the snowfall, I prepared a meal of some of my dried fruits and nuts, and tended a small pear sapling I'd grown from a fallen limb in one of the fields I'd be working. I hummed songs to myself as I was wont to do and I would spend the evening preparing a supper to celebrate the New Year of Trees -- the only holy day I could remember; the keenest memory of my mother.

Chapter 0.9

A knock at the door interrupted my joyous chorus. Thinking nothing of it, I walked from the fire and opened the door. My hospitality was met with the simper of a mild-mannered man who didn't look so unlike myself.

"Fionnghall, sir. Pleasure to meet you. I saw the smoke from the chimney and wondered if I might bother you for warmth?" he asked kindly.

I opened the door to him, and he followed me to the modest meal I had prepared. I offered him a seat, and he obliged. We sat, we chatted, and we broke bread with one another.

After the meal, I cleared the scraps and saved what could be saved before donning my cloak and picking up a folded cloth from the corner.

"Please, make yourself at home, I'll return shortly. I have a small bit of business to tend on the banks of Garbh Uisge", I offered to the wanderer.

With a courteous nod, I collected my coin, agate and a seed from a pear, and set out to the riverbank to find a plot for my dear mother's ritual. The New Year of Trees will surely be bountiful and the pears symbolizing abundance will certainly see to that.

At the river's edge, I washed the dirt from my hands in the brisk water. I heard twigs breaking behind me, rocks under boots' soles. I turned to meet the gaze of Fionnghall, once again, only this time it was considerably less kind.

Behind him, a mob of farmers and townsfolk, many of which I knew and had sold goods or services to. Fionnghall stood tall in front of them, turning his back to me.

"This man, Evescha Heller, may look like any other man in our great land", he began. "I can assure you he is an immigrant!"

I was confused at what was happening. I narrowed my gaze to the crowd and walked towards Alba.

"Fionnghall, my friend, what is this about?" I inquired, reaching a hand toward him.

Swatting my hand away with haste, he launched himself backward.

"This Jewish swine is who has brought this Black Death to us. All of his kind are infectious with the thing and his presence here has damned our whole land!" he shouted, commanding the crowd to jeer and hiss.

"If we don't kill him now, surely his caustic existence will kill each and every one of us!"

The crowd swelled with agitation, and hands were raised demanding I be sent to my death.

"Kill the man! Rid us of this necrotic plague!" one man screamed.

"Who will have the honors, then?" Alba asked.

But no man stepped forward. Nervously, Fionnghall looked over the crowd.

"Will no man save this land?" his voice echoed in the silence.

Again, no man advanced.

"Then it would seem I must do this myself. Cowards!" his final address rang through the hills.

The wanderer walked toward me and raised a hand, feigning aversion, playing to the mob of people. Bewildered by what was unfolding, I didn't have the time to move from his grasp as he took hold of my arms. Then, a man walked from the crowd. A tall, ominous figure with a massive scar across his forehead.

"I believe you've met my brother, Heller, yes? Grishman Malort, servant to the house of Alba. A brother in arms and in deed", he simpered once again.

Staring into the eyes of the powerful man, it occurred to me that Alba was the manor atop Castle Hill, Stirling I believe it was called. Alba was a recluse, someone no one had seen save for ostentatious moments such as these. These moments did not happen often, and when they did, they were promptly covered up.

Covered up with things like, say a plague.

This was, one, Fionnghall Alba.

The burly brother-in-bond opened his arms wide and clapped both hands over my ears. The next thing I remember is the feeling of water surrounding my feet.

"You're awake, Mister Heller! Good, good", Alba smiled. "They've all left, as you can see. They're all scared that your blood will be spilled and damn them all to their deaths. Serendipitous that this Black Death arrived."

I stared into his eyes, briefly, then flailed my arms and legs to get up from the water. Or, at least, I would have flailed had I not been bound with my arms and legs hogtied together.

"Mister Heller, you see, my associate isn't the sharpest man. He doesn't think before he acts most times and it hasn't gone unnoticed by me. But, he is still like a brother to me", Alba sermonized, as if the crowd hadn't all skittered away long ago.

"He stole something from you, as I understand it, through quite the brutal assault", he shook his head. "He ought to know better, but alas he's, again, not the most sensible man. As I have also come to learn, you were beaten in an alley in the market square as well. Not exactly inconspicuous if I do say so myself".

"What are you talking abo--"

A finger to my lips, Alba shushed me like a child.

"The problem here is the girl you saw him with in that tavern. She, and her family I should add, have been dealt with. The unfortunate fire that occurred in the middle of the night at their home, sadly, took their lives. Seems embers were blown onto the thatching and they simply couldn't escape the blaze." The smirk that slid across his face was sickening.

His hands wrapped around my neck and pressed me to my knees.

"Now there's just you, Evescha Heller, who knows of his... ill-mannered handling of the young lady", Alba's grip tightened. "Only you, Mister Heller. So, you see, you must go away lest anyone come sniffing around his and, incidentally, my own affairs".

My legs buckled. I was going to die.

Alba leaned close to my head as he bid me farewell. Reactively, I butted my head into his face. Connecting squarely to his jawline, his lip split open and teeth smashed together.

Angrily, he shoved me toward the water. My head quickly enveloped in the freezing river, aptly named for its rough waters, and I was thrashed about as the wake crashed over me. I writhed and squirmed in Alba's grasp, but it was to no avail. Sputtering as he choked me, drowning me in the beautiful Scottish river. A moment frozen in time, looking up from beneath the water as if in a mirror. The man who would undoubtedly be my killer could have been my own kin if I hadn't been the only bastard of a bastard.

I kicked and flailed, my head breaching water every so often. Alba, gritting his teeth, seething through a bloody mess, spraying blood and saliva into my face. My eyes stung, my mouth foul with river water and blood, the light of the night sky began to close in. My eyes struggled to focus as they rolled into the back of my head. I inhaled sharply, feeling my lungs expand with icy water. I could breathe no longer. My head spun and then everything just... stopped.

Zion, my mother called it. "Gan Eden" to some. Heaven. The great beyond. The gentle breeze on my skin and the calming burble of a riverbank. The sun brightly shining, warming my face.

This must be heaven, I thought.

Epilogue

I was wrong, obviously, otherwise I wouldn't be writing this at all. I woke up downstream from where Alba had ushered me to my would-be doom. As ill-fated luck would have it, something happened that night and I have remained ever since.

It had been nearly seven centuries since that day. Some two hundred sixty thousand two hundred forty-five days -- not that anyone's counting.

I've spent all of that time being as aloof as I can. In my favor, I don't look like anyone in particular. That is to say, I look like nearly twenty percent of the worlds' population. No one would miss me if I disappeared, and I have done so through the years. No one would notice I was gone from work, or that I'd slipped off of a boat in the ocean.

No one would notice that I wasn't a world-class corporate CEO with the darkest of underpinnings when a raid happened in his high-rise office. No one would notice, because he, too, looks like nearly twenty percent of the worlds' population.

No one would notice that I have been imprisoned for his crimes, serving out multiple consecutive life sentences. Twenty-seven thousand, three hundred fifty-three days have passed and, at least so far, no one has noticed that I haven't aged a day.

I mostly run this place now, from the shadows, dealing with as little as possible, but controlling as much as I can. No one seems to have noticed that either.

I am Grady Sachs, or rather Evescha Heller.

I am thought to be Doctor Waylan Scott, Esquire.

I am no one.

Soon enough, they are going to figure it out.

Part Two:

No One Gets Out Alive

Prologue

Two hundred sixty-nine thousand three hundred seventy days have passed since that evening on the shore of Garbh Uisge.

Thirteen forty-nine, the Black Death had reached Scotland. I, a young man of thirty-something, was cleaning myself up at the riverbank from a ritual of the New Year of Trees. A ritual my dearest mother had taught me, and her loving caretaker before her.

Some bastardization of a Jewish and gypsy tradition, maybe an incantation even.

A coin, a seed of a pear tree, and a stone of purple agate went over my shoulder into the river.

I spoke the words, just as I had for so many years before.

Când te întorci la mine,

astfel soarta mea va fi anulată

Romanian, my bastard mother's illegitimate father's mamzer mother's native tongue.

When you come back to me,

So shall my fate be undone.

I can still taste it. The rough waters washing over my tongue as my lungs filled.

Presumed dead. Pleasantly forgotten for nearly seven centuries.

Now... now I see his face right in front of me, just as I had from beneath the cool water that night.

Waylan Scott, or was it Frank Naylor, or perhaps Dr. Winston Curdy? More importantly: Fionnghall Alba.

We two are kin. Not of blood, but in something more ethereal. Kismet.

Two hundred sixty-nine thousand three hundred seventy days have passed since that evening on the shore of Garbh Uisge. Yet a day has hardly passed if one were to look at either of us.

We are two of a kind, tethered for all time.

Bound; eternal.

Chapter 31

Grady Sachs stood -- more specifically he was strapped to a dolly as if he were Hannibal Lector -- in front of Waylan Scott. The *real* Doctor Waylan Scott, Esquire. The man who he'd been framed as some seventy-five or more years ago. The man who, over seven hundred years ago, drowned Grady Sachs, Evescha Heller then, and left him for dead to cover the crimes of his brother lest they reveal his own nefarious businesses.

Waylan simpered at Grady, his teeth showing, but only just. Clearly a practiced face to play coy to any point of authority if he were to be questioned about an alibi. A brilliant charm that had, evidently, kept him out of harm's way and faceless for centuries. Faceless, just like Grady. Forgettable, unremarkable, and untraceable if a profile were kept low enough.

That very trait had lent itself to Grady's advantage over the years as he noticed he wasn't aging. It gave him immunity to certain socialalties like public recognition. It offered him the ability to fade into the background and come and go as he pleased without note that he'd even been there at all. Incidentally, this trait is also what allowed Waylan to pin his entire life's' work (this modern life, at least) on him.

Grady seethed, sure he was foaming at the mouth as the man before him chortled to himself and turned his back looking at the array of security screens on the wall. Raising his right hand, he flicked two fingers in the air.

"Transfer day, Mister Sachs. There have been quite a few upgrades to the system since you were last serving time with the general population. We will be transferring you upstate. A new facility, lots of upgrades to security. The most modern of technologies" Waylan spoke, quietly melodious, as if he were writing a song of Grady's fate.

Lowering his hand, he grasped his other wrist behind his back.

"Farewell, Grady Sachs, or should I say Waylan Scott. I doubt I'll be seeing you again. Best of luck".

That was that. Grady was ushered from the control room, Waylan's lair, and back up to the main floor of the prison. Paraded through the cellblock, he was met with spit, jeers, and disdain. Men threw objects at him and took swipes at his flesh if they were close enough.

A freight elevator, a box truck, and then darkness. The door was lowered and all light escaped the hollow emptiness that surrounded Grady. He exhaled for the first time in, what felt like, minutes. Utterly befuddled in disbelief at what had just transpired.

It can't actually *be him, can it?*

How is that even possible?

Grady, how is any of this possible?

It's been centuries and you haven't aged a day. Is it really so hard to believe that nobody else was the same?

Grady pondered to himself for the ride, which seemed to take hours. The darkness enveloped him and he embraced the quiet as he was always wont to do.

Chapter 32

Grady slammed into the rear wall of the box truck he'd been loaded into as it backed into a loading area. The building was a massive gray and white set of boxes and sharp angles -- a homage to brutalist architecture of the nineteen sixties and seventies.

As the dolly was yanked from the truck, Grady's eyes were flooded with LED brightness and he cowered from it briefly. Cracking his eyes, he noted flat white walls, white ceilings, white lights, and white tiled floor. His restraints were removed and he was politely escorted to a mantrap where he was asked to remove his clothing. Doing as he was told, he felt cold shackles snap to his ankles, another set around his wrists, and a final band around his neck.

Feeling his feet lift from the ground, Grady laid horizontal in midair held aloft only by the mechanical appendages coming from beneath the flooring. A cloud of mist blanketed him as it filled the man-sized tube, followed by a pinch in his left thigh. The lights in the tube glowed crimson and he felt warmth on his skin as the condensation evaporated into steam around him. The arms stood him back to his feet, released themselves and retracted back from whence they came.

"Mister, Scott, is it?" an intercom blared in the plexiglass encasement.

No use fighting this fight anymore.

"So I'm told", Grady replied, snidely.

"Mister Waylan Scott, we would like to welcome you to the Bandash Memorial Reformation Facility", the robotic voice began. "Here, you will be treated as a citizen of this great nation and we assure that no harm will come to you during your stay".

My stay*? They're kidding, right? What is this, a Hilton?*

"Please be advised that the steam bath you were just given was standard delousing and antimicrobial mist. The red lights impregnated your skin with the steam from this bath, you will no longer require daily showering intervals. This is for your own safety as we have found that most security protocols are breached during those times".

No showers, got it. This place is something, that's for sure.

The unvarying voice continued, "The device implanted in your leg will act as your restraints. There is no need, here, to be handcuffed, or monitored personally. If an incident occurs that would jeopardize the lives of another of the Penalized, the capsule will release a two-point-two millimeter calcium pellet, followed by two-point-nine standard atmospheric units directly into your femoral vein. Upon introduction to your bloodstream, approximately thirty seconds later, an embolism will be created in the posterior communicating artery followed immediately by an aneurysm of the same blood vessel. The prognosis for this systemic operation is fatal."

Step out of line, get brain blown up. Got it.

"Please step forward through the glass. Once again, welcome to the Bandash Memorial Reformation Facility". A click and the placid voice was cut off.

Grady stepped forward and was given his garments, a thin silver thermal blanket, and a small pillow. A guard stood at the door like a sentry. The door whisked open and showed a green-lit hallway behind it. Another guard approached Grady, took hold of his right elbow, and led him through the portal.

Chapter 33

The green hallway pulsed as light flowed in the direction of "proper conveyance"; a docile voice from the facility intercom repeated this anytime a body was in motion. Red hallways were prohibited, orange were restricted, blue hallways were common areas, and yellow hallways were privileged zones.

Grady was escorted down a few green hallways, through a yellow room where men were playing billiards, and finally into a massive blue atrium where the guard released his grip. Every bit of fifty stories high, the walls were covered in plexiglass walls with sliding doors that partitioned off each of the Penalized from one another. Single bunks to each room, white lights flooded each eight-by-eight foot box.

A lift raised to the thirty-first floor and Grady followed the guard closely as he walked off of the platform. They walked down the corridor and Grady took note of the railing, the depth of the catwalk and the spacing of the doors. The walls were dense enough that you couldn't hear your neighbor, and the doors and front-facing walls were so thick, there's no way anything could get through them. The guard halted his stride, turned to his right like a soldier, and raised his left hand straight over his head. The red cell in front of him flashed green, then white as the door cranked open on its mechanism, an airlock gasping upon release.

Like being let into a high-end suite in a Vegas hotel, the guard stood beside the opened door and held a hand out, almost as if expecting a tip. Grady stood idly at the door and surveyed the three walls behind the pane of everything-proof glass. His leg emitted a small tone and he felt heat beneath his skin.

Obedience, that's what that little pinch buys them.

No sooner had he stepped into the cell when the door slid shut and locked, pulling air through the seal until completely closed. Grady sat on the edge of the floating plexiglass slab protruding from the wall. Placing the pillow against the wall, he laid back, closed his eyes and exhaled.

Relax now, Grady. Silence.

Hang back, figure this place out. Then we'll figure out how to get Scott. He's got to pay for this, all of it.

Somehow.

A tone of bells crackled through the intercom system. A relic of the past, preserved in a file somewhere in the machines that ran this place -- even the dirty record under the sound was intact.

Grady's eyes, once more, cracked open to the violent lighting of this sterile building. He rubbed the sleep from his eyes as he sat up and looked at the glass wall. An image appeared on the door, a silhouette of a man, built in stature like Grady. Entirely featureless; faceless, just like Grady had come to be. He stood at the doorway, the nothing-man mirroring him in the glass. The door breathed open as the silhouette glowed green.

No guards? They really do just let you roam around, huh? Interesting.

With no one to escort him, Grady walked freely from his cell and turned down the corridor that pulsed toward the lift. Keeping in mind the colors denoted to accesses, he wandered through the various hallways and rooms. Blues, greens, yellows. Grady searched for reds as he hugged corners and meandered trying to look aimless in his mannerisms.

Two rooms east of the cellblock. Three to the west. Sixteen floors down, another twelve floors up. That's just this wing, Grady, but it's a start.

Another tone sounded from the intercom and the hallway Grady was in turned orange.

Restricted. What happened?

Grady's leg suddenly seared with pain. The tone he'd heard wasn't from the walls of this facility. His leg was warning him of his curiosities and the consequences they could bear. Grady turned and walked with purpose to the nearest green area he could find. The lights pulsed as he entered the room, indicating he was to follow with their flow. He did as suggested and the pain in his leg subsided.

As he followed the pulsing chartreuse lights, Grady compliantly found himself at the cafeteria. At the smell of food, his stomach lurched. It was painfully apparent that he'd not eaten in quite some time. He grabbed a tray and got in line with the other Penalized. A capsule was placed on his tray and an empty cup. Nothing more.

The hell am I supposed to do with this?

Watching the other Penalized, Grady noted the machine at the end of the line people shuffled towards and away from in equal measure. A fellow inmate set his tray under the machine and it was lifted into a void. Five seconds later, the capsule had vanished and in its place was a meal, of sorts, on the tray. Grady stood at the machine and followed suit and, just as before, the machine produced something he was meant to eat.

As if prison food could get any worse. What even is this?

Pudding-like substances. Shades of green and yellow.

"What the hell is this stuff?" Grady muttered under his breath.

"Protein, fat, carbohydrates", an old man muttered back from the other side of the steel table. "Say its macro nutrients; all we need to survive. Water's funny tastin' too; wouldn't drink it. Makes the lights go funny; gives me the spins."

The emaciated codger stood from his seat and poured his glass over his head and smiled at Grady. Grady nodded at the old man and politely smiled back. The old man unsteadily walked toward the door of the courtyard, his head lolling around as if disconnected from his neck.

All of the years inside must've gotten to the poor guy.

Grady shook his head at the thought of spending so much time in a place that a person's mind would slip. The irony was not lost on him. He hunched in his seat and took a long guzzle of the cool water.

Chapter 34

Euphoria. A feeling Grady hadn't felt in decades. Tastes of comfort, moments of calm, sure, but nothing as pure and pristine as this.

His stride was airy and his head was light as he followed the pulsing green strobe along the guided path. The blue area he arrived at was throbbing with people. The warmth of the room was palpable and Grady felt the desire to lay down. The floor, he found, was carpeted in a plush and luxurious pile. Nestling his face into the floor, he rolled facedown against it. A peaceful smile turned the corners of his mouth, just slightly.

How did I get here? Where, even, is here?

Grady's voice echoed all around him.

Is this a dream?

As he'd heard his own narration, suddenly a rush of water took him over and he was barreling through the current, unable to right himself. Over and over he turned, smashing arms, legs, and head into craggy rocks and debris underwater. A final blow to his head and then there was nothing.

Grady jolted awake and scrambled to get to his feet. His head swam, spun, and he fell back to the floor as he retched violently and vomited the same green ooze he'd eaten back up as though untouched.

Attempting to stand again, he gingerly braced himself on his hands and knees. A cold sweat washed over him and he began to shake almost as though he'd had the flu. He stood, wearily, and held his stomach now lost of its contents, and stammered toward the green hallway. The blue light in the room turned to orange and Grady's leg emitted the familiar tone which indicated he needed to find an exit.

Unable to move with much haste, Grady limped to the hallway just as the room snapped red. He reached down and held the searing flesh of his leg trying to dull the pain. A head rush overtook him once more and he tripped over his own feet slamming his shoulder into the wall as he tried to stay upright.

The green light ticked forward showing him the way. Grady tried to move, but everything was spinning around him. The light blinked orange intermittently every fourth or fifth pulse.

Hallways are restricted too?

Trying to follow the lights' instructions, he ambled forward, limping and holding his stomach with one arm as the other hung limp by his side. It was all he could do to get to the blue lit cellblock where he resided.

Barely making it to the doorway, Grady retched once again and spewed the rest of his stomachs' contents all over the corridor. A small chime sounded and Grady let himself fall inside the door just as it slid shut. A small mopping robot attended to the mess he'd left outside of his cell and skittered away as quickly as it came.

The white lights faded in his vision once more.

Chapter 35

Awakened by the pre-recorded tones of the morning, Grady raised a hand and held his head. He'd gone to push himself from the bunk only to find the other wasn't exactly cooperating just as he'd taken note of his shoulder being, very obviously, out of socket, dropping towards his ribcage. He stood and searched the room for his sink, unable to open his eyes for the migrainous pain behind them.

As he fumbled around the unfamiliar walls, he found purchase on the faucet and turned on the cold water. He splashed handfuls against his face trying to wipe the sick feeling from his body. He blurrily looked into the mirror and assessed the damage to his shoulder through slitted eyelids. Grady inhaled as he held the dislocated wrist, pulling the arm ninety degrees into his torso. He set his elbow on the edge of the toilet-sink, turned his body to rotate the arm outward and then dropped his weight out from under himself. Crashing to the floor, he shuddered an exhale as his shoulder snapped back into place.

Pulling himself to his feet, he sat on the edge of his cot and hung his head, suddenly not hurting nearly as much by comparison.

What in the hell happened here, Grady?

The food? Are they poisoning the food?

No. No, no, wait. This is Waylan, it's got to be. "No harm will come to you", yeah right. This whole place is probably another part of his network of lackeys.

The song remains the same, Grady, be careful. This isn't over.

The day came and went. Grady stayed in bed, and to his relief, he was left alone to do so without any issue. He pulled himself from his bed the next day and shuffled from the door as the airlock released. The blue cellblock led to a green hallway, which led to the blue cafeteria. Wary to eat anything from the prior days' events, he got himself a cup and dispensed water for himself and necked the first two cups as though he'd just left a desert.

Chapter 36

Grady's vision cleared as he stared up into the sky. The sun was either rising or setting, -- he couldn't quite be sure -- and the air was brisk.

What time is it? How did I get outside?

He rolled to his side to prop himself up. Grady felt the same swimming sensation, then the spinning, and then the ejection of his guts into the grass. Wiping his mouth, he pushed himself to a seated position and stared at the building in front of him. Massive and rigid. Unique in the many angles and aggressive lines, but somehow still entirely shapeless, lost in its own design.

This place is going to try and kill you, Grady. Waylan will not make this easy, this is only the start.

Grady looked skyward as rain started to fall. Drops touched his skin and he could smell something in the air as the rain fell to the ground and steam rose from the heat of the day. He opened his eyes and the liquid burned slightly, and as it fell over him, he licked a droplet from his lip.

Chlorine.

The sky... it's not. It's not real. This place is a self-contained biome.

Quickly, he got up and rushed beneath the awning and watched the courtyard as the steam billowed from the turfed ground and a fog of mist formed nearly two feet high and stagnated in place. He smelled the chemicals hanging in the recirculated breeze.

No need for showers, they pump that mist through the entire system.

Before Grady could put the entire thought together, thunder boomed and lightning struck -- red lightning. His leg began to burn, a light glowed under the skin. He dashed to the adjacent wall toward the door. He reached his destination, but the door didn't open. He banged on it and a guard stood just inside turned away, ignoring him entirely.

"Open the door! Hey! Open the damn door, you prick!" he shouted.

Crimson lightning streaked the courtyard again and his leg pulsed with scalding pain. Frantically, Grady slammed his fists into the door like a panicked gorilla. Lightning darted directly to the center of the turfed area and his leg shot a spasm of heat through him that radiated his entire body.

"I didn't put myself out here! Open the goddamn door, pig!" he screamed against the thick, soundproof glass.

Another lightning strike, another boom of thunder and Grady fell to his knees as the pain seared so keenly he was sure the flesh would melt from his bones.

The door opened, the sky parted immediately back to dusky blue, and the guard stepped aside, refusing eye contact just as they all were trained to do. Grady crawled on his hands and knees into the vestibule. He watched a surveillance camera turn its gaze directly toward him. Grady raised his right arm and gave the camera the finger as he stood up, walked toward it, and met its leering stare with his own.

Not today, Scott. Not today.

Chapter 37

Grady had limped back to his cell after he'd stopped at the cafe for a cup of water and some bread.

We can't trust anything else. Bread and water, Grady. We've made it through on less.

Grady leaned against the wall as he sat on his bunk. He sipped the cool water and ate small pieces of the bread. Careful not to indulge too much, just in case he had to ration himself.

They are watching. He *is watching, Grady. Always watching. He'll take bread out of the food rotation if he sees you only eating it, or eating too much of it.*

Grady searched his cell for cameras, but there's no way he'd be able to find them at the rate of technology. He was grossly unfamiliar with a lot of the advances that had occurred in the last seventy-five years. Cameras could be all but invisible at this point. Pinholes, bolts, screws, maybe even something attached to a bug.

Hang on, bugs! Wasn't Waylan's whole modern world empire created off of a camera drone bug? Surveillance bugs, that's got to be how he's watching!

Scanning the area as casually as he could, Grady found no sign of an insect. Not even an ant crawling across the floor. He sat back and relaxed in the thought that, for now at least, it seemed as though he wasn't being watched. He took a few gulps of the water and laid his head against the wall.

Grady's eyes shot open and he found that daylight had faded from the corridors and common areas in the cellblock. He'd clearly taken quite the beating from the impromptu rainstorm-slash-torture session from earlier that day. His neck ached from being bent against the wall as he'd slipped down it in his slumber.

He splashed water on his face and looked into the mirror as he stood at his meager prison vanity. The water ran down his forehead and cheeks, dripped from his jaw where he saw stubble. As he studied his chin, flesh gave way to muscle, sinew and bone. His face began to melt in his reflection. His eyes bulged as the water ran down his face, chunks of skin and his forgettable features with it.

Grady turned to his bunk and grabbed the pillow and wiped his face as quickly as he could. Feverishly he tried to scrub the acid-water from his face and neck. His skin burned and he hissed in pain. He pulled the pillow away and found there was nothing on it. No gore, no blood... nothing. Grady looked back into the mirror; everything was fine. His entire face was just how he'd left it before he'd fallen asleep. He sat back on the bunk wrapped in confusion.

Grady, you're losing it. If the water was acidic, everyone would be dying. Wait...

Grady recalled the old man in the mess hall the first day he'd arrived at this new facility, something out of a science fiction novel.

"The water", he muttered to himself.

He held the glass to the light and noticed nothing peculiar about the liquid. The cup seemed normal, nothing smelled of chemicals. He tasted the water and noted nothing more than a typical chlorination-and-something-else flavor of most any tap water. He'd always chalked it up to fluoride -- isn't that what they added to municipal water works? He took a long swig of the water, emptying the cup, then stood and stared into the mirror.

Nothing happened.

His face remained the same. The skin hung on his skull as it always had. He stared at himself, positive he had lost his mind. But then, he watched his eyes dilate in his reflection. Grady turned his head away. He stared at the bright light in his cell, then back to the mirror.

No change.

His eyes remained dilated.

"You bastard. There *is* something in the water, isn't there?" Grady whispered to the mirror. "You're micro-dosing this whole place with something. For what? Compliance?"

Smirking to himself with smug pride, Grady laid on his bed. He'd figured out the crux of the game, he thought. He laid his head down on his pillow and found it soaked and cold.

"Little prick, and now I have a wet pillow too", he snickered as he let the involuntary drug take him into the night's sleep.

Chapter 38

Alarms blared and Grady sprang from his comatose slumber. The door of his cell slammed open and the corridors flashed orange to red epileptically. His eyes couldn't focus as he ran from the door and into the hall, nearly toppling over the railing. He found the green catwalk at the end of the wing and sprinted for it. His leg started to signal and he felt the all-to-familiar burning in his thigh. He took a diving leap out of the strobing proscription and slammed into the unforgiving floor of the green hallway.

He gasped for breath as he rolled over and propped himself on his elbows. The cellblock alarm ceased and the entire area was blotted out into a crimson hue. Then something curious came to mind. In all of the panic, Grady had been the only one running through the cellblock. He shared the area with hundreds of Penalized. How it was that he was the only one running for his life, he wondered.

He brushed himself off as he got to his feet and edged towards the cavernous red room. He craned his head around the corner to take a look into the cells. His leg pinged its warning as he gazed upon dozens of glass walls. Behind each of them, a prisoner, unaware of any emergent situation.

He turned back to the green hallway as the lights began to pulse, guiding the way to somewhere. Grady cautiously obeyed the emerald navigator.

Alright, new variable. Next piece of the puzzle, Grady.

The green hallway gave way to a yellow room behind a massive set of glass double doors. The doors pulled inward on their tracks and

Grady stood at the entryway looking around. The lights along the hall blinked orange intermittently.

Yeah, yeah. I get it. Go into the room.

Stepping into the room a few paces, the doors darted shut. The room was entirely empty save for a single metal chair in the middle. An absurd sight given the sheer size of the room, but then again, absurd and over the top was Waylan Scott's modus operandi. Grady walked the hundred or so feet into the center of the mammoth space.

He sat, crossing his arms and raising an eyebrow.

"Well, what now?" he demanded after a few silent minutes passed

A screen appeared midair a few yards in front of him, nearly as wide and as tall as the room. Grady craned his neck to take it all in. A chair appeared in the middle of the screen. Then a man from far across the room. Then the man walked closer and sat in the chair, facing Grady. But, the man in the chair *was* Grady.

A recording?

The man crossed his arms, spread his feet, and sat back raising an eyebrow, mirroring Grady's posture.

Am I still high on whatever's in the water? What's going on here?

The may uncrossed his arms just before Grady uncrossed his.

Hold on. How did that…

"Mister Scott, or rather mister Sachs", the hologram spoke.

"Waylan, you bastard! What's going on here?" Grady shouted into the room, the image miming him.

I'm hallucinating. I have to be. The thing spoke, but its mouth didn't move.

"Tsk, tsk, tsk... haven't you learned by now that my only objective here is to watch you squirm?" Phantom-Waylan's smile dripped from every word. "Almost eight hundred years to find you, now another eight hundred more to keep you captive and bat you around like a cat with a cornered mouse."

Grady went to stand up from the chair to address the ghostly screen and the figure within followed. Then, the man in the hologram fell to his knees. He folded over and writhed in silent pain. Grady felt the sting in his leg and quickly took his seat. He was, as Waylan had stated, good and well cornered.

"What do you want with me? All of that was so long ago, how could I possibly be a threat to you anymore?" Grady pleaded. "How is there anything left to settle?"

"Evescha Heller, there *is* nothing left to settle", Waylan addressed Grady by his birth name. "I simply want to understand, much like yourself I'm sure, how it's possible that either of us are even in this position. Timeless, unaffected by the ebb and flow of the continuum; life passing us by as we plod through it."

The screen glitched and the man in the chair stood up and walked towards Grady, growing larger. The mouth suddenly matched Waylan's voice as he spoke.

"You must be bored by now, aren't you, old friend?" he continued. "I have been *so* bored through all of these years. Living many lives, under many names, but always coming to a similar end until I moved on. Someone, like you, always found out something and uncovered a small thread of truth that could have unraveled everything."

Again, Grady shouted, "What the hell does that have to do with me? You've gotten so good at disappearing, blending in, why make me pay for everything you've done this time around? You've already killed me once. Isn't that enough?"

"Ah, but I didn't, did I?" Fionnghall's words hung in the air, and Grady's head hung on his shoulders.

"Alba, I am old, I am tired, and I am bored. You're right. This life, if you can even call it that, is not natural. We aren't meant to live like this. We aren't meant to *keep* living", Evescha softly admitted.

The lights in the room blinked red. The screen disappeared. Grady heard the tone from under his skin, then a beep followed by a pop. His leg jolted and the pain forced him to his knees. He doubled over screaming in agony just as the hologram had moments before.

"Goodbye, Heller. For good this time." Alba's voice was followed by a low click.

Grady was alone, as he'd always been. Alone, afflicted, and dying.

A shock of numbness followed by incredible, horrific pain in his skull. Grady tried to stand, to move, to do anything as he grabbed either side of his head and attempted to scream and vomited instead.

Falling to the floor, Grady's eyes rolled back in his sockets.

A seizure, then a twitch. Then nothing.

The eternal Grady Sachs was dead.

Interlude

A light? He did it! He actually did it!

I don't know if I should be grateful or furious with him.

Finally, silence. Eternal, blissful, heavenly silence.

Who is that in the distance? M-mother? Mother is that you?!

Standing next to her… is that… me?

Când te întorci la mine,

astfel soarta mea va fi anulată

Those words. I know those words. My mother's prayer for the trees. Life for the trees.

My life flashing before my eyes -- if that's the case, we may be here awhile.

Când te întorci la mine,

astfel soarta mea va fi anulată

Those words again, but who's that at the rivers' edge now?

Me, again? But I'm older now…

Alba!

Evescha turn around, turn around!

Evescha, guard yourself!

Când te întorci la mine,

astfel soarta mea va fi anulată

The water is so cool, so refreshing.

Heavenly.

Fateful.

Chapter 39

A body bag is loaded into the back of a truck, stacked beside sixteen others. Exports from the Bandash Memorial Reformation Facility. Two bangs from the palm of the guard inspecting the truck, the doors were closed and the vehicle drove through the gates and toward the highway.

Grady opened his eyes and inhaled too quickly, coughing and sputtered against blackness. All he could see was black. He tried to move, but found he wasn't able to lift his head very far, nor his legs or arms. No room to his sides, a flat, hard surface below, and no space above him. Just pitch darkness.

He began to hyperventilate. Grady inhaled sharply through his nose and exhaled through his mouth. Again, and again, and again. He felt his heart calm with his breathing.

Alright, Grady. What's going on here?

Is this purgatory?

You lived long enough that there's no place for you among the rest of the dead?

A bump forced Grady's body from its rest. Another shifted him to the side. A third followed by a long rumbling, vibrating his whole body. He could smell the vinyl now, as his senses were shaken into consciousness. He reached in front of his chest and felt a seam. A zipper.

Not dead after all, huh?

The movement around him halted and Grady heard voices muffled through layers of whatever was surrounding him. Two loud bangs and the ground seemed to slip from under him.

A truck. You're in a bag, in a truck, Grady.

The vehicle halted once more, a beeping sound drew Grady's hands to his thigh reflexively. No warmth met his palms.

It's gone. The tracker, the node, whatever it was, it's gone.

Waylan must have thought destroying my brain would kill me.

What does he think this is, Night of the Living Dead?

The sound of a bay door opening, a cargo door following that, and Grady's head slammed into the flooring under him as he was yanked from the truck by his feet. Two sets of hands grabbed the short ends of the bag and he was swung, then flung on top of a pile of something. What felt like cadaveric knees and elbows jutted into his ribs and back and he was carted to god knows where.

Bangs of doors, jolts to his head and neck, slams to his feet and ankles. Each threshold and expansion joint jostled him about. Again he was unceremoniously hoisted from the pile of bodies and then laid on his back on a cold surface. The sound of sliding metal halted as Grady skidded forward, his feet touching a wall. A soft thud, latching, and then complete silence.

Cold overtook the air around him.

Shit! They think I'm dead. I must have been transported to a morgue offsite.

Hold on. He truly thinks you're dead, Grady.

You're in a morgue offsite.

Get out of this bag, get out of this meat locker.

Get Waylan Scott.

Chapter 40

Grady panicked for a moment feeling claustrophobic and utterly trapped. Wiggling in the body bag, he nudged himself to the left and found about six inches of space. Back to the right, about the same. He raised his head and found he'd had a little bit of a ceiling to work with. Grady wedged himself against the wall to one side and he was able to get his arm over his head. He searched for the zipper on the bag.

Hardly able to get a finger between the teeth at the edge of the zipper stop, Grady was able to prise the slider just enough to move it downward on the teeth. After a few painstaking seconds, he was able to get a hand out of the bag and grasp the zipper awkwardly and push it downward until his head was uncovered and he could breathe a bit better.

The thirty-six degree air sent chills down his spine as he pushed the zipper downward towards his chest and finally made enough of a hole to get his entire arm out. Grady pulled the slider down as far as he could and shifted against the opposite wall to free his other arm from the bag tucking the vinyl under his neck as he craned his head backward.

Upside down, he was able to note a small piece of metal bolted to the door. He fidgeted with the small rectangle and it shifted counterclockwise and he kept turning until it met some resistance. He gripped it firmly and twisted as hard as he could and heard the door latch pop. Grady pushed the door open, grabbed the hatch and slid the drawer out of the locker.

As he sat up on the slab to free his legs from the black bag, the shift in weight caused the entire drawer to pitch backward and crash to the floor.

Blinking the black from his eyes, his ears rang from the impact. Just then, Grady heard heavy footsteps from outside the room. He clamored to his feet and tried to right the steel gurney into the locker. The footsteps stopped outside of the door and two voices could be heard, but not understood. Grady gently slid the drawer into the locker and closed the door as quietly as he could. It was then he realized there was nowhere to hide -- this came just a second before he'd also realized he was naked as the day he was born.

A small hatch on the wall at the end of the cold storage lockers caught his eye as he heard the second of two series of beeps at the large insulated door. He dove for the hatch, twisted the tiny knob and crawled inside the cramped shaft just as the door whined open.

"You heard that, right?" one of the voices asked.

"Unless we're both losing our minds, something is in here, and it's alive." the second man's tension evident in his tone.

"Guess we should start opening the lockers?"

Latches were pulled and doors were opened. Grady listened intently as the men silently inspected the cadaver storage.

"Sixteen full, four empty. Just like we left it." A relieved sigh followed the statement.

"Let's get the hell outta here then. This place gives me the creeps."

The large door swung open and shut with a slam. Grady crawled from his hiding place into the large autopsy room. A steel table in the center with massive flood lights overhead and a wall of storage lockers for twenty bodies. Grady opened and closed each door, just as the men had, and counted sixteen shrouded bodies and four empty units.

They weren't counting me. I am not supposed to be here.

Waylan Scott, always keeping his secrets.

Grady took a chance and cracked the massive entrance door to look out into the hallway. To his good fortune, he'd found that no one was manning the door. A typical mortuary, he guessed.

Not much need for armed guards for a bunch of dead people, Grady.

Waylan's hiding you in plain sight. Does he own this place, or is this so far off the grid that you can't be traced back to anything?

Then it dawned on Grady.

I'm Doctor Waylan Scott. As far as anyone is concerned, he's got to be dead by now. There can't be a file saying he's dead again.

It would seem Waylan had truly believed the aneurysm would spell the end for Grady Sachs. He'd intended to dispose of him in secret, rid any record of the no-name body of the unremarkable man who took the place of another plain-looking man some seventy-five years ago for horrific crimes against humanity.

Waylan Scott was likely dead, many years ago now, as far as the public knew. Grady Sachs never existed in any way that anyone would remember. Now, as far as the only man who would have known who he was, Grady Sachs was good and well deceased. Fionnghall Alba and Evescha Heller remained.

Chapter 41

Grady had a problem, it had occurred to him: he wasn't supposed to be here *at all.* Sneaking out of the underbelly of a mortuary wasn't exactly an easy feat considering this was a one-way-in one-way-out kind of operation. Doubly hard considering he wasn't exactly clothed for any occasion beyond a bath or, un-ironically, cremation.

He cautiously walked around corners in the unfamiliar understructure and found a staircase. He could hear low music playing from somewhere at the top of the steps.

A regular funeral home.

Retracing his steps, Grady went back to the refrigeration room and leaned against the cold steel autopsy table. The huge door to his left, a massive rollup door behind him, the lockers to his right and another door, he'd finally noticed, in front of him. Grady put an ear to the door and listened for a minute to see if he would hear anything. Deciding the coast was clear, he pushed the door open.

Softly lit, Grady walked inside and saw a desk, a lamp and a coat rack. A sweater hung from the rack, a pair of sneakers and a gym bag sat beside it. He rummaged through the bag and found a pair of shorts, some socks, and a t-shirt. Sitting in the office chair, he donned his costume, laced up the New Balance six-oh-eights and walked back to the entrance.

Grady, this is a funeral home, idiot. You can't exactly go walking out of the morgue into a room full of mourners wearing the funeral director's gym clothes.

We need to find another way out, pal.

Turning back toward the room, Grady noted another doorway on his left. He heard a roaring behind the door as he listened for voices. Opening the door, he found three metal facades with doors in the center.

Crematory chambers. This was Waylan's plan.

How was he going to play this? John Doe just shows up in a morgue and he expects no one to question an undocumented body?

The room swelled with heat as the furnaces roared consuming the bodies inside. The air was acrid and smelt of death and smoke, even beyond the well-sealed chambers. Grady stared in wonder into the porthole in one of the units and watched as the flames danced inside. Then he'd seen it. Out of the corner of his eye, an emergency exit.

Straight out the back. That might just work, Grady. Now how to get it open without sounding the alarm.

Grady went back to the funeral director's office and dug through his bag and found a small card, probably an ID card to get him into a twenty-four hour gym. Hurrying to the emergency door, he stuffed the card into the jamb and fished for resistance near the center where the break-bar was. Careful not to lean into the door, he pulled the card back and shoved against the small obstacle and the door dislodged just enough.

Hot air blasted past Grady as he walked through the portal. It was evening, the sun was setting and Grady hoped that would help his escape from the property. He took off from the back of the building up a small tree lined hill. He surveyed the area and found he was directly in the center of a grand and expansive cemetery.

Mausoleums and headstones as far as the eye could see, he started walking through the forest of death. His gait went from walk to jog and soon from a jog to a sprint. Noticeable as this may have made him,

Grady was terrified to be so close to death. Ever since he'd awakened on the riverbank so many years ago, he never trusted the buried truly remained so.

Chapter 42

Running through a cemetery at dusk is probably not the best way to keep your head down, Grady. At least we're out of there though.

Now, to find out where the hell we actually are.

Grady had taken what felt like a short cut through the cemetery only to find himself on the side of a winding country road. He looked towards the sky and decided to follow the path of the moonrise. The waxing crescent hardly shone light on his path. Grady stayed close to the road, but buried himself behind the tree line. An eerie fog spread across the ground and stretched over the roadway.

As if waking up dead and running through acres of a graveyard wasn't enough for one night. What is this, a Stephen King novel?

Taking advantage of his new shoes, Grady paced himself into a light jog trying to make up some ground to wherever it was that he was headed. Completely unsure of his whereabouts, he saw the glow of civilization in the sky ahead of him. He cut through the woods and came upon a lone chrome building.

A diner in the middle of nowhere? Come on, this can't be a thing, can it?

He walked through the clearing and towards the parking lot looking over his shoulder. A few older trucks, mid-eighties sedans and a conversion van sat sparsely spaced outside the building. Grady walked to the door and looked inside. He didn't notice anything particularly peculiar so he opened the door and walked in quietly and slid into the booth closest to the door.

How far away did they take me to make me disappear? This place is lost in time. Must be some podunk backwater in the sticks somewhere.

A waitress walked towards him and paused at his table and tapped her foot impatiently. Grady noted the agitation and ordered a coffee and a glass of water. She rolled her eyes, turned away with a huff and went to fetch the drinks.

Grady grabbed the menu and peered over the top of it at the other patrons. All of them seemed to be alone, spread across the bar seats and a few of the booths. He didn't notice anything specifically odd about them, but something here felt off.

Flo brought his coffee and water to the table, both of which Grady found were tepid. He sipped the coffee and picked up the glass of water. Staring at the cup, he suddenly felt skeptical of the entire situation. He looked around the diner again, paranoid he was being watched. He sat the glass of water down as he recalled the laced water from the Reformation Facility.

Sweat beaded across Grady's brow and he stood up as calmly as he could and backed towards the door. He reached an arm behind him to push it open, but felt what was clearly not a door against his palm. Warm and cottony, he pulled his hand away quickly and turned on his heels. He was face to face with a man he recognized but couldn't place. The man looked Grady up and down before grunting at him and shoving him aside with his massive forearm.

Against his better judgment, Grady walked toward the restroom and shut himself in a stall.

This is like a fever dream. Is Waylan still messing with me? Does he know his plan didn't work?

How would he even be able to know that, Grady? Unless...

Frantically, he stripped his borrowed clothes from his body and started frisking himself for strange bumps, nicks, cuts, or even moles that weren't there before. He searched his skin with his hands and found nothing. He exited the stall and slammed the deadbolt on the door closed. He looked in the mirror and spun in circles, positive he'd find something and still came up short.

Grady, you're losing it. This is what he wants.

Keep it together, old friend.

Waylan Scott thinks you are dead.

The world thinks Waylan Scott is dead.

No one here is looking for you.

No one here knows who you are.

You are no one.

Putting his clothes back on, he walked from the bathroom back to his seat in the corner near the door with his head low. He slithered into the booth and looked up to take another sip of his coffee when he noticed the man he'd bumped into was sitting across the table from him.

"Far ways from West Elm, ain'tcha?" the man asked, his eyes on his own mug.

"I dunno what you're talking about, friend. I'm just passing through on my way to a funeral tomorrow." Grady fabricated a story as quickly as he could.

Looking up from his coffee, the man stared directly into Grady's eyes. "Seems to me you just come from one...friend."

This is not possible. You've lost it, this is all a dream, a hallucination, something. Grady, wake up! Wake up!

The man sat down his cup and placed both of his hands on the table. Grady watched as he slid from his bench and stood at the end of the table. He nodded toward the door and walked outside, lighting up a cigarette as he walked through the doorway. Grady asked the waitress for a hot refill at the bar top. With her back turned, he palmed a knife and then took the cup with a small smile.

"I'll be just outside having a smoke." Grady tilted his cup towards her and she rolled her eyes and turned her back once more.

Chapter 43

He walked towards the door, which seemed like a death sentence. Grady wasn't sure why, but he felt like he'd been here before. The door closed behind him and he walked towards the streetlight pole where the man had propped himself.

Smoking coolly, he took a drag and flicked the butt directly at Grady's chest. Grady jumped back from the taunting gesture and sipped his too-hot coffee. The man lit another cigarette and straightened himself up. Pulling his jeans up, tucking in his shirt, and rolling his sleeves to his elbows, he didn't make a single sound before he launched toward Grady.

Reflexively, Grady threw the scalding coffee at the man. The giant doubled over holding his burned face and Grady took the opportunity to shove a knee directly into it. The man took a knee and reached, blindly, for Grady, his eyes slammed shut from the caffeinated napalm.

Another kick to the man's head and he fell over, limp. Grady looked around the parking lot frantically and didn't see anyone. No one had left the diner, no cars on the road, nobody in sight but him and the unconscious man.

Grady rummaged through the man's pockets and found a ring of keys. He went to the nearest vehicle and tried the valet key. Nothing. He ran to the next car and still nothing. He knew if he'd kept running from car to car trying keys and handles, someone was bound to come out and question him. They would find the unconscious man and god knows what would come from that.

Grady tried one more door of a pickup truck and it was unlocked. He jumped inside and tried to put the keys in the ignition, but it was no use. Whatever he'd stolen from the man certainly wasn't for a vehicle. He took a minute to try and regroup his mind in the silence of the truck. Holding his head in his hands, eyes tightly closed as he pushed on his temples.

You're fine, Grady. This was a fluke.

You're an outsider in a small town in the middle of nowhere.

You look like you just left a Zumbathon on top of that. You aren't exactly blending in.

You're being paranoid. No one knows who you are.

No one cares that you're here.

Just figure out where you are and get out of this place.

Abruptly, there was a tapping on the window of the truck. Grady's mind flashed back to sitting in the parking lot of the West Elm Shopping Plaza. A mysterious nobody of a man. Frank. The agency. Inventaratus. It all flew through his mind like a bolt of lightning.

Another tap on the window and Grady snapped back to reality. He opened his eyes and turned to see a nobody of a man standing outside of the vehicle. Rolling the window down, Grady addressed the man with a smile.

"Can I help you, sir?" the man asked.

"No, thank you. No problem here. Just trying to wake myself up before my drive home", Grady lied.

"It's just that, well, you're in my truck, sir", the man politely stated.

Grady looked around the interior and turned to the man as he scratched his head. Luckily, he didn't have to fake the look of confusion on his face.

"Guess that's why these keys didn't work, huh?" Grady tried to choke a chuckle out. "I've got one just like this parked over..."

Grady pointed and there were no cars in the parking lot. Everyone had cleared out of the area. The building was empty, and the lights were all off.

No. No, no, no, no. No!

The man backed up from the door as Grady let himself out of the truck with as much composure as he could muster. Backing towards the tailgate, Grady watched the man close the vehicle's door. He turned his head to Grady and then looked up at the sky. He raised a hand above his head and pointed two fingers in the air.

Grady watched as the man made a meaningless gesture to nothing and a cold chill ran up his spine. He looked to where the man was pointing and saw the moon, now fourteen days further along to a full orb in an eerily clear sky. The halo around the moon swelled and grew brighter until the entire sky was flooded with white light.

Grady heard a ringing in his ears and it kept getting louder and louder. He squatted on the ground shielding himself from the brightness and holding his ears as he screamed in agony and doubled over as he vomited. His field of vision dimmed, tunneled to a pinhole surrounded by blackness. Through a needlepoint of consciousness, Grady saw the same face that haunted his dreams looking down at him, simpering as always.

Grady looked around the interior and turned to the man as he scratched his head. Luckily, he didn't have to fake the look of confusion on his face.

"[illegible] that's why these [illegible] don't work, huh?" Grady [illegible]. "I've got one just like this parked over[illegible]."

Grady counted and there were no cars in the parking lot. Everyone had cleared out of the area. The parking lot was empty, and the [illegible] were off.

[illegible] No.

The man looked up from the [illegible] and [illegible] of the truck with [illegible] as he [illegible] towards the [illegible]. Grady watched the man [illegible]. He turned his head to Grady and then looked up at the sky. He raised a hand above his head and pointed two fingers in the air.

Grady looked at the man [illegible] the sky, [illegible] only [illegible] a full or [illegible] sky. He [illegible] around the moon [illegible] and then the entire sky was [illegible] with white light.

Grady heard a ringing in his ears and it kept getting louder and louder. He collapsed on the ground shielding himself from the [illegible] and holding his ears as he screamed in agony and [illegible] as he [illegible]. His field of vision [illegible], [illegible] in a [illegible] surrounded by [illegible]. Through a [illegible] of consciousness, Grady saw the same [illegible] looking down at him, smiling as always.

Chapter 44

"Goddammit, Heller! I really thought that was the one", a voice guffawed.

Grady attempted to open his eyes but could barely see anything. He was nearly blind as he heard the all-too-familiar voice of Doctor Waylan Scott, Esquire. Grady blinked as his vision returned bit by blurry bit.

Waylan stood over Grady's fetal body, curled from the pain he'd just endured.

"Aneurysm and all, and you still are alive and kicking. I'm amazed, honestly. I really thought I had it this time. Cut off the flow of oxygen and trigger a full brain death. I had an inkling it might not work, especially when you started screaming." Waylan shook his head, pondering his chin.

"That's the most humane way to handle the Penalized. Usually they just slump to the floor and it's a done deal. We pack them in a truck, ship them off to a crematorium in the hills, and that's that. But you..." he looked at Grady in wonder.

"I cou-" Grady struggled to speak. "I could've tol-told you that, prick", he choked out.

Shivering the cold hands of death from his body, Grady unwound himself from the knot of pain he'd formed on the floor. He tried to sit up and managed to only roll onto his back and stare into the industrial ceiling of the cavernous room. Scott looked down at him from above, surreally as this was how he had looked when he'd killed him the first time.

Feebly, Grady reached for Waylan's ankle. Waylan stepped backward a few inches evading his grasp with nonchalance.

"Evescha, you will have to tell me how you surmise this all happened someday, our shared condition. Perhaps we can meet regularly and regale one another with our histories and the feats we've accomplished over these many years. For now I think however, you will go back to the hole where you belong. Guards." Alba waved a hand and Grady was pulled from the floor and carried out by his underarms.

Tossed into his cell, the door glided shut and Grady laid on the floor and wept for the first time in as long as he could remember. His life ended centuries ago. He was a man from nowhere with nothing. A man at the wrong place at the wrong time. He'd found out early on in his immortality that he could not surround himself with people, and he'd have to leave a place after long before anyone started talking.

Evescha Heller was a vagabond of time. Without the hope of anything other than loneliness. He had no one. Through centuries of time, he had no one. It was only then, in that moment on the floor of his cold prison cell, that he realized he had always had someone. He always had Fionghall Alba. This thought made him heave with sorrow, feeling more loneliness than he'd ever known before.

Chapter 45

Nemesis.

This word kept repeating over and over again in Grady's mind.

Nemesis. Waylan Scott -- Fionnghall Alba is your nemesis. Through all time, he has always been there. Watching, somehow always watching. When did he first suspect we were akin in this curse? How long has he been counting the days like I have?

Grady grinded his teeth as he sat in the mess hall staring a hole straight through the steel table. It had been months since Alba's failed attempt to rid himself of Evescha once and for all. Another one hundred seventy-two days, to be exact.

Waylan left Grady alone. There were no coups in the Reformation Facility for his life. No guards allowed Penalized to enter his cell. No lights changing overhead and spelling his imminent, yet constantly foiled, doom. Grady was, quite simply, invisible to the machine that thrummed around him.

The Reformation Facility teemed with criminals just as any other prison would, but all of these men were docile. Calm as Hindu cows. They befriended one another, but not by means of gang affiliation or moronic tattoos. They intellectualized, or at the very least conversed, with one another and found common ground in things like their own pasts, the follies that brought them to this place, and the families and loved ones they inevitably left behind from their poor judgment.

Grady watched all of this unfold day in and day out. He observed and made mental note of the men that seemed to be approached most often. Grady decided he'd need to socialize if he was to make any headway in this place. *This place is like any other place, Grady. These men can be bought. They can be traded.*

They can be employed.

He got up from his seat and walked to a table where men were discussing, to his shock, philosophy, of all things. Discussions of Marcus Aurelius lectures on Stoicism and concerning oneself only with that which he can control. Neitze's philosophy of Perspectivism: that there can never be a singular universal perspective on anything, meaning that truth wasn't real, but only a figment of the beholder's mind. Jung's concepts of interpersonal relationships and how people relate to one another as a reflection of how they relate to themselves.

Most curiously, though, were the discussions about William of Ockham, the man responsible for the philosophy of Occam's Razor. William of Ockham was a man of Grady's, or rather Evescha's time. An agent of the Catholic Church, a philosopher that returned from Italy to his home in Germany in the early thirteen hundreds after being excommunicated from the clergy. Occam's Razor is the thought that, quite plainly, the simplest explanation is likely the best one.

Grady spent weeks waxing these topics with the Penalized. Grady even started to feel as though he'd formed a rapport with them after weighing in on these great philosophers and their thoughts. Little by little, Grady started posing questions against these philosophies to the men for consideration.

"If a person's consciousness was to become eternal, let's say, clearly that would prove the Death of God Neitze believed in so heavily. If God is truly dead, ironically through the belief that a god can only exist through disbelief, how does that reflect how a person interprets their own reality?"

"You're mixing and matching here, friend" one man interjected.

"That's the point of philosophy, Gerry, to debate and grow the whole damn thing" another retorted in Grady's defense.

"If a god cannot be proven, there is no god to disprove."

"Yes, but, god can only be disproved if one believes he exists at all." Grady replied. "So a god has to exist to the non-believer in order to prove that he can't exist."

"But if the mind is eternal..." a third man's words hung in the air.

"Nothing can be true other than what the mind knows, then", Gerry stated matter-of-factly.

"Nothing can be true other than what the mind *experiences*", corrected Grady.

All four men sat silently until one of them took a breath and asked the question that was idle on everyone's tongues. A question that no one dared to ask after all of these weeks and months passing talking of eternal consciousness and immortality. A question that, among these prison scholars, seemed beneath them.

"How would someone *become* eternal?" finally, one of the men asked.

Grady replied, inquisitively "That is the question, isn't it?"

Interlude

What can you control here?

How are Fionnghall's taunts and musings with your life reflective of the way he perceives himself?

If he truly believes he is immortal, but he also believes I can be killed, where's the line there? What's the truth of the matter?

The simplest explanation, Grady. You can figure this out, but keep it simple.

Thirteen forty-nine, Scotland. Fionnghall Alba visited your home on the eve of the New Year of Trees.

You left him in your home. You walked to the riverbank with your tokens.

A coin. A seed. Purple agate.

It was there that Fionnghall found you, deceived you -- turned the township against you.

But no one wanted to get their hands dirty. The man that stayed in the background was forced into action.

His hands were around my neck. He held me underwater. He taunted me, told me I was being framed for his brothers' crimes.

I head-butted him in the jaw.

He forced me under the current and I flailed to break free of his grip. My head bobbed above water.

I can still see his face when I sleep. Maniacal eyes, bearing his teeth in a murderous sneer. Shouting with a mouthful of blood from the blow to his face...

There has to be a simple explanation for all of this.

What are you missing, old friend?

Chapter 46

The years since his imprisonment had been eventful in modern medicine. Psychology leaned into micro-doses of naturally occurring substances. Western medicine had taken a similar approach and started working with blood borne pathogens and commensal countermeasures for all sorts of ailments, some of which involved cutting-edge nanotechnologies.

Cancer was being controlled through circulatory manipulation and the introduction of certain non-pathogenic agents. Hybrid medications with low doses of MDMA and LSD were able to revitalize the minds of Alzheimer's and dementia patients, even causing full remissions in over seventy percent. Psilocybin was used in psychiatric facilities regularly and pain management through blood infusions amassed staggering results.

Grady poured himself into researching all of these advancements and he uncovered quite a few studies that seemed to line up with Waylan's facility.

> Psilocybin is used in psychological and pharmaceutical rehabilitation facilities worldwide. The micro-doses of this substance are introduced through varying means, however the oral route of diluted concentrations has proven to be the most effective. The dulling of negative human emotions, most notably agitation and consequent anger, has proven to ostensibly instill compliance among the convalescent. Furthermore, the use of hypodermal implants of Five-HTP and L-theanine increase the effects ten-fold.

Adverse side effects of the hematological supplementation range from psychosis to mania, the most common of which is paranoia and hallucinations. These side effects are monitored closely as dosages are incrementally increased until the desired medicinal reaction is achieved.

Nanotechnology has also proven unreservedly effective in controlling hallucinatory episodes in patients with schizophrenia, psychosis, and rudimentary detoxification. These technologies, also introduced hypodermically, when utilized properly can alter the communications to the brain from the amygdala satiating fear responses and outbursts. The technologies have also proven to be effective in altering the perception of basic senses of touch, sound, and even sight.

Experimentation with light therapy and different wavelengths of UV radiation have been introduced to these studies and are returning with astonishing results. Red lights breeding fear, yellow lights instilling a sense of solitude; orange increasing the body's nervous reaction and creating tension, and blue lights rousing a sense of calm and aiding in communal activities.

The water...Waylan is using the water to control everyone in here.

That's why there are no assaults. That's why they all talk like people to each other. That's why no one cares about who someone is in the company of.

No one cares about their clothes, scars, tattoos or dialects.

It's the water and those implants they administer during processing.

Grady rubbed his leg where his implant had been inserted when he'd arrived at the Reformation Facility. It occurred to him that he no longer had it. Waylan had forgotten to shoot another one under his flesh. He wondered if that was a mistake, or a purposeful move on Waylan's part.

Assume it was done on purpose. Stay vigilant, old friend.

Grady spent a few months buried in research of psychedelics and the effects on the human body. He spent his time in the common areas, the courtyard and mess hall watching the inmates intently. He saw psychotic breakdowns as dehydration caused men to down liters of the prison's water during a sitting. He'd realized that these outbursts went unnoticed by the other Penalized. The guards simply cleared the body as they slumped over, having been deemed a danger to others by the automated aneurysm induction system. Everything else in the Reformation Facility just continued to move around the events as they occurred.

Drooling messes of men, nearly comatose with serotonin syndrome would seize in their cells at night. The light in the corridor would simply glow brighter as an indicator for men in white jumpsuits to gather a body and carry them away on a gurney. Again, unnoticed by anyone other than Grady, it seemed.

He made note that, while he could see the lights fluctuate, he was no longer seeing hallways and rooms changing colors. Grady had also taken account of the fact that he was, seemingly, unfazed by the water supply. What was more interesting is that his sparing consumption -- only enough to stay hydrated throughout the day -- kept his mind from racing and allowed him to concentrate on the task of Fionnghall Alba's downfall.

Ozzy rubbed his leg where his implant had been inserted when he'd arrived at the Reformatory. Suddenly it occurred to him that he no longer had it. Waylan had forgotten to shoot another one under his flesh. He wondered if that was a mistake, or a purposeful move on Waylan's part.

Assume it was done on purpose. Stay vigilant, old friend.

Ozzy spent a few more hours online in research of psychedelics and the effects on the human body. He spent his time at the common areas, [illegible] and his [illegible] window [illegible] the new psychoactive [illegible] caused [illegible] down [illegible] the [illegible] were used by the other inmates. The inmates simply ignored the boys as they slumped over, talking [illegible] automated [illegible] [illegible] finally [illegible] the events as they unfolded.

Feeling [illegible] emotions [illegible]

[illegible]

[illegible] anxiety [illegible] induced by [illegible] pressure.

He made note that while he could see the lights flicker, he was no longer seeing rainbows and neon-glowing colors. Ozzy had also taken account of the fact that he was seemingly unfazed by the [illegible]. What was more interesting is that his soaring concentration [illegible] only allowed him to stay hydrated throughout the day — kept his mind from racing and [illegible] led him to come [illegible] on the tasks [illegible] Alba's downfall.

Chapter 47

On the anniversary of Grady's second death, he was escorted from his cell through a maze of hallways by one of the guards. The white hallways all blended together -- everything looked sterile, lifeless, and identical. Grady felt calm for the first time in a long time, surrounded by inordinate sameness.

His escort stopped at the end of a hallway and folded his arms behind his back. Grady took it to mean they had arrived at their destination, or rather *his* destination. A door slid into its pocketed frame with a hiss and closed behind Grady as he walked forward. A small, carpeted room with light wood paneling and a solitary oak table in the middle. Two chairs and either end of the table and nothing more.

Hesitant to take his seat, Grady stood by the doorway and watched as the opposite wall split open and Waylan Scott walked in with his arms out at his sides greeting Grady with unnatural warmth.

"Evescha, my friend! How have you been? Settling in nicely, I hope?" Alba exclaimed.

"Waylan". It was all Grady could muster in response.

"Please, please, let's drop the charade of these adoptive names. We are among kin here, are we not? Fionnghall, if you will".

"Fionnghall", Grady feigned cordiality, "to what do I owe this esteemed pleasure?"

Alba paced along the back wall of the room, a hand held aloft as if he were about to recite a passage from Hamlet.

"Evescha, it has been a year since your sophomore un-death. What should have been a time of celebration and relief of the end of your long suffering became something more... curious. Instead of dying, or at least completely, you rose back to life as if touched by the gods."

Grady couldn't help but recall Jung's theories on interpersonality.

He believes we are of the gods. Killing me was a test.

"I wonder, Evescha, what was it like being on death's door?" Fionnghall inquired with genuine intrigue.

He's scared of dying, isn't he, Grady?

"You left this mortal coil for nearly twenty minutes" Alba claimed. "Something must have happened in that time. Tell me, what was it you saw? What did you hear? What was it like being on the precipice?"

Grady's dream replayed in his mind. Awaking in a body bag stark naked, escaping a mortuary. The graveyard, the forest, the clearing and a lone diner from the past. The smoking man, the death, the truck, the paranoia. All of it rushed through his mind as Fionnghall's diatribe continued.

"I wonder, Evescha, what would happen if we tried it again? What if we celebrated your anniversary with ceremonial homicide? Wouldn't that be fun?" Alba snorted a stifled laugh.

Grady sat alert, very aware of what was just suggested.

"If you're going to do it, just do it. I'm tired of this conversation, Alba. Get it over with."

Waylan walked to Grady's end of the table and placed his hands on Grady's shoulders. Grady winced slightly at the sensation and sat patiently, awaiting his fate. Waylan, however, just slapped him on the shoulder like an old friend.

"No, I don't think so, Evescha. Not this time at least. I think, this time, we'll part as friends", Waylan mused. His next words, he spoke quietly, just loud enough for Grady to make out.

"Agus nuair a thilleas tu, tig an dàn maille riut"

Chapter 48

Grady was unescorted once he was out of the elevator from Waylan's quarters. He was lost in thought and waved to the guard as if they were acquainted in a past life.

Those words... Gaelic. Is Scottish his mother tongue, or is that a coincidence? Agus nuair a thilleas tu, tig an dàn maille riut. An insult? An inside joke to remind me of where this all began?

Grady found himself, once again, in the library, but this time pouring over books of medieval Scotland, archaic Gaelic dialect, and translations through the ages.

Agus nuair a thilleas tu, tig an dàn maille riut.

It took some time to dig through language as it evolved through the ages, but he'd pieced together the puzzle after a few days.

And when you return, fate will come with you.

Grady puzzled as he sat back in his seat and stared at the ceiling repeating the translation to himself.

And when you return, fate will come with you. And when you return, fate will come with you.

Return? To come back. Fate...death? And when you return...

Maybe you isn't formal, maybe it's just speaking personally of something inanimate?

Grady was reminded of his dear mother, Marioziota, and the words she would speak over her son -- the words that young Evescha would cling to after his mother abandoned him.

Când te întorci la mine,

astfel soarta mea va fi anulată

When you come back to me, so shall my fate be undone.

Surely Waylan Scott -- Fionnghall Alba, hadn't held onto his Scottish heritage all of these years. The man hasn't let a grudge go on behalf of his business partner for eight centuries, Grady.

Holding onto his lineage though… that's a risky play being removed from time as we are.

Research of Gaelic evolution and geographic dialects turned into the medieval faiths of Scotsmen. Polytheism, in particular, stood out to Grady. A reverence of a variety of deities and ancestral beings, Scottish polytheism wasn't so unlike Greek mythos. Gods of war and peace, light and dark, heaven and hell, sky and earth. The more Grady read, the more he couldn't stop thinking about the words Alba spoke -- the words that were un-ironically so similar to those which he was taught as a boy.

Grady had carried those words as a memory of his mother to whom he never got to wish goodbye. To a man like Waylan Scott, however, it was almost as though those words haunted him through time. Fionnghall Alba had always been a white-collar criminal, a splendidly allusive one at that.

The words fate and return weighed on Grady's mind as he dove deeper and deeper into these gods of an ancient religion. The Morrigan and The Dagda, the gods of the gods, were of the highest revered in that time. The Mother and Father gods who had control over life and death itself intrigued Grady most over the weeks of reading.

Prayers, ceremonies and rituals were carried out to appease these gods. The Irish druids spent weeks in prayer to them, built monuments to them. Scotland's adoption of this faith was something of a direct insult to the growing footprint of Christianity in the thirteenth century. By the thirteen hundreds, many highlanders had taken it as their own.

Tokens were buried in the soil with seeds and saplings with words of return being chanted over the turned earth. Trinkets were buried with the dead and songs of fate were sung in hopes that the families of the deceased would prosper long lives once the gods were paid their tributes.

Fionnghall Alba is afraid of dying.

Waylan Scott, that immortal and infamous bastard, has spent his whole life waiting for his comeuppance.

He has willed his fate into something and knows that death is lying in wait to take him.

He believes The Morrigan and Dagda have been sitting patiently for him to slip up.

Grady closed his books and held his head in his hands and laughed to himself. His laughter grew until he was cackling in the middle of the library filled with silent Penalized. The guards looked over at him with confusion and the inmate responsible for the area asked Grady if he would mind leaving so as not to disturb other Penalized.

Crying with laughter, Grady saw himself out of the suddenly stuffy room and walked to the courtyard. The day was balmy and clouds were rolling through manufactured blue skies. Grady looked up and saw the pseudo-sun and closed his eyes as he tilted his head upward. The men in the courtyard hurried past him as the rain started to fall. Remembering his last time in this area, Grady felt pity for the men as they rushed inside. He knew they had all seen red, heard alarms, and felt unbearable burning in their bodies.

Grady stretched his arms to his sides and smiled. A peace washed over him that he hadn't felt in twenty-seven thousand eight hundred ninety-four days.

Chapter 49

The simplest answer is usually the best answer.

Grady had found the theories of William of Ockham much more helpful than he'd ever thought they would be. The answer, Grady had decided, was to return that which Fionnghall left behind. Now the question was what had Waylan forsaken for his gift?

Grady's days returned to the norm of walks, reading, and mess hall conversations. Mostly, he kept to himself otherwise. The Reformation Facility provided him little in amusement, or anything beyond simple pleasures. Grady didn't go looking for a return on his investment of time in the place either. The druidic histories he'd read had offered him a new lane of literature to delve into, however. He'd found he enjoyed reading about the history of his homelands quite a bit.

Magic and mystique was as thick as a morning fog over the hills of Scotland. The same was true of Grady's own birthplace, Germany, and that of his mother's, Romania. The stories of druids and gypsies, Judeans and pagans littered Grady's cell walls as the books stacked up. He'd all but stopped his socializing and allowed himself to be enveloped into the worlds of his past.

The Romani, he had learned, were an intertwined people with Jewish religion and culture. They were often persecuted for the same reasons throughout history, and it wasn't unheard of for excommunicated Jews to join the nomadic ranks of the gypsies. Grady's mother, as it turned out, was one such person. Her mother had traveled from Romania to Hungary, and her mother before her from Turkiye.

The bloodline of these people, both Jews and Gypsies, was very important to their culture. As far as what Grady could remember from his mother's stories, his lineage was entirely maternal until him. He was the only boy to have happened among the generations of illegitimacy he'd been born into. Raised by different parents and caretakers, somehow the traditions had continued throughout.

Grady read of pacts with the dead, amulets and trinkets to ward off evil, and most curiously, the similarities between the pagans and polytheists, Romani and Celt, druid and gypsy. Both of these faiths would make offerings and bargains to their deities, and their deities would do the same with them. Gods, however, were not as specific as those farmers asking for a good reaping.

Celtic gods, and most higher gods of polytheism, were tricksters. They would wrap words in beautiful packages and spin the minds of their subjects to make them believe that they were getting something they asked for. In reality, the gods have always been selfish and wouldn't dare grant any good graces without levying a heavy tax. Some would promise a hearty crop for land, but then a flood would erode the farm from the mountainside. Some would assure safe travels, but would not divulge the devotee would be interned along the way.

Men are fickle and shortsighted. Gods have existed for eons. Boredom led them to swindling the devout for entertainment. Boredom and spite.

Waylan thinks he is *a god.*

Eight centuries, and he'd left me alone. Suddenly he decided to play with me like a cat with a trapped mouse.

He'd been watching me for some time, perhaps, but he never made a move until I got too close.

The thing with games, though, is there are incursions and reprisals. A person can observe a game from afar and master the plays. Someone watching close enough can determine a way to overthrow a master with their own strategy. Grady was reminded of Sisyphus and his humiliation of the Greek gods. Sisyphus thought himself smarter than the almighty Zeus and after cheating death on two separate occasions, he was forced to serve his time in hell rolling a boulder up a hill. The issue being that Sisyphus smugly believed this wasn't a curse, just another opportunity to show how stupid the gods were.

Sisyphus watched the game the gods played and beat them with their own moves. Sisyphus went too far by playing his hand three times, though. The gods were on to him and they, in turn, defeated Sisyphus with his own grand design.

This is not the gift you think it is, Waylan. You are cursed just like I am, you're just too smug to realize it.

Chapter 50

Another year had passed and it was early in the morning when a guard stood at Grady's door as it slid open.

"Happy anniversary, sir," the man uttered.

It was the first time Grady had heard any of the guards speak. He slid on his shoes and walked down the corridor. The guard stepped out of Grady's way and allowed him to take the lead.

"You know the way, Mister Heller. He's expecting you."

Grady walked through the halls at an unenthused pace. He looked into the cells and recreational areas as he walked by and watched the early risers take part in their morning rituals. Some worked out, doing endless push-ups and crunches, others on their knees praying and chanting.

Coming to the end of the corridor, Grady boarded the elevator and took it to Waylan's sub-basement floor. He startled for a moment before he walked into the hall where Waylan was waiting for him. In his hand, he held a small monogrammed box with Grady's, or rather Evescha's initials on it.

"Please, come with me. I've had lunch prepared for our visit." Alba smiled as he bowed with an arm extended showing the way.

Untrusting of anything that could come from Waylan Scott's mouth, Grady walked cautiously into the large hall. The same table with chairs on either end in an otherwise barren room. Grady took his seat and placed the box on the table in front of him.

"I suppose you want me to open this," inquired Grady. "I also assume whatever this is is meant to kill me?"

Waylan hung his head and exhaled with a chortle. "My friend, we are beyond that now I think. Don't you agree?"

Grady nodded with a raised eyebrow and unwrapped the box. Inside was a handkerchief, also monograms in golden thread, with Evecha's initials.

"Second Anniversary is cotton, as I understand it," Waylan took his seat. "I can appreciate the lack of creature comforts in this place, cushy as it may be. I figured a man such as yourself would appreciate some facial linens."

Grady held the kerchief up to the light, stared directly in Waylan's eyes and picked his nose with the cloth. Intending to show his disdain for Waylan, he realized all he'd done is prove that it was useful instead.

"I appreciate the gesture, Wayl-- Alba. I don't know that we're at the gift stage of our relationship." Grady held the handkerchief up as a toast and placed it back in the box. "Maybe we should take this time to get to know one another instead", Grady played into the ruse.

Waylan waved at the guard and a small staff of men and women brought finger foods and sandwiches to the table. The only thing missing was tea and it would have been a garden party. Grady helped himself to some refreshing cucumber sandwiches and a glass of water.

Grady, keeping his endgame in mind, began by asking Waylan a simple question.

"How did you wind up here, Fionnghall?" Grady asked as he shoveled a sandwich into his mouth.

"Ah, well'" Waylan began, "penitentiaries was a business that I hadn't gotten into over the years, if you can believe it. I wan--"

Grady interrupted him, for once. "No, no. Not *here*, Alba. How did you end up here, with me, in this impossible scenario?"

Waylan folded his hands on the table and smiled as he closed his eyes. "Only fitting you understand why I'm here since we're both aware of your background. Curious as it may be precisely *how* you're here at all. Perhaps that's another conversation for another time."

Fionnghall spoke to Evescha about The Dagda and The Morrigan and their disdain for humankind. The need for sacrifices to appease them and the games of life and death they would play with mortals. Grady had figured their conversation would get here eventually. He was pleased that his theory may have been true after all.

"You see, the lineage of a Scotsman is patrilineal. The father's blood is passed to the son. The first born, in legend, would be bestowed the blessings and curses of the father as well. The name carried a great weight, Heller. We only have our names, after all", Waylan pontificated.

"Alba is one of the oldest names in Scottish history", Grady affirmed.

"It is", agreed Waylan, "yet it was not the one I was born with." Waylan's eyes stared into the distance as his words quieted.

Grady's posture sharpened at those words.

"I think that's enough for today", Alba commanded.

Waylan waved a hand in the air once more and the table was cleared as Grady's chair was pulled out and he stood up.

"I appreciate your time, Fionnghall, truly", Grady smiled as he showed himself out.

Grady interrupted him, for once. "No, no. Not here, Alba. How did you end up here with her in this impossible scenario?"

Waylan folded his hands on the table and smiled as he closed his eyes. "Only fitting you understand why I'm here since we're both aware of your background. Curious as it may be precisely how you're here at all. Perhaps that's another conversation for another time."

Fionnghal spoke to Caescha about The Dagda and The Morrigan and their desire for control [illegible]. The need for sacrifices to appease them, [illegible] and use in their [illegible] play with [illegible]. Grady had figured the conversation would get here eventually. He was pleased that [illegible] they [illegible] at all.

"You see, for the eye of [illegible] [illegible] the [illegible] [illegible] to the [illegible]. The [illegible], both, in legend, would [illegible] for the [illegible] and curses of the former as well [illegible] a great [illegible] weight. Hence we only have ourselves [illegible]," Waylan [illegible].

"It's one of the oldest [illegible]," Grady [illegible].

"It's [illegible] Waylan, and it was not the one I was [illegible]." Waylan's eyes stared into the distance as his words quieted.

Grady's posture sharpened at those words.

"I think that's enough for today," Alba [illegible].

Waylan waved a hand in the air once more and the table was cleared as Grady's chair was pulled out and he stood up.

"I appreciate your time, Fionnghal, truly," Grady smiled as he showed himself out.

Chapter 51

Pagans, druids, splintered bloodlines.

Grady thought of his own history and the similarities it shared with Waylan's as he walked back to the general population cellblock. Arriving at his cell, he stood for the familiar beep and whirr of the door, yet there was none.

He looked around at the cameras and guards, but no one seemed to be paying attention. His cell remained closed, curiously.

He walked to either side and came back to his cell, but the door remained shut. Grady stared, perplexed by his cell door just as green arrows scrolled along its face. His heart sank and he felt a cold chill run up his spine.

What did he do to me back there? I haven't seen the colors and indicators in two years now.

Grady frantically searched the corridor for proof that he had been drugged or somehow embedded with another capsule. The lights remained white and with slight relief he walked the direction of the arrows.

Finding his way through the corridors to the library, Grady stood at the entrance which was closed off with double doors. He hadn't even realized there were doors on the library, but he hadn't ventured here at this late an hour either.

He walked inside and the doors closed behind him. Grady surveyed the area. The grand hall now eerie under the sparse emergency lighting, wasn't the welcoming room he'd visited so many times before.

The PA system clicked and Waylan's voice echoed through the room.

"Evescha, my friend. I'm sorry to say that I may have divulged too much to you in our visit", Alba declared. "I don't think there's any harm in knowing what you've been told. After all, we are kin. However, this will be the final visit to the Reformation Facility's library."

Grady felt a heat swelling from his side.

"It would seem the scholarly endeavors of the Penalized have gotten to a level that is disparaging to the penal system. As such, we will be digitizing and monitoring all content that is available in the Reformation Facility."

The heat grew and Grady saw a glow from the right side of the massive room. As the glow grew, he saw the fire licking forward and upward through the library. The old books and tomes of knowledge bursting into flames and the shelving buckled and crumbled.

Grady ran to the doors but they remained shut. He turned to face the blaze covering his mouth in the monogrammed kerchief Waylan had given him moments ago. He had walked into a trap, one that he should have assumed would be waiting for him given the ominous day.

Waylan's voice, barely audible over the inferno, came through the loudspeaker. "Enjoy your books, my friend."

A display on the far wall scrolled words that read: The simplest answer is the best answer, Mister Heller. Ashes to ashes. Farewell.

Chapter 52

Grady was running through a forest, sticks and branches smashing into his arms as he shielded his face. Heavy footsteps followed him and shouts burst through the midnight air.

Only lit by the waning moonlight, Grady ran as fast as he could before he reached the edge of the trees. If he ran out of the tree line, he'd definitely be found. He doubled back and darted through the trees in the direction he'd come from. Hiding as he heard the footsteps, he knelt down as they passed and he took off once more.

The canopy of foliage blotted out the little light the moon had provided. Grady couldn't hear the footsteps any longer and the shouting had died some time ago. He took a knee to catch his breath and rested.

The light roused him from his sleep first. The heat that followed alarmed his senses to wake completely. Grady turned his head in panicked circles and found he was helplessly surrounded by fire. He screamed at the top of his lungs as the flames engulfed him.

A stone slab underneath him, Grady startled awake. Bars surrounding the room, the sound of cannon fire booming through the barred window. Shackles around Grady's wrists and ankles, he launched off of the slab and dashed for the cell wall. His ankles ripped out from under him as he fell to the floor.

Fuzzy-headed, he heard dampened explosions all around. Just as he opened his eyes, he felt the floor give way and he fell with the block and shrapnel through the next floor. Rubble piled on top of him, Grady heard cracking and popping and felt his bones bursting as the weight on top of him became greater and greater. A painful shriek escaped his throat as another explosion surrounded him and the world went black.

Grady looked down at his blood-soaked hands. In the background, blurred from adrenaline, a body lay lifeless on the thatched floor. Grady burst through the archaic door and vomited in the grass. Wiping his mouth on his bloodied cloak, he went back inside and assessed the scene.

What happened here? What have I done?

Grady's body was hoisted into a hay cart and shuttled towards the shoreline. His head lolled on its neck, barely attached. Reaching the river bank, his body was unloaded and dragged as far as it could be before letting it go.

Agus nuair a thilleas tu, tig an dàn maille riut.

Agus nuair a thilleas tu, tig an dàn maille riut.

Agus nuair a thilleas tu, tig an dàn maille riut.

Three times the words were spoken, but the voice was not his own.

Agus nuair a thilleas tu, tig an dàn maille riut.

Agus nuair a thilleas tu, tig an dàn maille riut.

Agus nuair a thilleas tu, tig an dàn maille riut.

Three more times he heard the voice mutter.

Agus nuair a thilleas tu, tig an dàn maille riut.

Agus nuair a thilleas tu, tig an dàn maille riut.

Agus nuair a thilleas tu, tig an dàn maille riut.

Grady pooled the cool river water in his hands and brought it to his face to wipe away his transgressions. He drank from his palms and opened his eyes. Looking back at him was Fionnghall Alba.

Chapter 53

Grady opened his eyes, squinting from the bright white light flooding the room. He attempted to roll over and felt a pressure on his arm. He craned his neck from his horizontal posture, he couldn't see much beyond the white cloth, white bandages, and white room. His legs and arms were restrained, his head strapped to the hospital bed.

"He's awake, sir."

A silhouette of a man appeared in Grady's strained vision. Waylan Scott stared down at him.

"Water won't kill you, cranial destruction won't do it. Fire won't kill you, but I will say you are in bad shape being caught in the library during its controlled demolition." Waylan's devious smile eroded to a slight frown.

Grady's garbled voice crept from his smoke-ruined throat, "You... you killed him, didn't you?"

Waylan took a step back from Grady's bedside.

"You'll have to be much clearer, Heller. Many men have died as a result of my life's work", he smugly grinned.

"It was...Alba. You..."

Grady thrashed in the blackness. A sharpness pried at his skin and clothes. He was crammed into a space with his knees to his chest and a tepid liquid pooled down his front. A rumbling, then what felt like the floor dropping out from under him followed by a bone-shattering crash.

The smell of soil in his nose, vision from one eye obscured with red. He attempted to move his legs and only felt pain. His shoulders burned as he tried to push himself up, one arm giving way completely. His head bobbed to the side as his jaw fell open, clearly unhinged. The glory of New York's High Bridge overhead and the screams of horror erupting around him.

"Sir."

"Evescha, please try and stay with us." Waylan sat on the edge of the hospital bed. "It would seem that pain causes you to lapse in consciousness, but your body just continues to keep ticking. One hundred percent of your body, covered in third degree burns, yet only fifteen days in the ICU and you're all but healed."

Grady tucked an elbow under himself and rolled to his side sitting on the edge of the bed. Bandages wrapped his arms and legs and he could feel the itch of a sunburn as new skin grew in place of the sloughed damage beneath his gown and gauze.

"How many times?" Grady coughed as he tried his voice out. "How many times did they try to kill you? How many times were you Frankenstein with his monster being run out of a country?"

Waylan leaned into Grady's side and spoke lowly into his ear. "Where have you been, old friend? What have you seen?"

"A forest ablaze, cannon fire in an ancient prison, a barrel off the side of a bridge in New York." Grady stared at the floor, his eyes wide as he slipped into the vivid scenes. "You killed him. A man -- so long ago. You washed his blood from your hands in the river and spoke those words."

"Agus nuair a thilleas tu, tig an dàn maille riut," both men recited in unison.

Waylan's eyes widened as if he'd seen a ghost.

"I haven't thought of that day in a very long time, Heller." Waylan stood from the bed and walked through the infirmary doors. "Perhaps we can discuss it when, next, we meet."

Chapter 54

The blood of the father bestowed on the son.

Grady toiled over the visions he had seen in the blackness. The gates of death were sealed to him regardless of the attempts to open them. Now he was given fragmented insights to Fionnghall's time on this plane. He had seen the many times throughout history that Fionnghall had died. He had been shown the times that his Morrigan and Dagda caught up with him, outsmarted him at his game.

He was found out. Everyone has to slip eventually, Grady. Somehow he evaded death over and over, though.

And when you return, fate will come with you. The words that Fionnghall had spoken to Evescha on his anniversary. The words he'd recited in triplicate as he cast a body into a river. Those words ran through Grady's mind over and over.

The blood is a birthright, from father to son in his faith. Was the man in the vision his father?

Pieces of the puzzle were missing and Grady was too exhausted from his immolation and resurrection to consider them. The elevator doors opened and he made his way to his quarters to sleep. Sleep, however, did not come easy for Grady Sachs.

He dreamt of washing his hands in the cool river water but the red never came off. He felt the cold air on his face as it skimmed his damp skin as he drank from his blood soaked palms. He felt the mud under his feet as he pulled the body through the rain soaked fields -- the dead weight pulling at his tired shoulders.

Chapter 55

The rain outside of a stone hut fell harshly. A howling wind rolled through the hills in the Scottish lowlands. A candle flickered in the draft. Midnight approached and a man snuffed the light as he knelt by the door. Footsteps squelched in the mud and the man burst through the door, out into the harsh storm.

Two men grunted and groaned into the night. Hands prying at rain-soaked clothes in the downpour, clawing for grip. A sharp blow to the head and the man fell to the ground. Another smash to his skull of his enemy's own head and he slipped in and out of consciousness.

His shirt snagged on the briars as he was dragged through the fields. He could feel the blood streaming from his head and warming his face. He trashed and rolled to his chest and kicked the man from the shadows knees from under him.

The cloaked man fell to the ground and grabbed the ankle of the other. Mud caked on them both as they grappled one another. Rolling on the sopping earth, the storm swirling around them, neither man saw the approaching bluff until it was too late.

Their bodies crashed to the shore beneath them. The cloaked man got to his hands and knees and pulled a knife from his belt. As he straddled the man from the hut's chest, the man looked into his eyes with terror.

"Please, don't. What have I done to you? Let me make it right!" the man pleaded.

"That child doesn't deserve your gift! The Morrigan and Dagda were wrong to place this burden on your bloodline!" the cloaked man shouted over the rolling thunder.

The man looked up from the ground as the blade was placed against his throat.

"These words will be your last, Alba. Make them concise. Your name will live on, but not in that child", the cloaked man snarled.

"Please. Without me, he will not live. Please!" he begged.

The knife punctured the skin under his ear and he felt it drag through his flesh and sinew. His throat buckled as the blade was pulled through his neck.

Cool river water ran over his face. He took drinks of it from his blood soaked palms. Removing his hooded cloak, he stretched his arms to his sides.

Agus nuair a thilleas tu, tig an dàn maille riut

Agus nuair a thilleas tu, tig an dàn maille riut

Agus nuair a thilleas tu, tig an dàn maille riut

He took another drink from his bloodied hands, lapping the water from his skin.

Agus nuair a thilleas tu, tig an dàn maille riut

Agus nuair a thilleas tu, tig an dàn maille riut

Agus nuair a thilleas tu, tig an dàn maille riut

"There will be no return for you. As of this day I, Baird Muir, have died with your body. From this day forward, I shall carry your burden, Fionnghall Alba, and your name will henceforth live on through me."

Grady shot bolt-upright from his slumber. Sweat beaded on his forehead and soaked his shirt.

That thief! He stole a child's birthright! He denied this man his chance to pass on his legacy.

Furious, Grady pushed himself from his bunk and stared into the mirror. The face he saw was his own, but it was also Waylan's, it was Alba's -- the *true* Alba.

He died. Alba died. His blood was taken, Waylan drank it from his hands.

With the blood goes the curse. But how has he gone so long without it being taken from him?

Agus nuair a thilleas tu, tig an dàn maille riut. When the body returns?

When the blood returns...

Fionnghall Alba was dead, his identity was stolen. Now Grady knew the truth of the matter. The blood that Waylan stole passed the curse with it. Power hungry, Waylan carried on under this fallacy evading death. Childless, without spouse, without siblings. Surrounding himself with business partners and brothers in bond, but never in blood.

Childless, just like Grady. Partner-less, and without blood ties to any single person. Alone, isolated, and afraid to garner anything more than infrequent acquaintanceship to anyone.

Chapter 56

The door released Grady from his cell and he took off for the mess hall. He had dreamt of Waylan, Alba… Miur. The real culprit here, his true identity. Just like Grady, Baird Miur had evaded time and its natural progression. He had stolen many things throughout his years. He had outsmarted his fate every step of the way. Grady Sachs, however, knew the truth now. He was Baird Muir's retribution.

As he entered the cafeteria, he shoved his way to the front of the Penalized. He pulled himself on top of the service counter and kicked a stack of metal trays to the floor. The entire room fell silent at attention.

"Baird Muir!" Grady shouted.

The Penalized looked around among themselves with confusion.

"Baird Muir!" Grady repeated.

The guards looked equally bewildered at the scene. Conflict was the lowest risk in the Bandash Memorial Reformation Facility and, as such, no one quite knew how to deal with what was unfolding.

"I am looking for Baird Muir. I hear he's taken issue with me and I mean to settle it once and for all." Grady demanded as the men began whispering to one another.

"Let me be clear", he continued "I am going to take this man's life. He has wronged everyone in this place. He has taken the livelihoods of many, and the lives of many more."

The guards began to approach with trepidation. Prods at the ready, they formed a wide semi-circle berth around Grady. He surveyed them all, looking them up and down one at a time, and smiled. His plan was coming together.

The guards searched one another for a shred of bravery. They'd been trained to deal with these kinds of outbursts, surely, but those muscles were cold and atrophied. The implant did all of the work in these scenarios. Waylan Scott had foregone the formality after it proved ineffective in Grady's case.

One of the uniformed men stepped forward from the siege of guards. His face was determined, but his hand wavered as he raised it above his head.

"Penalized One-three-four-nine, stand down or you will be neutralized", his voice feigned confidence.

Grady clenched a fist at his side as the man approached.

"I'm only going to ask one more time. Bring me Baird Muir and tell him there's hell to pay."

The guard edged in on Grady with his electrified baton raised high. Grady launched himself onto the man, feet first, stomping him to the ground. The other guards closed tightly around the men and Grady stood up with his foot on the guard's chest. Two brave guards approached with prods forward and Grady took the hit from both, falling to a knee. He swept under one of the men and toppled him over, taking his knees out from under him.

The Penalized, still silent, stared at the altercation like cavemen discovering fire. They searched one another before grimaces and rage painted their faces. All at once a frenzy broke out through the entire room. Men clawed and punched and kicked at one another. A full brawl ensued as the lights blared overhead.

There it is. Finally.

Grady knew the brightening lights were glaring orange to all of the Penalized. To his delight, all of them were so busy trying to tear each other apart that they weren't paying attention in the slightest. Blood spattered through the air as screams echoed against the white walls. The lights pulsed brighter.

Red.

Cutting through the ruckus a thin, whining sound started to build. The sound a transformer would make charging a flash on an old camera.

And now for the finale.

Grady lowered his arms and allowed the guards to detain him. They pulled him to his feet and pinned his arms behind his back. The mob surrounding them grew in volume -- the men newly imbued with a virulence they'd not been allowed to display for the duration of their sentences.

As Grady stood with guards surrounding him, the high-pitched whine cut through the cacophony and suddenly bodies began to slump to the floor. One after another, the horde thinned as the whites of the Penalized's eyes rolled into view.

The lights overhead flooded white forcing Grady to squint. The guards that held him let go as they dropped their arms to their sides and stared at the leveled battlefield. Every last one of the men laid on the floor, lifeless. Grady smiled, staring into the large domed camera in the ceiling.

He turned to the nearest guard grabbing his arm and pulling him in closely. Face to face, Grady spoke very concisely. "Find me Baird Muir. This will not be the last massacre otherwise."

Grady stepped through the ocean of death towards the exit. Looking over his shoulder, he sternly repeated himself. “Baird Muir. Find him.”

Chapter 57

Grady dashed down the corridor towards his cell. The lights overhead pulsed dimming and brightening.

Good, the alert is at least traveling already.

Carving the corner into his cellblock, the lights flared a blinding white. Thrumming echoed through the long, tall hallway as Penalized hands smashed against the plexiglass doors. Panicked looks spread over their faces, unaware of what had transpired in the mess hall moments ago.

Behind clear panes, every range of emotion was on display. The rumble of hands was almost soothing to the ears, muted by the thickness of the sound-dampened doors and walls. He stood in the middle of the ground floor and looked around, turning in circles completely in awe.

If they are all panicking, Waylan is panicking.

Grady climbed the flights of stairs to his floor and found his cell was the only one open. He stood against the railing and faced his cell door.

Most definitely a trap. Waylan's trying to contain the threat.

Grady leaned against the railing and watched as the lights pulsed to an impossibly bright white. The room washed of all color and the wild drumming of hands stopped nearly all at once. The lights dimmed in the room and Grady squinted to see inside the cells of his neighbors.

Bodies twisted and contorted in the corners of the cells against the doors. Faces smashed against the glass with eyes rolled back in their skulls. Some of the bodies convulsed the last few nervous twitches of life and then silence fell over the block.

He's willing to throw away every single life in this place, Grady.

To prove what?

Is this all truly a game to him?

Grady walked through the empty corridors and cat walks and saw the bodies all laying on the floor. Each and every last Penalized in his cellblock was dead. Dead because of Grady.

His mind reeled as Grady took off to the courtyard.

There shouldn't be anyone out there this time of day. Open air, get somewhere you can bait him out to you.

Grady walked toward the eastern entrance of the outdoor common area and found it to be swarming with Penalized. Men gathering in conversation, working out, playing basketball sitting alone reading. For the first time ever, Grady noticed that these men -- all of the Penalized -- were enjoying themselves.

They had all become so institutionalized, so complacent to their fates that they just settled into the life they had left. The drugged water kept their minds clear and offered them peace despite their permanent incarcerations.

Grady reached a hand out to the door to push it open and saw the faux sun's glare change. The men all looked skyward in unison. The basketballs fell to the ground, weights were re-racked on benches and stands, books were slowly closed. All of the men stood as they shielded their eyes from the growing brightness.

They don't know it's fake, Grady. They don't know what's about to happen. It's safe out here for them.

Grady backed away from the door and watched the sun's brightness begin to mute. The men gawked with confusion another moment and then went back to their hobbies and conversations.

He's toying with you, Grady. It's a game. He's showing you that these men, their lives, are in your hands.

Grady fell to his knees and held his head in his hands. His shoulders rose and fell as he sobbed in the empty hall. Waylan had made his move and cornered Grady. He stood slowly and wiped his face before turning back and making his way to his cell.

He walked past all of the death he'd caused and stood outside of his open door. Inhaling deeply, he walked inside and sat on his bunk. Folding his hands in his lap, he hung his head.

Check.

Chapter 58

The door slid shut on Grady's cell and the glass went from transparent to completely opaque. He watched as the back wall split in half and the portion with his toilet and vanity rotated to a bare wall. The halves came back together seamlessly just as Grady felt the bunk beneath him pull into the wall.

He stood in his barren, white cell, then sat on the floor as he looked around.

Solitary confinement.

Grady wondered how long it had been since this protocol was called into play at the Reformation Facility. The lights dimmed overhead until the room was engulfed in total darkness. Grady could only hear his breathing now, but even that was muted somehow.

He snapped his fingers and there was barely a sound at all. The lights had gone out entirely and with it, the room had gone completely anechoic. True, deathly silence surrounded Grady as a panic started to take him over.

Calm down, old friend. This is what he wants.

Waylan wants you to freak out.

He wants you to break down.

It's all a game.

Grady laid in the middle of the isolation chamber his cell had become. Folding his hands on his chest, he closed his eyes and let the void swell around him until he fell asleep.

Grady felt his eyes open, but there was no light. He rubbed his face and flashes of phosphenes bolted through his vision. Opening his eyes once more he found there was still no light. He sat up and felt around the room for his bunk, his sink, anything to help him get his bearings. There was nothing.

He spun around frantically and began to shout but his voice hardly made a sound. He smacked his hands against the walls and floor and screamed at the top of his lungs. The silence was deafening.

Grady sat back on the floor and backed himself into a corner. He hugged his knees to his chest and tried to stop himself from hyperventilating.

"I've gone blind. I'm deaf and I've gone blind", he muttered to himself.

His breathing sped up as tears streamed down his face.

"Where am I? How long have I been here?"

Grady screamed once more.

"How long are you going to keep this up, you bastard?!"

Grady choked on his breath as he gasped between sobs. He felt lightheaded as he laid on the floor fetally. His heart raced in his chest. He tried to hold his breath to calm himself but it only made the blackness swirl around him.

As the room spun Grady couldn't inhale deep enough to make a sound. His breaths were quick and shallow as he yanked his shirt from his chest. He wrapped the cloth around his neck and pulled both sides as tightly as he could.

Gasping, raspy breaths escaped his throat as flashes of light entered his periphery. He pulled the garment tighter as he felt his temples throb and swell. His lips felt like they would burst. Grady leaned against the wall and slid to the floor. His legs began to twitch from oxygen deprivation and white blotted out his entire field of vision.

Another long, stifled attempt at inhaling and then...nothing.

Chapter 59

"One hundred five hours, Evescha." The voice sounded like it was underwater.

Grady's head jolted to the side -- a slap burned into his cheek.

"Tsk, tsk, tsk", the voice condescended. "Suicide, really?"

Another strike against the other side of his face.

"Now, now, Heller. Stop the charade and wake up. We both know that wasn't going to be enough. I am sorry to see that you can be driven to madness so easily", Waylan emotionlessly stated.

Grady shot up from his lying position on the floor. He scrambled backward away from Waylan as far as he could before abruptly smashing his back into the wall. His eyes bulged and scanned the area wildly looking for an escape but he found none.

"Please, Alba, please..." Grady pleaded. "Enough, please. I can't do this any longer. Just put me out of my misery."

"Two hundred sixty-nine thousand six hundred twenty-five days in this world, Heller", Waylan said. "Seven hundred thirty-nine years, almost, of being entirely alone. Isolated from the world and its pleasures and just over four days breaks you? Pitiful, really."

Waylan approached Grady slowly. Grady's pupils were so wide it looked like his irises had gone black.

"S-stay away from me, Alba. Get away!"

Waylan stopped mere inches from Grady as he knelt down and backhanded him across the face harshly.

"I expected more from you, Evescha, truly."

Waylan almost sounded disappointed as he took a step back and unleashed another swift backhand. Grady was knocked to the floor momentarily. He perched himself on his elbow as he rubbed his jaw.

"I thought it would only take the cafeteria falling to their knees to keep you in line, Evescha", said Alba. "When you took to the counter and started rallying them against one another, it must have been quite the speech. Tell me, what did you tell them to counteract everything we've worked for here?"

"Sisyphus", replied Grady under his breath.

Waylan turned his head curiously like a dog.

"Come again?"

"Sisyphus", Grady repeated. "Sisyphus thought that he was smarter than his gods. He tricked them many times and humiliated them."

Waylan smiled at Grady's musings.

"Sisyphus showed the gods that they were idiotic and vain. He showed them they were no better than mortal men", Waylan proudly declared.

Grady took a knee as he wiped the blood from his lip.

"The story didn't end there though, did it Baird?"

Grady smirked as he deftly lunged at Waylan and tackled him to the floor. He held both of his hands overhead and threw a hammering blow into Waylan's face, breaking his nose causing blood to splatter down his chin and neck.

Waylan grabbed at Grady's wrists and kicked wildly underneath him, rolling to his side. He clawed at the smooth tiled floor trying to get out from under Grady, but Grady landed another blow squarely into the back of his head smashing his face into the ground.

Grady rolled Waylan back over in his stupor and grabbed him by his collar, smashing his head into the floor repeatedly. Waylan reached for Grady's neck, scratching at his chest and shoulders. He took hold of his throat and squeezed as tightly as he could, causing Grady to recoil.

The movement backward was just enough for Waylan to shuttle himself away from Grady's straddled hold on him. He mustered himself to his feet.

"Heller, you know this won't do either of us any good. We can do this every day for years and we'll both still be here", Waylan shouted.

Grady fired back, "Yes, but only one of us is Sisyphus, Muir."

Waylan ran at Grady as Grady stood firmly in place. He threw a wild haymaker at Grady's jaw, and another into his ribs. Grady doubled over as Waylan's knee came up into Grady's chin. Grady would feel the blood pooling in his mouth from the blow.

Reeling backward, Grady looked up at Waylan and smiled a bloody, toothy smile. He launched toward Alba once more and grabbed him behind his knees as Waylan's arms wrapped under Grady's shoulders. They both tumbled to the floor, Grady's weight knocking the wind out of his adversary.

Pulling himself from Waylan's grasp, Grady straddled him once more and punched Waylan's jaw hard. Waylan let out a groan as his mouth locked open, his jaw obviously dislocated.

"You stole Alba's blood -- his son's birthright", Grady snarled. "You stole everything from him and you recited those words. The body slipped away from you and you thought you had outsmarted your gods that night!"

Waylan thrashed under Grady grunting and attempting to swear through his ruined jaw.

"Those words, you thought you were in the clear from your Morrigan and Dadga! You thought your fate was sealed in that body as you cast it to the waters", Grady continued. "You thought that was it, didn't you, Muir?"

Waylan laid still beneath Grady now, his eyes wide with rage as a wet snicker crept out from his bleeding maw.

Grady leaned his own battered, crimson face close to Waylan's. His mouth tightly closed as he inhaled sharply, furious with vengeance.

Grady spat into the mouth of his lifelong enemy before he spoke.

"You stole the blood from Alba. On that night on the banks of Garbh Uisge, you intended to steal my life", he said.

Waylan breathed through his shattered nose as he swallowed wetly through his broken face.

"Your blood, Baird Muir, *Alba's blood*, soaked my eyes that night. It mixed with the river water that coursed through my lungs", Grady hissed.

Waylan's eyes grew wide as he, once again, tried to prise himself from under Grady.

"You gifted me this curse, you bastard. You made me who I am, *what* I am!" Grady simpered at Waylan, mockingly.

"*I* am your fate, Baird Muir, and I have returned what you stole."

Grady grabbed Waylan by the collar once more and raised his head from the floor. With a guttural scream, Grady slammed his head into the ground. Blood sprayed across the pristine white floor from the back of Waylan's head as his body convulsed. Grady let his hands drop to his sides as he looked into the white lights flooding the room and sighed as tears rolled down his face.

It was finally over.

Chapter 60

Grady took great care in removing the bloodied clothes from himself and from Waylan Scott's corpse. Changing into the garb, he walked toward the back of the room and stood in the middle of the white wall. He held his hands to his sides, palms soaked in blood, dripping to the floor.

"Open the blasted doors. It's done. Heller is gone for good this time. Get someone in here and clean up this mess."

Three men in white coveralls collected the cadaver from the middle of the room and robots spilled from the walls to clean the biohazard from the floor. As the men exited through the door, it slammed shut and an automation spoke over the intercom.

"Facial verification invalid. Please step away from the doors", it commanded.

"That bastard ruined my face. Just what am I supposed to do about that? Now, open the damned door and get me to the infirmary", Grady shouted.

Nothing happened.

Grady walked toward the front of the room and pounded on the gigantic glass doors. He looked down the corridor at a guard standing by. He furiously pointed and waved him over.

"Take me through the gates to my quarters", he commanded.

The guard didn't move.

"Now, or I'll rip your face off and do it myself!"

The guard turned on his heels and pinned a code into a blank space on the wall. The doors slid open and the guard escorted Grady to Waylan Scott's wing of the Reformation Facility. As the elevator moved down the shaft through the sublevels, Grady looked at himself in the mirrored walls of the car.

You are Evescha Heller, not Baird Muir.

You look like Waylan Scott, but you are not Fionnghall Alba.

You are Grady Sachs.

You are Grady Sachs.

You are Grady Sachs.

"Sir? Your floor", the guard's voice rattled Grady to reality.

Walking off of the lift, he turned to the guard and smiled at him, but only slightly.

"Let the staff know things are changing around here. I feel like a new man -- I think it's time to turn this place over to someone else." Grady waved him off as he walked away.

The doors closed and Grady made his way to Waylan's quarters. His office was as opulent as any time he'd seen it. The massive oak desk taking up a quarter of the space, paintings and tapestries on the walls.

Grady stopped in front of the tall painting of Doctor Waylan Scott, Esquire in a modest suit that hung on the wall at Inventaratus.

"Damn you to hell, Scott. Damn you for the eternity you've damned me to!" Grady spat on the painting leaving a trail of blood as it ran down.

Exhausted, Grady walked to the plush office chair and sat down. He sighed heavily as he laid his head against the headrest.

Looking down, he saw a small red light blinking under the desk against his leg. He leaned over to look under the drawer and saw a small button blinking on and off. Warily, he pressed the LED and the sound of an airlock broke open behind him. He turned and saw a small compartment in the wall open with an old combination locking mechanism adorning it.

More secrets, Alba?

Grady went to the safe and stared at the four wheels. He dialed the numbers one, three, four, and nine and the safe popped. As he opened the door, Grady's eyes grew wide as he held his breath. A closed envelope was propped against three items.

A purple agate, a seed, and a small medieval coin.

Epilogue

Evescha, my dear friend,

Once thought to be permanent, I discovered hundreds of years ago that this gift of eternal life could be stolen like so many other possessions. As you are reading this letter, I can only assume you've been able to connect the dots of our ineluctable, kismetic lives. What's more, I can guarantee that you've solved the riddle of my, or rather our mother tongues.

The words I spoke, mockingly, over your body in this prison, I spoke over Fionnghall Alba's so many centuries ago. The words I spoke, as it turned out, were not so dissimilar to those you chanted that night on the riverbank.

My gift was stolen and for this crime I have been interned in a dance with death throughout my days. I never married, I knew no siblings or children. My blood, or rather Alba's blood, was only ever to be mine and through it, I would live eternally.

Superstitious and gullible with my everlasting gift, I collected tokens from the delta of the Garbh Uisge. An ancient coin and an iridescent purple agate -- memento mori for you, my friend.

I spent countless hundreds of years with no concern for you until nearly one hundred years ago.

I recognized your face as if I were looking at my own. In passing on a street one day, another as a new tenant applied to rent one of my properties. It couldn't be that Evescha Heller in that courtroom sitting mere feet in front of me some eight hundred years removed from that fateful night.

You never saw my face, not until that day you were arrested.

Your presence in my life shook my confidence in my own immortality. I traveled the globe, retracing my footsteps until I came across a flourishing tree on the banks of the Garbh Uisge. I picked a pear from the tree and blissfully enjoyed the sweetest nectar until I found myself choking on a seed.

I kept that seed as a reminder of my intentions for you.

I transferred you to this technological mecca of penitential enterprise. I toyed with your mind, assaulted your body, and killed your spirit. Yet, somehow, in that time you managed to put together the pieces that I'd never thought to seek. I was so busy trying to end your life that I had forgotten to protect mine entirely.

But you figured it out, didn't you?

The blood.

It was always in the blood. My fate always rested in you, coursing through your veins.

If you are reading this, I have finally reaped what I'd sown for so long. So, Evescha, as you have presented me with my fate, I now present you with yours.

Please do be careful, old friend. Your life was always in my hands, but now I know it had to be in yours all along.

Când te întorci la mine,

astfel soarta mea va fi anulată

Checkmate,

W.S. Esq.

Part Three:

No One Has To Die

Prologue

How is this even possible?

Finally, after all this time -- after two hundred sixty-nine thousand six hundred twenty-five days, it was over.

It was finally over, Grady!

What does this even mean?

This letter… these curios.

They can't be from that day.

Can they?

He'd known all along. He'd known all along and he exploited you into putting together the pieces.

You solved his puzzle and were so foolhardy you didn't even stop to think that you may have been helping him solve your own.

Is this your puzzle? After all of this time…

Time to live.

Time to die.

It's always been a matter of time, hasn't it?

Chapter 61

Doctor Waylan Scott, Esquire spent the last potential century acutely aware of his immortality, but keenly fearful of his fate. As it turned out, his fears had been coursing through his veins all along. Quite literally, his blood bore the marks of his demise. The words of his ancestors resonated throughout his years.

Agus nuair a thilleas tu, tig an dàn maille riut.

And when you return, fate will come with you.

Grady Sachs had done Waylan Scott the favor of returning what was his. By spilling his own blood and reintroducing it to Waylan's system, Grady's nemesis found the hands of time suddenly in lockstep with him once again. A blood borne transference between immortals seemed to negate Waylan's gift, just as Grady had theorized it might.

Grady Sachs sat in an opulent leather chair behind a massive oaken desk. Blood soaked through the bespoke business suit he was wearing. Much like the clothing, the blood did not belong to Grady, at least not all of it -- not anymore.

As he stared at his open palm, his vision blurred. Flashes of a river, of a tree, office buildings, courtrooms, and prisons went through his mind. The red on his flesh echoed the pool of crimson refuse being mopped from the white tile floor somewhere stories above him. The man masquerading as Waylan Scott was dead.

His fate had returned for him, and by Grady Sach's own hand. A hand that incidentally held a posthumous memento from his psychopathic enemy. Three small tokens: an iridescent purple agate, a medieval coin, and the seed of an ancient pear tree from the shores of Garbh Uisge in Scotland.

These things cannot exist. They cannot be those *things.*

Grady stared at the objects as a cold, sinking feeling settled in. He'd spent his entire life, all seven hundred thirty-eight years, complacent in the knowledge that he would outlive everyone. In fact, until close to eighty years ago, it hadn't occurred to him that he had any company in his unique plight until he was framed for Waylan Scott's criminal enterprises.

You should have known he was watching you, Grady. You were foolish, just like you always are.

You got comfortable in your quest and focused on your trajectory and forgot to survey the landscape.

This is how you got here in the first place, old friend.

Shortsighted and foolish.

Grady sat the items on the desk and wearily held his head in his hands. As he closed his eyes, he couldn't shake the images of the life draining from Waylan Scott's body. A shudder ripped up Grady's spine as he sharply inhaled and shakily exhaled, damming the tears from flowing down his face.

One thing at a time, old friend.

For now, it's over. This part, at least, is finally over.

He laid his head back against the cool leather and let the relief wash over him. The tears fell of their own free will despite Grady's efforts. As he closed his eyes, a smile came to his face. When he opened them back up, however, he saw the three objects on the desk in front of him and his expression faded. Relief had come for Grady Sachs, but for Evescha Heller, fear began to set in.

Grady spent the next few days exploring the luxurious and immodest quarters. As their kismetic fate had tied them together through history, it also added the lucky perk that they shared the size and fit of most things. Grady had found his consolation prize for taking the life of his eternal adversary was a rather extensive and extortionate wardrobe. He found this to be particularly useful when traveling through the back halls and administrative wings of the Bandash Memorial Reformation Facility.

It became more evident than ever just how many similarities Grady and Waylan shared, physically at least. As he silently observed the inner workings of Doctor Scott's penal stronghold, he was greeted by his doppelganger's name repeatedly.

They really have no clue that he's gone and that I'm here in his place. It's no wonder he was able to continually reinvent himself over the ages.

No one has any concern for what happens around them.

Chapter 62

Grady had found freedom, at least to some degree. For all of the technological advances in the complex, Waylan Scott had evidently cleared himself from most biometric security protocols like retinal scams or fingerprint readers. As such, Grady was able to come and go as he pleased through the various wings and offices of the prison solely on facial recognition. He'd even found himself on the observation deck watching the Penalized as they milled around through their daily lives.

It's like watching an ant farm from up here.

The Penalized all had routines they adhered to rather strictly. Even though there was no single measure of enforcement, each man went about their days in exactly the same order. Some would take time in the new digital library, some would study and take exams of various scholarly endeavors. Others would spend hours lifting weights or producing works of art. Every last one of them would stop at their exact same times every day, though. No presence of clocks, no indication of anything that Grady could note.

They all just... stop and go back to their cells until the next task.

The compliancy implant and the threat of immediate death notwithstanding, Grady was well aware of the tainted water supply and how the lights interacted with it. None of those measures seemed to be enough to cause thousands of men to act like the inner workings of a Swiss pocket watch, though. But the more he observed, the more apparent it was that something was forcing an eerie timeliness to the place.

Grady had also taken note that the guard rotation was sporadic at best. Each station was manned twenty-four-seven, but there was no rhyme or reason behind the shift lengths. Some guards would spend forty-eight hours in place while others would be posted for all of thirty minutes. In two weeks' time, he never saw the same guard at the same post twice. Even more perplexing, after a month, he realized he hadn't seen the same guard twice at all save for two. One stood outside his suite all hours of the day, and another outside of the blank white room where Grady had unwittingly assumed the identity of Doctor Waylan Scott, Esquire once again.

Both of these men were as stoic as royal guards at Buckingham Palace. Grady had attempted conversation with the one outside of the suite, but the man didn't even offer a nod in return. Gargoyles in the guise of men. Put in place, no doubt, to ward off the dues that Waylan would eventually have to pay. Still, Grady thought it was very strange that they seemingly never left their marks regardless of the time of day.

One morning, Grady set off on his daily rounds. As it turned out, he too fell into a bit of a routine in the walls of this palace of internment. He found himself at the doors of the blank room, a place he hadn't returned to since he'd murdered Waylan and freed himself of his endless torment. As he approached the doors, the statuesque guard stepped between Grady and the entryway. Without making eye contact in the least, he bolstered his stance indicating Grady wasn't to enter the area.

"Step aside, guard", Grady commanded.

The guard remained rigidly in place as Grady approached to push past him.

"Get out of the damn way!" Grady pressed, irritated.

"No can do, sir", the guard spoke.

Grady was lost for words momentarily as it registered that this is the first time he'd heard *any* of the enforcers speak. He put an arm forward to brush the man aside. The guard stood in place like he was made of concrete and rebar.

"I said *move*", Grady shouted and he shoved his full weight into the guard.

The guard remained completely still as if Grady's body was no more than a gentle breeze.

"Warden Scott made it clear you weren't to enter this area again, sir", the guard spoke matter-of-factly, still staring blankly ahead.

"I'm Warden Scott", Grady almost choked on the words. "I'm Waylan Scott. I run this place and I cut your checks. Now let me through."

"Warden Scott said you'd say that, sir", the guard blithely replied.

"*I* am Waylan Scott!"

"Please step back, sir, or I'll have to force you back." The guard met Grady's enraged eyes with complete indifference.

Grady moved toward the guard once more and the man reached for his baton. As he raised it in front of him, a whining sound started to ramp to a shrill tone. Grady rushed the man from a few paces away and suddenly found himself flat on his back. His ears rang and his chest felt heavy until the feeling of pins and needles set in. The sting caused Grady to wince as he got to his feet and eyed the guard, his brow furrowed.

Grady crouched to one knee and sprang toward the enforcer again. Staying low, he went to take the guard's knees from under him and found himself knocked back to the ground. His head swam and a numbness set into the entire left side of his face. His jaw went slack almost like he'd been injected with Novocain. He propped himself on his elbows and lashed out a kick to the guard's shin. This time he was able to catch the gargoyle's almost inhuman movement as his leg raised and stomped Grady's own shin to the ground.

Grady yelped in pain as he tried to pull his leg from under the guard's booted foot, but there was no return on his investment. The crushing weight on his leg threatened to snap it in half. The guard looked down at Grady with dead eyes and pointed his baton toward his face. A small pop and then the whining started again.

"You are not permitted into The Brink by orders of the warden Waylan Scott. Please withdraw from the area immediately."

Grady's leg was released by the guard as he returned to his station beside the entryway. Grady got himself to his feet and limped away looking over his shoulder at the guard. Through the panoramic glass wall, the lights pulsed with effulgence as if they were mocking his failure.

Chapter 63

Grady hobbled to Waylan's quarters. His leg throbbed and his mind raced.

Why would Scott have restricted himself from areas of his own prison?

As he approached the suite, the posted enforcer sidestepped toward the door blocking Grady's gait.

Not this again.

Grady slowed down and stood a few feet from the guard. The man extended his hand and presented an envelope to Grady before turning militaristically and replanting himself.

Grady walked through the door and sat on the edge of the plush bed -- another spoil of a centuries' long war between him and Waylan. Rubbing his leg, he studied the envelope he'd been handed. No markings of any kind were present; nothing to discern the sender, contents, or intent. Disquieted, Grady pried the envelope open. Inside was simply a tri-folded piece of paper.

A letter?

Dearest Evescha,

I do hope this has found you well. If you are reading this, it has been three months since my untimely demise. By now you have, no doubt, searched my quarters and perused my effects. Please, by all means, make yourself at home. I bequeath to you all of my worldly possessions and accounts.

Knowing your curiosities, you have undoubtedly tried to re-enter the scene of the crime that allowed you these fortunes of fate. The Brink, as I call it, is a technological wonder of a room. I have used it for many years as a means for reformation of our more… difficult inhabitants.

The Brink is a hyper-realistic holographic interface that is designed to interact with the compliancy implant administered upon ingestion to the reformation system here. As such, the operator is capable of prompting scenarios based on the thoughts and fears of the Penalized in order to force complacency with their providence. If those measures do not work, the ulterior protocol of the implant would be triggered.

For us, however, The Brink is so much more. Having lived the lives we have lived -- having been set free of the bounds of time and tied to one another throughout our days -- this room has gleaned powerful insights of past and present to me. I can only imagine it will suffice the same results for you. You can see, then, how I cannot permit you to enter the room.

My affairs have been paused until you've received this message, at which time Waylan Scott must return to his schedule. Considering you have done so well to settle into my worldly delights, it's only fair you should minister my underworldly prospects as well. Be wary, dear friend. I may have been faceless in life, but my reputation has made me quite the villain to a great many people.

The artifacts you found weeks ago have granted you with a unique dilemma, you see. Though lashed to my routines and business involvements, you are otherwise a free man to roam the world at your leisure. However, with those items returned to you, your fate is now sealed. While you are able to live your life, you are now susceptible to expiration.

Just as you repaid my fate, I have returned yours. I always saw our mutual circumstance as a gift, yet you always regarded it as a curse. Well, Evescha, I have gifted you freedom from that curse. A drunk driver, a freak lightning strike, a gunshot wound of murderous revenge, even something as simple as choking on a midnight snack could spell your death. You may find that, although you are able to roam free, the threats outside of these walls are overwhelming in these new times.

My dear Evescha, you may have freed yourself from my grasp, but I have always been a step ahead of you. Beyond the grave, I still surpass time. You will be indentured to me for eternity one way or another.

See you in hell, old friend,

W.S. Esq.

Grady's stomach roiled as he stared at the letter. The color flushed from his face and he felt like he was going to be sick. The room spun around him as he tried to process what had just happened. He had spent the last ninety or so days walking in the footsteps of Waylan Scott trying to come up with his next move for his escape from this fraudulent incarceration.

Two hundred sixty-nine thousand seven hundred fifteen days, Grady, and an eternity more to go.

Chapter 64

Before Grady could recompose himself from the bombshell Waylan had plotted in a brilliant postmortem play, there was a knock at his chamber door. Grady got to his feet and shakily hobbled over to answer it. Opening the door, both of the stoic guards stood beside one another, but dressed in black business suits instead of their typical enforcer uniforms.

The men entered the room and stood on either side of the doors.

"Doctor Scott, please clothe yourself so we can get today's events underway", one of the guards said monotonously.

The second enforcer approached the walk-in closet and pulled one of a dozen gray suits from the rack and laid it on the bed. Both men turned on their heels and left the room swiftly. Grady thought it best not to shake the confidence that he was, once again, Waylan Scott to these droning soldiers of the real Waylan Scott's empire.

Meeting the men outside of the room, they escorted Grady to one of the upper sublevels and out to a private parking garage. A few collector cars and some blacked out SUVs were parked side by side and the guards walked to one of the more modest vehicles. Opening the door, Grady got inside. The interior was illuminated upon his entry and there were benches of seats and a head's up display on the windshield, but nothing else.

The men entered the front of the vehicle and it silently moved forward without the slightest inkling of a lurch. As the car sped up, it neared a cinderblock wall. Grady looked at the men to steer the accelerating SUV from hitting the wall, but neither man seemed concerned, nor did there seem to be a way to *steer* anything. Grady sat back in his seat and as the wall approached more quickly, he closed his eyes accepting this was Waylan's plan all along.

Sunlight blared into Grady's eyes as he opened them and found they were on a highway. The vehicle silently traveled at an impossible speed. The world rushed past the windows and Grady began to feel motion sick just as the windows blacked out and the lights in the cab brightened seemingly as a reaction to his discomfort. With the windows opaque, there was an illusion of sitting still in the car.

This is not the same world you remember, Grady.

After five minutes or so, the guards opened the doors and exited the vehicle.

A moment of panic. Grady thought he was hurtling down a highway that he couldn't see like an unguided missile when his door opened.

A new world, Grady. A brand new world with brand new threats.

The car had been parked just as fluidly as it had taken off from its spot at the Reformation Facility. As they walked through the garage, lights glowed and dimmed with their strides.

A voice greeted the men at a set of double doors.

"Welcome back, Mister Scott."

Grady straightened his tie nervously as the threesome traversed the long hallway to a massive, empty conference room. The doors opened automatically and Grady was seated at the head of a table fit for twenty or more. His bodyguards stood at his sides as a holoscreen appeared in the middle of the room.

"Gentlemen, welcome back", a man spoke on the screen. "We trust your time away was productive, Mister Scott. Please feel free to interject at any point. We are eager to hear a full debrief once we've finished with new business."

Debrief? What debrief? Business as usual, huh? Well played Waylan.

Grady sat back and listened as various men summarized their last three months of business. They all addressed Grady, or rather Waylan, directly.

This must be a council of his conglomerate.

Men covered defense efforts, technologies for commercial and personal travel, and medical advancements worldwide. The briefing lasted nearly an hour and Grady had a hard time keeping up with all of the jargon. These men were not cut from his cloth, and he was certainly not from their world.

"Gentlemen, if I may", Grady's voice escaped his throat before he'd fully realized he started speaking.

He stood and tried to calm his self-induced panic. Straightening his jacket cuffs and brushing his lapel trying to look confident, he continued.

"I trust all of you have been doing exactly what you are all paid to do. Now, if we can hurry all of this along, please? I have just spent the last ninety days dealing with a thorn in my side and need to get back to more pressing matters."

That sounded official, right?

The room was filled with dead-air silence as all of the men on the conference call stayed silent.

A voice finally spoke up after what seemed like an eternity.

"Sir, please take your seat." One of his guards placed a hand on Grady's shoulder.

Grady sat down in his chair unsure of what had just taken place. The men on the call started in on their briefings once more, but now the subject matter was more to Grady's understanding. The tech-speak and defense slang, acronyms and business law idioms faded away. With the terminologies, the benign faces also gave way to more animated expressions.

Wars started by Waylan's cohorts to insure bottom lines. Murders of countless millions of people in the name of domination and money. Blackmail of state and federal officials from scandals instigated by his own workforce. Prostitution, child trafficking, drug cartels and arms races.

It had been nearly eighty years since Doctor Waylan Scott, Esquire had been publicly outed for this very same list of crimes. The very same list of crimes that he'd been guilty of over centuries of time.

Grady tried to look like he was confident, even pleased, with the reports from Waylan's clan of despots. His blood boiled as he clenched his fists below the table, fingernails digging into his skin.

"That brings us to you, sir", a voice shook Grady back to the room.

Shit. Think fast, Grady.

Grady put his hands on the table and pushed himself to his feet once again only to find a hand pressing him back down to his seat.

"Please take your seat, sir", the robotic voice of his sentry reiterated.

"Mister Scott, if you would please indulge us on your time away, we can wrap things up and begin your debrief", the proctor of the meeting said.

Think, Grady! Think!

"Everything went as planned. I was able to obtain the artifacts and the threat has been neutralized", he feigned.

Silence on the line, again.

"Needless to say, I think we're in the clear to continue business as usual, gentlemen. Now, if there's nothing else, we can call this meeting adjourned."

A man's face appeared on the screen that Grady hasn't seen yet.

"Did you say all of the artifacts, sir? We have them all?" he said.

"That's correct", Grady replied. "All of the artifacts have been obtained."

Chapter 65

The man in the holoscreen looked off camera with wide eyes and quickly turned back to face forward. Concerned, it was suddenly very apparent to Grady that something was off about all of this.

A small clicking sound was coming through an open mic on the call and Grady heard a low hum in the room with him. He went to stand again and his enforcers both pressed him to his seat and held him in place. The humming sound was accompanied by a rattling and the room began to shake. The glass doors and walls cracked and Grady was flooded with raw fear.

The glass shattered, throwing shards through the room. The table quaked as the entire room seemed to sway. The legs gave out on the heavy piece of furniture and it came crashing to the ground and narrowly missed crushing Grady's lower extremities.

Adrenaline coursed through his veins. The room shook violently around him, yet the men behind him remained perfectly still. Their grip was tight on Grady's shoulders preventing him from standing. As the walls began to crumble, Grady slipped out of his chair towards the floor and managed to shake the grasp of the men.

He bolted through the broken glass and down the long hallway. The enforcers turned in unison and took off after Grady. He was only steps ahead of them when he came to the double doors at the end of the hall. He pushed on them, pulled with all of his might, but they didn't budge.

The drone-like men closed in on Grady and he ducked to try and escape their clutches. He managed to dodge one of the men, but the other caught him by his wrist and yanked him away from the doors. Holding him under both arms, he wrenched Grady's shoulders behind him, nearly pulling them from their sockets. The second guard righted himself and approached them and just as he was within reach, a chunk of concrete and steel fell from the collapsing ceiling.

The man fell to the floor under the ball of rubble and Grady saw sparks fly and he shielded his face as best as he could. Liquid poured from the body of the enforcer and Grady could smell oil, suddenly.

Androids! Of course!

The ceiling continued to drop chunks of the floors above them into the hallway. The floor below them heaved as the building convulsed horrifically.

"Can't you see he's dead?! We're going to die here. Waylan Scott is going to die unless you do something about it!" Grady screamed at the robot holding him hostage.

"Independent sentry protocol activated", the golem-man uttered.

All at once, Grady was picked up and both he and the robot crashed through the doors into the garage. The ground started to fall from beneath them as the android deftly maneuvered through the craggy upheavals and reached the SUV. The doors swung open automatically and the droid threw himself into the vehicle with Grady in his arms.

The lights in the vehicle started to illuminate as Grady felt his stomach lurch upward. He could feel that the ground had fallen from beneath the car, but there was complete silence inside. The guard seemed unaffected as always as he sat in the front of the vehicle staring straight ahead.

Grady felt a jostling and then there was nothing. He suspected the building collapsed on top of them and they were likely buried alive. Grady found himself wondering if being buried alive after having his trinkets returned to him would equate to dying or not. As he sat in the seat he began to sweat and hyperventilate. Trying to gain composure, he reached for the door handle and found there was none.

Trapped in a car, trapped under a building. This is it Grady, this is how you die. In agony, of starvation. Torturous and slow just like Waylan would have wanted.

The android exited the vehicle and Grady's door opened up a few seconds later. They were back in the same spot at the Reformation Facility and Grady was entirely confused.

He ran through the labyrinth of hallways to his suite and frantically searched for a television, a radio, anything to find out what he'd just miraculously lived through.

"Where the hell are the TVs in this place?" He shouted to no one, distraught and bankrupt of emotions.

It had never occurred to Grady that there were no televisions in the quarters at all. In fact, the only screens he'd seen his entire imprisonment here were the ones that appeared in The Brink and on the thick doors on the numerous cells. He paced in Waylan's office trying to calm himself down.

The Brink...

Now that his sentinels were down by one, he thought it might give him a chance to infiltrate the restricted area. He walked through his quarters' entrance and, to his delight, found his guard stationed at the door, his suit covered in concrete dust.

"You, clean yourself up. What do you think this is, a county dump?"

The guard didn't move.

Grady didn't care.

Chapter 66

Grady walked as quickly as he could without causing alarm. He was confident no one was watching, but it was increasingly obvious that, even in death, Waylan Scott was *always* watching. He turned a few corners in the wrong direction in order to throw off anyone following him. He made too many lefts followed by too many rights, followed by stairwells up and down in every direction.

Grady, you're losing it. You run this place. You're the only one here. Someone just tried having you killed. You're in shock. Calm down. Get to The Brink.

He slowed his gait and settled his mind. He wasn't sure what he would find when he got to The Brink, but it had to be worth keeping away from him. As he neared his destination, he saw a man standing at the end of the hallway. Not in front of the blank, white room, but close enough to make Grady skittish. Grady turned away and started down the hallway in the opposite direction.

Coward.

Bolstering himself, he turned down the hallway once more and started toward The Brink. As he approached, the man looked up at him and made a few steps in his direction. Still more than two hundred feet away, Grady kept moving with purpose toward the empty room. The man kept moving toward Grady.

He's looking right at me and he's walking too quickly. Not an android.

Grady stopped in the middle of the hallway and the man followed suit. Grady started toward his destination again, and the man advanced on him. Grady stopped, as did the man.

What is this guy playing at?

Standing as tall as he could, Grady walked toward The Brink with determination. The man straightened his posture and kept walking toward

Grady. As Grady closed in on the man, he raised his right hand to his side, fist clenched. The mysterious figure did the same. Twenty feet apart, Grady set into a run and reared his fist back to subdue the man. The man had evidently meant to do the same as he reared his arm back as well.

Hold on a minute. The Brink.

Grady stopped mere feet from the man and put his arm down and the man mimed the movements in return. Grady turned his head to his left and the man turned his to Grady's right. He recalled the first time Waylan tried to kill him in this place. The holoscreen, the premonitory movements, the foreshadowing of his foiled death.

Grady walked toward The Brink and passed through the man at the center of the doors.

Clever, Waylan.

Grady smirked to himself and approached the massive glass doors and pushed on them. An alert buzzed inside and then stopped. Grady tried to pry his fingers between the two doors, but they were plumb to one another, almost impossible to discern as doors if he hadn't already known about them.

"Now what, Grady", he muttered to himself.

The doors hissed open and the robotic female voice said "passcode accepted".

Grady walked into the cavernous, bright white, empty room.

"Now what, indeed, Evescha", Waylan's voice echoed in the vacant space.

Interlude

Waylan had enough time to prepare for you.

A game, no doubt. A cruel, unscrupulous game.

Grady, you need to be a step ahead of him. You need to be cautious. He's dead now and he could have only planned so far.

If you can figure out the game from the inside, you may be able to unravel it, but mind the view from thirty thousand feet. You have to be vigilant, old friend.

You can't play this game as a twentieth century man -- you cannot be Grady Sachs here. He is taunting Evescha Heller. He has always been following Evescha Heller.

This plot isn't going to be played out in modern advances alone, no. Fionnghall Alba... Baird Muir will be playing along, just as much as the good Doctor.

You are both -- were both -- transcendent of time.

Keep an open mind, Grady. You and Waylan may have been without bounds, but this world isn't grounded in the fantastic. The tangential can only achieve so much, even in these new times.

Every move needs to be calculated. You have to match him until you can make a break for it.

He's fooled you before.

He cannot have that luxury again.

Chapter 67

Grady hesitated before he walked through the entryway. The doors quietly slid shut behind him and Waylan's voice echoed through the cavernous chamber.

"Evescha, my dear friend. No doubt you have returned to the scene of the crime."

Grady seethed at the sound of his voice, turning in place to make sure he was, in fact, alone.

"I trust you've received your gifts? It took some time to put your pieces together but once you began to retrace your steps to the Garbh Uisge, it all started to make sense." Waylan's voice oozed self-righteousness just as thick as when he was breathing. "I'd walked that river countless times after ridding you from my periphery so many centuries ago. Months after your supposed death, I found the purple stone and the small coin washed ashore in the midst of a drought."

Grady grew impatient at Waylan's speech.

"Get to the point you pri--".

"Once you'd sorted out Baird Muir, it was all clear that my time on this plane was limited." Even in death, he was still cutting Grady off. "Very clever, Heller, though I must admit, I'm not entirely sure how you came to your revelations."

It was a point of peculiarity that Grady had pondered as well. Through all of it, the only thing he could ever come up with was the blood had something to do with it.

"I'm sure, in time", Waylan quietly said "you will reveal that to me as well. Safe travels, my friend. Do keep in touch."

Reveal to a dead man? Keep in touch? This man is nothing unless dramatic.

Chapter 68

Grady stood in the empty room alone. The white walls blended seamlessly to the white floor and ceiling. The more he looked around, the more dizzying the room became.

"I need to sit down", he muttered to himself.

He heard a whirring sound behind him and leapt to the side expecting a trap of some sort. A simple chair slid into place on invisible mechanisms. Grady kicked the side of the chair and it fell over. He booted it a few feet away and nothing happened. As he walked to the chair cautiously, he righted it and took a seat.

Sitting down helped him find his bearings a little better. He studied the room from its center looking for any hint of a door, control room, anything that may help him use this space and find its secrets.

"Control room", he stated aloud.

Nothing happened.

You have to assume nothing is generically automated, Grady. Waylan would have made things personal, just like opening the doors with a question only you would ask.

"He thinks he can still control me?" he asked the room.

Still nothing.

It won't be that easy, old friend.

Grady reclined in the chair and looked at the ceiling. He scanned the wide area but saw nothing but white and integrated LEDs washing everything above him out. His eyes watered at the sight after a minute or two.

"Not too bright, staring into the sun like that", he quietly said to himself.

The lights dimmed and Grady perked. He wasn't trying to do anything with the room, but some combination of his words had triggered a response.

"Too bright", he said again.

Nothing happened above him.

"The sun", he paused.

Nothing.

"It's like staring into the sun", he said and the lights dimmed further.

The sun makes them dim. The moon should make them brighten.

"Staring at the moon", Grady clearly spoke to the room.

The lights above continued to dim until he could barely make out his feet on the floor.

You don't stare at the moon, Grady. You gaze at it.

"What a night for moon gazing", he said, sheepishly.

The lights in the room rose to full intensity again. Grady smiled to himself and straightened in the chair.

Opposites. Remember that, pal.

Grady spoke the words that dimmed the LEDs as he stood to take a look around the room in the dusky light. He walked the walls running his hand slowly over them looking for any indication of a seam or depression. He inspected every reachable inch of the walls and found nothing. The floor held no secrets that he could gather either.

He sat on the floor and looked all around him once more before laying down on his back with his hands under his head. As he laid there, he felt a wave of fatigue wash over him and he closed his eyes.

No one else can get in here and I run the place. Rest, Grady. It's alright to rest.

He focused on his breath as it resonated quietly through the empty room.

Chapter 69

Grady stretched as he awoke. He looked around the room and found that nothing had changed and wondered how long it had been that he'd slept. He got himself to his feet and started for the door. As he approached the front of the room, he realized there was no door.

Wake up, Grady. Other wall.

He turned to the room and found three white walls looking back at him. He turned to face the doors once more and found the glass wall had gone opaque. Grady backed up to the center of the room and found there was no longer a chair there either. He was trapped in the room with no exit. The lights dimmed around him and he began to panic.

"Nice n-night for moon gazing", he stammered.

The lights went out completely. Grady was surrounded by darkness. He snapped his fingers and the sound spun around his head bouncing off of the walls.

"What a night for moon gazing!" Grady shouted, trying to invoke the automation with the exact words he'd used before.

His voice was choked off in the room where it should have otherwise reverberated. He snapped his fingers again and the sound bounced with a Doppler effect. As it resonated, it was amplified by its own noise and Grady felt as though his eardrums would burst until, suddenly, it was deathly silent.

"Keep it together, old friend", Grady mumbled under his breath.

"Keep it together; everything's alright", a voice crawled from the ether around Grady.

The room burst into light as thunder cracked overhead and rain poured down on Grady. He ran for shelter under a nearby tree a few yards from a building in a pitifully dilapidated state. He heard a child crying in the distance and watched as a cloaked figure walked toward the structure.

The figure stepped over rubble and into the stone corner of the building and walked back out a moment later with their arms wrapped tightly around a small child, no older than a toddler, if that. Grady stepped out from under the tree and watched as the figure removed their hood and looked around.

Grady knelt to the ground trying not to be seen. But, as the man searched in the downpour for something to explain the baby in his arms, Grady leaned out from the shadows.

"Kérem, vigye el. Neveld őt a sajátodnak. Nem tehetem – nem érdemlem meg. Kérem?"

Please, take her. Raise her as your own. I cannot -- I do not deserve her. Please?

He felt a pang of guilt in his stomach and his chest tightened. He turned his back to the little girl as the man shielded her from the downpour. Grady cried as he raced up the hillside and down the worn dirt road. Hot tears ran down his cheeks as the cold rain soaked him through to his bones.

He found the candlelight of a field stone building flickering ahead and he ran toward it. As he approached, three men spilled from the doorway carrying on with one another before one stumbled to the ground. The other men helped him up, roaring with laughter as they swayed down the street.

Grady walked through the door and sat in the corner, shivering under his clothes. He looked down at his hands and found they were much smaller than he recalled. He felt his face and, even under numb fingertips, noted the softness of his features. He stood and walked to the bar top against the wall and asked where he could find the restroom.

"Hol van a fürdőház?"

"Du bist zu jung, um hier zu sein!" the man behind the bar pointed to the door screaming.

Grady understood the gesture enough to take off without another word.

As he bundled himself into his wool cloak, he found a nook in an alleyway that was out of the way of most of the weather. The night grew darker and colder. Grady couldn't feel his fingers and toes anymore. Again, tears streamed down his face as he laid his head back against the stone wall and cried himself to sleep.

Grady woke to a painful feeling in his chest. He opened his eyes wearily and tried to inhale, but there was no breath to be drawn. His gaze was fixed on a window of a stone building just in front of him. The daylight surrounded him and he felt an emptiness where his lungs should have been. The sun grew brighter and brighter until his vision was thoroughly bleached.

Grady startled awake and got to his feet quickly sprinting from the spot on the floor. He backed against the wall furthest from the glass doors and looked around. The chair was exactly where it had been. The lights were dimmed to the same dusky tones.

What in the hell just happened?

Grady walked toward the great glass doors slowly.

"What a night for moon gazing", he said.

The lights rose and the room was illuminated just as it had been when he walked in. As he approached the doors, they separated and the air from the room blew out into the hallway. Grady turned back toward the room and stared at the vast white nothingness and wiped his face as he backed out the doors and watched them gently close behind him.

Chapter 70

Waylan said the room was something special for people in our special circumstances. What was it he said? He could glean things from his past.

Was I reliving something from mine?

Grady, how could you be? What language was that, German? Hungarian? The buildings were far older than anything you could remember.

That voice, your voice was female, wasn't it?

As Grady took the scenic route back to his quarters, he couldn't shake the feeling of emptiness he'd felt in his chest.

It was so real. Hearing that child cry, the pangs of guilt and sorrow.

The frigid cold.

The rain.

The building and the man. Wait...

Grady recalled a story his mother would tell him when he was younger of a man named Carl, her father. Though not truly her father, he was as good as any father could be. The German shearer and spinner that took her in as a small girl and raised her as his own until a horrific night that changed her life forever.

As he neared his room, the android gargoyle backed away from the center of the doorway as they parted for entry. Grady stopped in his tracks and fell to his knees.

Mother...

The thought of his dear mother flooded his mind and he was overcome with emotion. He held his face in his hands as he crumpled into his own lap and sobbed. The vision he'd had in The Brink was of his mother. More accurately, he had seen through his gypsy grandmother's eyes the events of the night when she had abandoned her child.

He pulled himself to his hands and knees, unable to muster the strength to stand. Exhausted from the lucidity of The Brink and the crushing visions of his mother as a baby, he drug himself to his bed.

"What did you see, old friend?"

The room spoke with Waylan's voice -- Grady seethed at the sound.

"Damn you to hell, you bastard!" Grady shouted into the emptiness.

"Now, now, Evescha. Is that any way to talk to your only confidant?"

The simpering smirk was weighty in the air on his words. Grady upended a nightstand and launched to his feet.

"You're dead! This nightmare was supposed to be over!" Grady clamored at the nothingness. "All of this was supposed to be over..." Grady whimpered as he sat back on the bed with his head hung low.

"Tsk, tsk, tsk", Waylan's condescending voice scolded, almost as if he were sitting beside Grady. "I will always be a step ahead of you, Evescha. The afterlife cannot compromise that, not with the advent of such modernities as advanced artificial intelligence."

Grady looked up toward the ceiling with a menacing look in his eyes.

"Baird, I will be rid of you somehow", he snarled through gritted teeth.

"You saw your past, didn't you?" Waylan cooed, almost melodiously. "Tell me, dear friend, what was it you saw? Your death? *My* death?"

Grady allowed the silence to swell, Waylan's words hanging in the air.

"Tell me what you saw, Evescha!"

Grady startled at the sudden outburst.

Impatience. That's not like Waylan at all.

The AI can't regulate itself; it can only react.

Grady sat silently a moment longer, testing the program.

"EVESCHA, TELL ME EVERYTHING!" The AI's voice clipped and glitched as it shouted in Waylan's voice.

It's afraid, same as Waylan was.

It doesn't know the things I know, only what Waylan knew or might have learned from keeping me in his sights.

It needs input -- input that Waylan couldn't provide. But for what?

"My past, Alba. I saw my past, the night you drowned me. The night you damned me to this cursed life", Grady told the apparition.

Silence fell on the room once more. Grady gathered himself and walked toward the doors of the quarters. The android detail stepped between him and the hallway and pointed behind him.

"Useless, Evescha. Useless as always", pseudo-Waylan's frustration evident in every syllable.

"Careful, Waylan, you don't want your emotions getting the best of you", Grady said as he smugly walked past the guard.

Chapter 71

Grady made his rounds through the facility and watched the Penalized as they took to their routines as usual. He walked the catwalk above the cellblocks and he noted a man in the corner pressed against the glass doors to the courtyard. Grady paused and watched the man, an anomaly amongst the rest.

As he stood twenty feet above him, he heard the man as he muttered to himself and then it all clicked. It was the old man who'd warned Grady about the water when he'd arrived. He looked different now, oddly misshapen and hunched.

"You, old timer", Grady called out. "Everything alright?"

The man stopped whispering to himself, stopped moving entirely and then jerked his body around and stared straight at Grady as if he'd known he was being watched all along.

"You aren't gonna make me one of them!" The man shouted, holding a hand up, blood streaming down his arm.

Grady stared in shock at the man and he shouted, over and over, that he wouldn't be turned into "one of them".

"One of them?" Grady, genuinely curious, inquired.

"None of these bastards are real! You're just playing a foul game! I'll never let you take me!" he screamed, staring with wide eyes at Grady like a feral animal.

He's lost it, Grady. He'll wind up neutralized like the rest, no reason for concern.

The crazed man held his bloody hand high with something pinched between his fingers. It flashed a small red beacon and then popped with a small puff of mist. It was then that Grady noticed the man's leg with blood pooling around his foot.

He figured out the implant! How long has he been here?

The man turned his back on Grady and started toward the administrative wing as fast as he would. Grady walked the catwalk above him and watched as he feebly made his way to the double doors at the end of the hall. The lights blared white on the other side of the glass, no doubt pulsing red to anyone still under compliance protocols.

The old man reached the doors and pushed against them and, to Grady's surprise, they opened.

Do the automations only work in conjunction with the implant?

Grady observed through the glass wall at the end of the catwalk as the man hobbled through the hallway looking to either side. Clearly lost, he spun in circles and made his way to the closest door. Grady took the flight of stairs downward and followed the man down the hallway and through the door he'd disappeared behind.

"You doing alright, pal?" Grady called into the hallway.

As he turned the corner and looked down the corridor he noticed that this particular passageway was very outdated, almost purposeful. Wooden doors, drop ceilings, incandescent lights. Beige and mundane.

"Sir, do you need some help?" He asked mindlessly as he looked around at the dated decor.

Just as he'd turned to look in the small window of one of the wooden doors, he felt a sharp pain in his side and a silent exhale of breath against the back of his neck.

"I know who you are. You aren't like the rest of them. You aren't like the guards or the maggots in this damned place. You're the showrunner, the puppeteer. But I figured you out."

The man groaned and Grady felt a twisting in his guts. It was then he realized he'd been stabbed with something. Small, but effective, the pain caused him to lean against the doorframe as he turned toward his assailant.

"Congratulations", he exhaled in pain, "you figured out the implant just like you figured out the water. I'm impressed."

Feigning his charade as Waylan, he winced as he tried to remain as patronizing as possible.

"You've passed the test, friend. You've even made it so far as to bait me into a trap. I commend your efforts in winning this game."

Grady played into the man's delusional state as he stood straight. The thought of his artifacts crossed his mind and he felt sweat beading on his brow, suddenly reminded of his precarious position.

"Let's you and I go to the hospital wing and we'll get you cleaned up. I have a business proposition for you", Grady offered.

The man stood and looked at Grady, confused.

"I can't stay here any longer. I can't", the man sniveled.

"You won't be with them anymore. Come, let's talk while we get stitched up."

Grady tried to walk as straight as he could as the man hobbled just behind him, clearly wary of the turn of events. As they exited the dated hallway, Grady has a sense of deja vu. He'd been in this hall before. He was ushered from this hallway before he was ejected from Waylan's office below the prison he was sentenced to some eighty years ago. He was standing in, seemingly, the exact psych ward that Waylan had spent countless hours doing god knows what to Grady.

The old man waved his hand in front of Grady's face jogging him back to reality. He shook his head and walked through the doorway at the end of the hall. Grady couldn't help but look over his shoulder as the hairs on the back of his neck stood on end.

It's all a puzzle, Grady. Waylan's toying with you.

Why would you save this room, Waylan? What happened here that you want me to discover?

Chapter 72

The old man was silent for the entire walk to Waylan's private infirmary. He looked around in awe at the corridors he'd never been authorized for. Without his compliancy implant, Grady had no problem taking him through the back halls and restricted areas of the Reformation Facility.

Frail and contorted, he edged himself away from the nurse when she attempted to stitch his leg suspecting a new implant would be inserted. The nurse simply applied skin adhesive and a couple of butterfly bandages and turned to tend to Grady's wound.

Grady laid back on his bed as a trio of medical staff went to work on the well the codger had dug into his side.

"How long have you been here, Mister..." Grady realized he'd never bothered to know the man's name even though they'd met when he first arrived himself.

The man looked at the ceiling and around the room for some invisible something. His eyes darted wildly before he jolted to his feet and made for the door. He wasn't quick, and he was clearly malnourished on top of it. The nurses looked to Grady for direction and he shrugged them off.

"Let him go, he won't get far, and he can't get out", he lazily waved his hand and adjusted himself while he was cleaned up and stitched together.

The feeling of falling rattled Grady awake. He opened his eyes and was surrounded by complete blackness. His stomach lurched as he fell through the nothingness flailing his arms and legs wildly.

He opened his mouth to scream but no sound came.

He inhaled and no breath entered his lungs.

He went to grab his chest and felt nothing on his fingertips.

Grady fell through the infinite darkness in complete numbness and paralyzing fear.

An alarm sounded and Grady woke up in his hospital bed. He looked around, bleary-eyed and groggy and saw a red light flashing overhead. He checked his leg frantically and saw no blinking diode. He leapt from the bed and toward the doors of the infirmary. It wasn't too far down the hallway he'd seen the cause for alarm. The old man had grabbed one of the staff by the throat and was dragging them out of the hospital wing as a hostage.

"You can't take me!" he shouted repeatedly.

"Let them go!" Grady shouted back over the alarm. "Let him go, they haven't done anything to you. If you want someone to pay for what's been done to you here, I'll go willingly."

The man paused, staring Grady down before he threw the nurse to the floor. Grady ran to the man and rolled him to his back just as his eyes rolled back into his head.

Murderer. Duly noted.

Grady carefully rose to his feet and approached the old man with his arms out at his sides. The old man wielded a scalpel like a fencing foil as Grady closed in on him.

"Come on, old timer. I stitched you up, you aren't in any danger here. These are my personal wards, no one here will do anything without my say so." Grady attempted to quell the man's rightful paranoia.

"Stay the fuck back you bastards. All of you, BACK!"

Grady neared him cautiously, almost close enough to reach him. The man lunged at Grady with the blade as Grady sidestepped the attack.

The gaffer swung wildly and threw himself off balance causing him to lose his footing and crash to the floor. Grady blanketed himself over the man and pried the instrument from his worn hand.

"Listen to me, you fool!" Grady sneered into the man's ear. "I am offering you your freedom from this game. You cannot leave this place, not yet, but you can cooperate and find yourself a sense of peace."

The man whimpered under Grady's weight and began to cry.

"Please, just let me go. Let me die", he sniffled between words.

Grady pushed himself off of the man and sat against the wall panting to catch his breath.

"I'm Evescha Heller. What's your name, friend?" Grady attempted to extend kindness to the man as the life spilled from the caregiver on the floor in front of him.

"I-I..." the man stammered, "I can't remember. It's been so long without speaking to anyone, I can't remember!" He sobbed as he realized he'd lost himself to the Reformation Facility whether he fought it or not.

Grady reached a hand out and kneaded the man's shoulder.

"How about I call you Pa for now? I'll try and help you find yourself if you can help me with a few things."

The man relaxed his head against the tile next to Grady and exhaled in concession.

"My grandkids would have called me that, I think", Pa sniggered to himself.

Chapter 73

Pa didn't ask how Grady came to be the warden, and Grady didn't ask how Pa wound up in the system. They respected the fact that they were free men confined to their fortress of conviction. More off, they respected that they were both due their privacies after being kept under the watchful eye of the Reformation Facility. As such, over the next few weeks, they'd built a bit of a rapport, albeit on shaky foundations.

"I need you to do something for me, Pa", Grady said over a shared meal.

"Whatcha got in mind, Ev?" The man replied through a mouthful of food.

"Let's take a walk. There's a room I want to show you."

They took to the labyrinth of hallways after their lunch. Grady found that he had grown very familiar with the maze. He felt a sinking feeling in his stomach -- the prison was starting to feel like home.

They cornered the hallway that held The Brink and Pa stopped dead in his tracks.

"You son of a bitch", he growled. "You said I was free of the games. Why did you bring me here?"

Grady walked to the doors and they slid open.

"Please, Pa. I know it's not what you expected, but you don't have your implant anymore. This room can't do anything to you", Grady bargained. "Trust me, if you can. The room was designed to use the implant for control. You're safe."

Pa fixed his eyes on the massive white room as he met Grady at the doors.

"You first", Pa commanded.

"Of course", Grady agreed.

Pa followed Grady into the room and the doors slid shut soundlessly. Pa looked around in wonder. Grady had recalled the room looked the same before his implant was employed and wondered if it was the same for all of the other Penalized when they were brought here.

"This room was used to intimidate you, wasn't it?" Grady asked Pa.

Pa nodded, tears forming in his eyes.

"This goddamned room showed me my children. My grandkids. Showed me my great-grandchildren -- I don't even have any." Pa dissociated as he recounted the experience. "Showed them all to me... all of them dying. Brutal, horrible deaths."

Pa wiped his eyes as he focused his attention on Grady.

"Why did you bring me here, Ev?" He nearly choked on his words.

"This is why I need your help, Pa."

Grady walked to the center of the room and declared a meeting was to take place. Two seats slid into the center of the room and a small round table accompanied them. Grady sat down and held a hand out inviting Pa to join him.

"Pa, this room isn't just for conditioning the Penalized. It can be used for so much more, but only to certain people. People with..." Grady paused searching for the right words. "...people with certain carnage in their pasts. It can provide a kind of therapy -- insight into the psyche. The compartmentalized and the repressed."

Pa leaned toward and cocked an eyebrow. "What are you hiding, Ev?"

"I just need you to watch the room for a little while. I'm going to dim the lights. I need you to pay attention to anything the room does, anything that happens to me." Grady laid on the floor beside the table.

"Not really time for a snooze, Ev. You're leaving me hanging here", Pa shook his head.

"It's so bright in here, isn't it Pa? Like staring into the sun."

Chapter 74

The warmth of the fire did little to stave off the bitter cold in the stone hut. A man shot from his bed and pointed to stuffed burlap bags stacked against the wall. A loud pounding came from the door and the man's large hand reached out and shook Grady wide awake. Pointing again at the pile of sacks, Grady felt a swell of panic in his chest.

Darting to the bags, Grady piled them on top of himself leaving a small opening to keep watch.

"Heller!" a shout rang through the night. "Heller, open the door. You owe me payment for your little secret!"

The man reached for the door as Grady watched through the small hole. A loud bang and the door slammed into the wall as it was kicked from the man's hand. Three men entered the small home and two grabbed the proprietor by his arms.

"Carl Heller. You've been keeping something here for quite some time, and dues are owed for it", the burly man scoffed, his voice sounding like rolling thunder.

Carl Heller? Mari's father? My grandfather?

Grady watched as Carl pleaded with the men to leave his house, that he had nothing to hide, that the girl he apprenticed was only that and she had gone to her own home just like every night before that.

The man shoved Carl to the side and took a seat as he claimed his debts will be settled tonight. Grady felt himself nudge backward and then felt the bags above him start to slip forward. Terror ran cold through Grady's veins as the massive man shot from his seat and closed the gap on him.

Before Grady could react, he felt his hair being pulled as he was snatched up by the man and threw him to the corner of the room. Grady felt a draft of air from the doorway as it closed and he watched the two men hold Carl tightly as the giant pulled Grady's leg, yanking him across the rough floor. Grady looked back at the man and noted his small legs and the hem of a night dress.

No. No, no, no, no!

"No, no, no!"

Grady's thoughts escaped his mouth just as the man's massive hand pushed his face into the dirt floor and he felt an impossible weight on top of him. Stars in his eyes, Grady felt a sharp pain between his legs and a pressure against his body. The sharp pain turned into a searing agony as he realized what was happening.

Cognizant of his own thoughts, he could not separate himself from what was happening to this small body. As the man laid on top of him a moment longer, he smashed Grady's head into the floor. Tears streamed down Grady's cheek as he stared into the corner of the ceiling. Muffled shouts rang through the house, but Grady's body was broken, his mind trapped. He couldn't move, he just cried silently and motionlessly.

Grady's eyes settled on the floor in front of him just as Carl slumped to his knees, his hands holding his stomach as blood flowed like a river through his fingers. He felt his body go numb and then his vision went black.

Falling again, his arms and legs flailing at his sides. Grady's eyes snapped open, or at least he thought they had, but he was in utter blackness once more. His stomach was in his throat as he gasped for breath but, again, found none. He closed his eyes and embraced the fall waiting for the eventual crash as he hit whatever he was falling towards.

Chapter 75

"Ev. Hey Ev. Ev!" Pa shouted as he snapped his fingers in Grady's face.

Grady's eyes focused on the man's hand as his eyes rolled back into place. He snorted a rough breath into his lungs as if he had awakened from the dead and sat up like he'd been prodded with electricity.

"W-w... What happened? What did you see?" He demanded of Pa.

"Calm down, take it easy. You had a seizure. Do you need me to get one of the nursing staff in here?" Pa asked as he put his hands on Grady's shoulders and patted his face trying to keep him jogged into lucidity.

"Pa, what happened?" Grady sighed, exhausted.

"You were out cold for a minute or two and then you screamed and started having tremors before you went limp. Thought you were dead, but then you started seizing again before I tried to snap you out of it."

Grady rubbed his temples and wiped the sweat from his forehead.

"How long was I out?" Grady asked.

"Two, maybe three minutes. Wasn't long", Pa offered a hand to Grady to help him stand. "Didn't look like you had any control over your body at all", he said with certitude.

A hissing sound cut through the air from behind them. Both men turned their heads, tense and ready to retreat. The Brink was anything but safe, no matter how much Grady lied to himself about it. A door opened from the seamless white wall.

"Great night for moon gazing", Grady commanded the room to illuminate.

He took Pa's hand and got to his feet already in stride toward the portal. As he neared the doorway, he saw that The Brink had revealed another entirely white, completely empty room. Pa followed Grady with trepidation and curiosity until they both stood beyond the threshold and the door closed behind them.

Grady could feel Pa's uneasiness as the room closed in around them.

"We're fine, Pa. Just give it a second." Grady feigned confidence trying to squelch his own anxiety.

A holoscreen blinked into view in the center of the room. Grady approached it and held out a hand. The yellowed interface blinked orange and then burst into full color.

"Welcome Evescha. I'm glad you made it!" Waylan's voice came through the walls.

Not this again. Another piece of the puzzle, Grady.

"I'm surprised it took you so long to figure out you needed a companion to get in here. The Brink isn't designed to be used as one person, at least not effectively. Tell me, who is your cohort?" Waylan's voice bounced along casually.

"Who is that? Who's there?" Pa's head darted from side to side.

"The puppeteer, Pa. Meet Waylan Scott, or rather, the program that is playing the part with annoying accuracy."

"Pa, you say? Fitting name coming from a man who never knew his own father. I suppose Freud had a point with the subconscious desires theory", Waylan quietly laughed to himself. "Greetings, Pa. Pleased to meet you. As Evescha mentioned, I am Doctor Waylan Scott, Esquire. I am the man who founded this lovely center and developed the reformation techniques we use here."

"You--You bastard! You filthy fucking bast--"

"Evescha, please, do quiet your companion", Waylan interrupted Pa's tirade.

Pa tensed in the middle of the room as he stared at the screen in front of them. Grady reached both hands out and began to move things around in midair until he pulled Waylan's disembodied head into view somehow.

"Ah, good to see you, old friend!" Wayland's smile sickened Grady as he stared at the hologram.

"What is it now, Baird?" Grady tersely replied.

"You are standing in the control room, the brain of this delightful apparatus. I'm sure you've spent a great deal of time wondering if there even *was* a control room considering what it can do with your mind in isolation, Evescha." Waylan's disgusting simper was painted across his face.

So there is a way to direct this thing, maybe?

Pa prodded at the holoscreen, careful not to press anything that looked important. Grady looked around the empty room as Waylan carried on in his typical monologuing ways.

No physical controls, no windows, nothing tactile in the least.

Everything must be controlled by this holoscreen. I'll need to figure out how it works and show Pa.

Christ, this will be like explaining lightning to a cavema--

The room went dark all of a sudden and Grady heard Pa's feet shuffling around.

"Shit, Ev. I think I messed something up. Ev? You there?"

"Over here, Pa. Stand still, give me a second", Grady assured the old timer.

Grady put his arms in front of him and scanned the area with his fingertips as he slowly walked forward. He touched the wall and walked to his left until he'd bumped into Pa.

"Lights out I guess", Grady sighed.

"Yeah, darker 'n a gorilla's armpit in here, ain't it?" Pa replied, matching Grady's exasperation.

"Whoa, whoa, wait a minute. Ev, you see that?"

Grady looked around and saw nothing but pitch darkness. He waved his hands in front of his face and could barely make them out.

Good, not blind at least.

"I got nothin', Pa."

"Hang on, I think I can... just one second", Pa's voice trailed off in concentration.

A low glow appeared in the wall from floor to ceiling and then separated revealing the larger chamber of The Brink. Grady looked around and the control room was still pitch black.

"Door oughta be open to get back out", said Pa.

"I see it", Grady replied curiously.

"Makes one of us. The hell's goin' on here?" Pa's voice was oddly calm given the situation.

"Hang back in here... I have an idea", Grady gestured to the blackness, unsure if Pa could see anything at all.

As he exited the control room, The Brink swallowed the seamless door and Grady was, once again, alone in the white void. He made his way to the center of the room once more and sat in the chair placing his hands on his knees. Looking forward, he concentrated on the thought of his mother. The rape, the murder she saw.

"Pa, can you hear me?"

"Loud and clear, Ev. I got that holo-thing in here. Looks different now that you're outta the room. Makes sense all of a sudden. Got a prompt on the screen, Ev. Says 'Initiate'. Whaddaya think?" Pa asked Grady, knowing the answer was yes.

"I'm ready", Grady exhaled a long breath before closing his eyes.

"No, Evescha, I fear you are not." Waylan's voice echoed through the room.

Chapter 76

Grady felt a great weight pulling against his arms as his heels slipped in the mud. His small hands were holding the ankles of a large man, stiff and bloodied.

Carl... mother.

A flash and then a hole being dug. Another and a body laid in the shallow pit. Hands in a river. Then crying himself to sleep.

This is all part of the machine, Grady. You're here to observe.

Marioziota Heller spent her days shearing sheep and reciting verses and songs to herself. Grady lived the experiences through his mother's hands. A swell of emotion came to Grady as he listened to her sweet voice singing herself lullabies.

"Father, I miss you", she whispered as tears streamed down her face and she held her belly as she fell to sleep.

Mother, I miss you.

Grady's vision went black as his mother closed her eyes before the floor slipped from beneath him once again.

Flailing, falling, utter darkness.

This again? What is this place?

The air around him was soundless, in fact, it wasn't air at all. The sensation of falling was the only thing Grady could feel. He pondered this momentarily before remembering words from one of his favorite authors, Orson Scott Card. In 'Ender's Game' it was noted by the titular character that "the enemy's gate is down" while in antigravity.

You are not falling, Grady.

You can't be falling when there is nothing to fall through.

Right yourself. Find your bearings.

Just then, as if he had willed it, Grady stopped falling. The blackness remained but it was as if he was enveloped in warm salt water. He could hear his heart beating in the void. The sound was loud, but calming. Calming until he felt the water drain from around him.

A tightness surrounded him now and he felt his legs press against his torso. There was pressure against his head and then cold chilled him from head to toe. His mouth opened and a shrill cry came from his whole body.

There was a peaceful shushing sound as he felt something rough rubbing against his skin. His cries lessened and then there was warmth against his face and warm, sweet liquid across his tongue. His vision was blurred as he opened his eyes and then he saw her -- his mother, sweet Marioziota.

His little body shivered as his mother wrapped him in her cloak and made for her house under the still of night. A small fire warmed the home, but only enough to not freeze to death. Mari held her baby boy tightly as she fed him. Grady's eyes grew heavy. He closed them as his mother sang him a lullaby and sweetly kissed his head.

Interlude

Bizarre, yes.

But that doesn't explain why Waylan would want to keep me from The Brink.

There's nothing in my past that could hurt him. Nothing that can make him any more dead than he already is.

What is it that he is so worried that I'll find here?

I have witnessed my mother taken in by a stranger.

The awful rape that resulted in my conception.

My own birth.

I know my life beyond this point, I've lived it.

What is it you're hiding Waylan? Can you manipulate how The Brink presents manifestations?

What have you put in this place for me to find?

Chapter 77

Grady retched as he coughed up blood onto the pristine white floor. A sharp pain shot through his chest followed quickly by the feeling of something snapping in half. Grady opened his eyes and saw Pa as he stood above him, foaming at the mouth as he kicked him in the ribs.

He tried to get out from under the codger, but he couldn't move his arm without his chest feeling like it was going to split open. He brought his legs up to a fetal position and swept them back down as he yelped in agony. Pa crashed to the floor, unable to catch himself from the sudden defensive maneuver. His head hit the white tile with a resounding thud and he laid still.

Grady got to his hands and knees as quickly as he could and cradled his broken ribcage. Straddling Pa's chest, he pressed his knees into his arms to keep him down. Pa laid on the ground muttering something to himself as his eyes moved around frantically in their sockets.

"Can't be. Can't do that. Can't. Tracy. Can't. Please stop. No! Freddy, Sharon! NO!"

Pa screamed and shoved Grady from his chest with a primal strength otherwise impossible for a man as frail as him. He scrambled to get to his feet but fell back to the ground before trying once more. His hands slipped from under him and blood splattered onto the alabaster floor from a shattered nose.

Grady tried to stand, still doubled over in excruciating pain and he mounted Pa again, pulling one of his arms back and wrenching it upward threatening to pull his shoulder from its socket.

"PA! Get a hold of yourself!" Grady shouted as he shoved his arm further upward.

Pa groaned a guttural noise and his shoulder distorted inhumanly as he rolled out of Grady's grasp. He shoved his good shoulder into Grady's torso and Grady screamed before falling off of Pa.

Both men clamored to their feet as Pa took off in a dead sprint. Grady ran behind him as quickly as he could follow, trying to straighten himself up. Pa blew through the doors at the end of the hall beyond The Brink and then ran up the stairs on all fours like a crazed animal until he reached the ground floor. Grady followed as closely as he could, lagging a floor or so behind Pa until he heard a wailing seemingly from outside.

There was a blaring of a klaxon, exactly the sound of World War Two air raid drills. Grady burst through a door that hadn't existed prior to now that he could recall. He found Pa standing in the middle of a grassy area with no fence as far as he could see.

Waylan had an exit just in case he needed to bail, smart.

Is this actually outside of the compound, or just another mockery of the world beyond the Reformation Facility?

The klaxon blared three times exactly and then abruptly ended. The air was still and silent. Grady could hear Pa rambling to himself as he held his head, pulling at his hair and spinning in circles. He squatted to the ground and turned to Grady, rage in his eyes as tears streamed down his age-weathered face.

Grady panted, propping himself in the doorway. Pa stared at him like a terrified animal. Grady remembered a night, long ago, when he'd seen the same look in a sickly wolf's eyes as it fended for its life. Pa stood slowly, backing away from Grady even though he was already yards away.

"Pa, what's wrong? What happened?" Grady called to the man just as he turned and made a break for the tree line.

Grady sighed and winced in pain. He was about to take off after the old man when there was a low hum that threatened to burst his eardrums. Grady ducked into the corner of the building trying to shield himself from the sound as it grew louder and then suddenly turned into a sharp whistling tone, almost like a kettle of hot water.

He opened one of his eyes just enough to see the landscape in front of him. A streak of light cut through the air and then Pa was gone from view. Grady pushed himself from the wall and ran to find his friend.

As Grady got closer to where he'd last seen Pa, he smelled something like burnt metal in the air. Just before the trees, there was a crater in the ground and steamed rose from it. Grady approached the pit and found nothing but a wet, red hole in the ground. The acrid smell of evaporating blood billowed from the earthen wound.

Grady backed away from the pit and heard the klaxon blaring again. He looked toward the building before it occurred to him, fully, that he was in the line of fire now. He sprinted toward the exit door and heard the siren wail a second, then a third time. Still thirty or so yards from the entrance, Grady felt the ground shake as the low rumble began to wind up.

Twenty yards and the tone began to whine.

Ten yards and the whine was too shrill to hear.

Five yards from the door, Grady dove to the ground just as the streak of light tore through the sky. He felt superheated wind whip over his body and only feet behind him the ground erupted covering him in singed grass and filth. The sub-tone started to wind up again and Grady crawled as quickly as he could until he was able to get his feet underneath him.

His vision blurred from the pain in his chest, exacerbated from throwing himself at the ground. He hobbled as fast as his legs would carry him, barely able to inhale. Just as the shrill sound disappeared, Grady slammed into the emergency door and saw the light flash and the ground in the path he'd just run burst into a cloud of dirt and ash. He slumped to the ground and laid his head against the doorframe as he tried to catch his breath.

The door opened and the guardian android came from behind it.

“Can’t be out here, sir. Not safe.”

The robot extended a hand and helped Grady up.

“I need to get to the infirmary” Grady’s voice strained to choke the words up. “I think I may be dying.” His vision began to narrow to a tunnel. Grady hoped that the droid would take his plea seriously.

Chapter 78

Blackness, once again, surrounded Grady. His senses were alive and he could feel everything, however.

There is no up or down, old friend. You are not falling, you are floating. If you are floating, you can move somehow.

He put his arms out in front of him and did something of a breaststroke as he hung in the void. He felt foolish as he tried such an elementary tactic, but everything was uncharted in the nothing.

Calm your mind, Grady.

If you are not free falling, you are levitating.

Levitation only works if you have something opposing you.

There is a down... somewhere.

Grady steadied himself in the ether and felt a pressure against the soles of his feet. Pillowy, almost like a gymnastics crash mat. His ankles and knees settled atop one another until Grady eventually felt his entire body succumb to something like gravity. He took a step forward like a fawn learning to walk, teetering with each step. As he gained his footing, he walked cautiously, feeling the surface with his toes for anything.

Just then, a thrumming sound whispered behind him. He turned and walked back the way he'd come, or at least the way that seemed to be backward. As he took one trepidatious step before another, the rhythmic sound began to build slightly.

Is that…rain?

As Grady drew closer to the sound, a small light flickered on the horizon. A pang of excitement shot through him. It took everything in him to not run to the landmark. One foot in front of the other, slowly he approached the faint light. The beacon didn't seem to grow as he got closer, however.

Another trick of The Brink, no doubt.

All at once, the light flew toward Grady with a blinding illumination, obscuring his entire field of vision. He raised an arm to shield his eyes from the brightness and then he felt it. A burning sensation spread through his entire body. Grady inhaled sharply and held his ribs, the pain unbearable.

"Doctor Scott, please, we need to restrain you. You are gravely wounded and we need to act quickly", a tranquil voice cooed through the blinding lights.

Grady's vision was blurry and distorted. He could make an outline of a person above him as he felt frigid cold coursing through his body now.

"We have injected you with a sedative, antibiotics, and an intravenous drip of morphine." The woman spoke with a kindness unlike anyone else he'd interacted with in months, years even. "We are rushing you to surgery, sir. We will do all we can to ensure a brisk recovery."

Grady's head lolled until he surrendered to the drugs.

The ground was plush beneath his feet again.

The nothingness.

The blackness seemed somehow lighter now, though there didn't seem to be any source of light.

This has to be The Brink.

I'm not hurt, there is no hospital. Pa is in the control room watching all of this.

Grady walked confidently through the blackness until he tripped over something and lost his footing. His head smashed against the ground, suddenly as hard as concrete, and the black flickered like a dying lightbulb.

He got to his feet and there was a flash above him. Then another. Grady rolled over as he felt blood streaming down his face from his unforgiving fall. He felt grass under his hands and wet ground all around him. Another light streaked across the sky above him, stars now plainly in view.

A bolt of panic burst through his chest and he took off away from the source of light. As he ran, his legs felt like they were going to give way underneath him. He was unable to keep his footing for more than a few steps at a time, falling and splashing in the boggy mire.

Grady's cloak snagged on the underbrush and he pulled himself from it, crawling on hands and knees. The whip of fiery arrows whisked overhead and Grady could hear footsteps sloshing through the mud and reeds behind him.

Hide! Hide!!

Grady sprawled in ankle deep water grabbing an arrow from one of the bodies nearby. He broke the shaft and quickly tucked it under his arm piercing his clothing. He laid as still as he could. Holding his breath, he watched as men ran over him from all directions, bottlenecking as they ran through the trees beyond the swamp.

"Muir, a mhuc! Bidh do chinn uile againn air sleagahn ro dheireadh seo!" A gigantic man stomped through the wetland as he took up the rear, sweeping the area for anyone left alive.

Pigs? Heads on spears? They're hunting.

The barbarian loomed over Grady as he booted each of the bodies that surrounded him. Grady did all he could to stop breathing as the man pushed on the stomachs and chests of each of the fallen. As the man's heavy foot pressed into Grady's chest, it took everything in his power not to gasp in pain. The boor moved on to the next body and stepped on it as he lumbered behind his people, the bones cracking under his mass.

Close call.

Grady waited until he couldn't hear footsteps and got to his feet slowly. He looked around as the sun cracked over the nights' sky and finally saw the devastation around him. Dozens of men in brown cloaks and furs downed from arrows and bludgeoned skulls. Animal skulls adorned their necks, fingers and heads -- jewelry and trinkets of teeth and claws attached to their bodies.

Druids. They are hunting his clan. They are hunting…

Under the waning moonlight, Grady saw his reflection in the murky water and confirmed his intuitions. Beyond the face paint and sullen expression, the furs and braided bear, it was Baird Muir looking back at him.

Chapter 79

As he traipsed through the swampland, his head hung heavy on his shoulders. Grady-as-Baird's people were slaughtered all around him. Men, too many to count, laid still in the shallow waters. Grady watched through Baird's eyes as he guided the deceased to the afterlife. He found himself feeling sorry for Waylan at that moment.

All of his people are being wiped out.

As the thought crossed Grady's mind, he caught something out of the corner of Baird's eye. A small trinket on his wrist, barely larger than a thimble. He would have missed it entirely had it not been for what Baird did with it next.

As he approached one of the more ostentatiously dressed men, he pulled a small crow's skull from his neck and pricked the wrist of the cadaver. Blood seeped slowly from the wound as Baird pulled the cork from the small vial and tipped the carrion beak into it. Drops of crimson collected in the bottom and he muttered words to himself that Grady couldn't quite make out.

Baird looked over his shoulder and Grady felt a pang of shame and then a smirk smeared across Baird's face. He watched as Baird surveyed the area for the more adorned corpses and made his way to them performing the same bloodletting ritual.

Agus nuair a thilleas tu, tig an dàn maille riut.

Grady knew the words well -- Waylan had recited them over his body a few times.

And when you return, fate will come with you.

These men are all of Waylan's druidic clan.

What could he possibly gain from the blood of the dead?

Baird sealed his vial and stowed it around his wrist wrapped under a leather cuff. He raised his arms to the sky and spoke an ancient tongue that Grady couldn't understand. Fire rained from the sky and each of the bodies in the bog were set alight. Baird watched the mass immolation with pleasure as he turned toward the tree line.

Full of selfish confidence, he did not hear the footsteps creeping through the forest. Grady noted the sound just as Baird's eyes became alert, but it was too late. A concussive blow to his head and Grady felt the earth slip from under him as Baird fell to the ground and everything blurred.

"Neach-brathaidh". A low voice spoke as a man crouched down and grabbed Baird by the hair so he could see him clearly.

Traitor.

Chapter 80

Grady opened his eyes but the lights above him were too bright to do more than squint. He moved to roll himself over and found his wrists and ankles were restrained.

"What's the meaning of this?!" He shouted at anyone listening.

"Sir, you're awake. Welcome back", a man in white scrubs said while calmly checking Grady's wrist for a pulse.

"What's going on here? Where am I? Get me out of these restraints!" Grady tugged at the cuffs wildly.

"Sir, we had to restrain you while you were in your induced coma. We found significant internal bleeding from your assault." The man checked a chart and then walked to a monitor by Grady's beside. "You've been out for nearly a month, sir. Your vitals all seem to be stable now, though."

Grady tried to calm himself, but the feeling of being tied to a bed brought back too many panicked memories of the asylum where Waylan had masqueraded as his psychiatric custodian.

"Please, if you could get me out of these restraints. They make me feel a bit claustrophobic." He tried to make himself as mild-mannered as possible.

The man approached his bed and loosened the ties around his ankles and wrists. To Grady's shock, he was released without question. He sat up slowly and was helped from the hospital bed. He looked around the beige room with drop ceilings and earth-toned tiles. The man in white held Grady by the arm like an invalid and helped him to a wheelchair.

Something's not right here. The colors are all wrong.

Grady snatched his arm from the man's grasp and tried to make a run for it, but he had no bearing on where he was running. The man was on top of him quickly and tackled him to the ground.

"Code gray! We have a code gray!" The man yelled as he tried to maintain his hold on Grady.

Grady pulled his arms from the man's grasp and threw a violent elbow into his body as hard as he could. The man buckled a bit but pulled Grady's arms behind him and shoved a knee into his back.

"Get off of me! Don't you know who I am?!" Grady screamed at the man as his ribs were pressed into the ground.

"Code gray! Someone get over here with five milligrams of lorazepam now!"

The man struggled to keep his grip on Grady as he thrashed underneath him. His arms were wrenched upward pinning his shoulders to the ground and then there was a prick in his leg. The room started to spin and then Grady stopped moving. He laid on the floor with barely-focused eyes and watched as three men collected him and sat him in his wheelchair.

They walked down the hall as they lashed his wrists and ankles to the chair. They turned the corner and walked through double doors at the end of the unremarkable hall. They paused at a wooden door and knocked.

"Yes, yes. Come in, Mister Carney."

That voice. I know that voice.

Grady was pushed through the threshold and the brakes were applied on the wheelchair. All three men exited the room before the large leather backed chair turned. Staring Grady in the face was none other than Waylan Scott under the facade of Curtis Winslow.

"What do you want from me, Scott? You're supposed to be dead!" Grady screamed, spitting his words as he seethed.

"Curtis Winslow, pleased to meet you. Montgomery, is it?" Doctor Winslow extended a hand before retracting it, almost jokingly.

He's dead. He's fucking dead! This can't be happening!

Grady lunged in his wheelchair at Winslow's desk. The man behind the desk watched Grady with a pitiful look in his eyes.

"Mister Carney, may I call you Monty?" Waylan asked as he read over notes in a file folder.

Who the hell is Monty?!

"You've been quite the issue since your arrival. We have tried to medicate your outbursts, and we have introduced numerous cognitive therapies. However, you seem to be very resistant to all of our measures."

Doctor Winslow sized up Montgomery Carney as he sat across from him and that all-too familiar simper formed across his face.

"We have a special project for you, as a result, Monty. We have built a state of the art treatment facility upstate and we'd like you to be the first to test it for us."

Grady sat silently. It was clear his fate was not his to determine either way.

"If you have no objections, we'd like you to accompany us to The Bandash Memorial Reformation Facility."

Chapter 81

Grady opened his eyes but the lights above him were too bright to do more than squint. He moved to roll himself over and found his wrists and ankles were restrained.

"What's the meaning of this?!" He shouted at anyone listening.

"Sir, you're awake. Welcome back, Mister Scott", a man in white scrubs said while calmly checking Grady's wrist for a pulse.

"What's going on here? Where am I? Get me out of these restraints!" Grady tugged at the cuffs wildly.

"Sir, we had to restrain you while you were in your induced coma. We found significant internal bleeding from your assault." The man checked a chart and then walked to a monitor by Grady's beside. "You've been out for nearly a month, sir. Your vitals all seem to be stable now, though."

Grady felt a strange sense of deja vu as he bargained with himself to calm down.

"Please, if you could get me out of these restraints. They make me feel a bit claustrophobic." He tried to make himself as mild-mannered as possible.

"Of course, Doctor Scott", the man replied as he loosened the restraints and freed Grady.

"What happened here? The last thing I remember is being outside of the Facility's walls. There were blasts. My partner, he'd had a breakdown and ran for the tree line." Grady recounted the events as he last remembered them trying to assure himself he was actually awake.

"Montgomery Carney, Penalized oh-four-nine-six-three. It was unfortunate that he was able to escape. Don't worry sir, our security protocols were able to neutralize the threat." The orderly spoke very matter-of-factly about the absolute destruction of a human.

"He was my partner! My friend! He's been with me for months now, why would you kill him?" Grady pried for some sort of reason for the mindless killing.

"We assumed you were enacting another protocol for his treatment, sir. The railguns are programmed to neutralize any threat entering or leaving the facility unless authorized by the adjudicating body." The man tidied the bedding and pulled the curtains open.

"Aren't I the adjudicating body?" Grady was genuinely confused.

"Of course, sir. You were in pursuit of Montgomery, however, and that was after he had brutally assaulted you in The Brink. The AI is programmed to work on assumptions based on the data it is given."

So was that Pa's past I was seeing?

How am I seeing any of that without being in The Brink?

I must still be in it. Pa's got to be watching all of this happening.

"You said I'm fine, my vitals are all good? I am free to leave?" Grady changed the subject -- he needed to get back to The Brink.

"Yes sir, everything is fine. We suggest you take it easy from any significant strain, however. You seemed to have inhaled the evaporative remains of Mister Carney and it caused a rather bizarre respiratory infection. Please take care of yourself, sir."

Grady feigned appreciation as he waved off the attending before hastily making for the door.

I could see through Pa's eyes, just like with Baird, just like with my mother.

I must be able to access their pasts through their blood, same as Waylan's. It's the only explanation.

Grady made a mad dash for The Brink. He hoped all of this was still part of the simulation and he'd find Pa in the control room after he woke up.

Get to The Brink.

Get to The Brink and you'll wake up.

Pa's fine.

You're not alone.

Get to The Brink.

Grady reached the doors and as they slid open he saw the chairs and small table in the middle of the room. Everything was as he'd left it when he ran after Pa.

"This has gotten out of control", he stammered, hopeful his command would reveal his friend behind the hidden door to the control room.

The door slid open from nowhere in the wall, just as it had before. Grady walked through the portal once again and found the room to be completely empty. The holoscreen was still in plain view as if The Brink was being used, though.

Grady sat down on the floor, his shoulders slumped as he stared into the monitor. On the screen were images and videos of Pa. His mugshot, pictures of a wedding. Children, roller coasters, birthdays. Bodies everywhere, rooms covered in gore. A man thrashing wildly in the arms of authorities on a newscast.

"It's too quiet in here", Grady sighed...

The volume increased and Grady caught the tail end of the editorial.

"...arrested this week on the grounds of mass murder. He lived with his daughter, Tracy, and her two children, Freddy and Sharon in the house he grew up in as a child. Montgomery Carney, once a prominent business partner of the defamed Doctor Waylan Scott, Esquire, recently escaped an institution for the mentally insane. Before authorities were able to find and apprehend him, he returned to his childhood home and brutally murdered his family. A statement was released by his attorney claiming that Carney has opted for a plea of no-contest and would like to file a motion to move straight to sentencing. This move may be recognized as the same plea that his mentor, Doctor Scott, made prior to his own multiple life sentences..."

Grady stopped listening as a picture of his face came across the screen. Not *his* face, no Waylan Scott's. It was in the right corner of the screen the entire time.

Pa was seeing this while I was in the simulation.

Pa thinks... Pa thought I did this to him.

Grady stood up and walked out of the control room, defeated.

A laugh quietly came from overhead.

"Heller, my dear friend. You didn't think it would be so easy, did you? You will only ever have me, Evescha." Waylan's voice trailed off as he laughed to himself.

He's right, Grady. You are only ever going to be alone.

You have to figure this out on your own. We have to be rid of him.

Chapter 82

Grady laid awake most of the night and finally sank into a dreamless sleep. As he awoke the next morning, he realized he hadn't had any visions which seemed to only come in The Brink or when he was unconscious. A twinge of panic set in as he walked towards the door. His sentry stood his ground like always.

"What day is it?" He asked.

"Thursday, sir."

"When did I come to my quarters last night?" Grady pried.

"Shortly after seven, sir. You left the infirmary and went to The Brink. We lost record of you for over an hour at which time you came to your quarters. Anything you need, sir?" The gargoyle stood firmly in place as he offered his services.

"I need to know this isn't a hallucination", Grady muttered under his breath.

The enforcer stood fast in place leaving Grady unanswered.

He walked back into his quarters and splashed cold water on his face a few times. As he wiped it, he looked himself in the mirror and saw his face, or was it Waylan's? He turned his head to the side and his reflection did the same. He turned quickly to the other side and his mirror image did as well.

You're losing it, Grady.

"Or are you?" Waylan's voice whispered behind him.

Grady whipped his body around and swung wildly at the air behind him. No one was there.

"What do you want from me, Muir?!" Grady's shouts echoed through the empty room.

He grabbed clothes from the wardrobe and shoved the door open. The sentry guard nodded his head as he passed him and made for the only place that made any sense anymore: The Brink.

Chapter 83

Days passed and Grady hadn't left The Brink. He paced the floor of the massive room countless times. He threw the chairs and table into the walls until they were in pieces. He cursed at the ceiling and challenged the commands of the room. The AI complied with his commands with no notion it could be broken despite his attempts to confuse it.

The doors opened and closed as he walked past them furiously. The command center door remained open, the screen playing Pa's unfortunate life over and over again. The sound of the news reporter was like a skipping record.

He worked for Waylan, the real Waylan, Grady.

How long ago were those reports?

Did you know Monty?

The sentry from Waylan's quarters relocated to The Brink. Meals were dropped off by a different staff member each day, and each day they were neglected. Grady's thoughts were consumed with rage and grief. He mourned Pa's brutal assassination, enraged that Waylan had plotted it all along. He toiled over the visions of Baird Muir's betrayal of his people. The blood he'd stolen from his clan.

It's the blood, Grady. It's always been the blood. It's got to be the blood!

Grady laid in the middle of The Brink and stared into the blinding lights.

"It's like staring at the sun", he commanded the lights to dim.

He concentrated on the thought of Baird and his treacherous deed. He tried to calm himself as best as he could and started to drift between being awake and asleep.

Grady's feet were planted firmly in a pillowy blackness.

Here again?

He pulled a foot from the fluff enveloping it and started to walk on the foam-like floor. Still no direction, but this place seemed different than the previous iterations. He walked for what seemed like miles until he felt something cold in front of him.

Grady reached a hand out and felt fingers interlace with his.

You're alright, old friend. Keep calm.

He embraced the frigid hand and pulled it toward him. The cold coursed up his arm and then covered his body from his chest to his feet. Grady instinctively put his other arm out and a body leaned into his, pressing itself into him tightly.

"M-mother?" Grady stammered.

The entity did not speak. The blackness remained as impossibly dark as it had always been, but Grady could *feel* light around him.

"Mari, is that you?"

The phantom squeezed him tightly before the sensation vanished entirely.

"Mother! Mother, come back, please!" Grady yelled for her, but his words barely made a sound in the void.

He fell to the ground and sobbed as another cold hand slithered over his shoulder and gripped it tightly.

"*You shouldn't be here.*" A voice swirled around Grady's head.

"Who are you?" Grady asked as he wiped his eyes.

"*You must go from this place*", the voice hissed.

"I didn't come here on purpose. Where am I?" Grady stood too quickly and his head spun. Cold hands grasped his arms, legs, neck and torso and started to pull him in all directions.

He struggled for a moment before he relaxed his body and let the apparitions have their way. They pulled him from the ground and ushered him like a dead body toward a deep blue light. The pallbearers of the void cast him into the pit and Grady fell through an illuminated nothing until the wind was knocked out of him from a sudden impact.

A cudgel crashed into his stomach as two men spoke an ancient language in front of him. Grady coughed up blood as he tried to catch his breath. His arms were bound above him and his legs tied together at the ankles with a great weight pulling downward.

Through a swollen eye, he noticed animal skulls, skins, and all manner of plants. A fire in front of the men glowed azure blue, the flames licking their fingertips as they threw things into the blaze.

Druids.

Grady tried to watch as the magus performed their ritual. The words were of no language Grady had ever heard in his long life. The man with the club reared back for another blow and smashed it across Grady's face. He felt the pain of his jaw shattering to pieces and the blood spilling from his gaping maw. The brutish man laughed and then joined the other two beside the fire.

Grady felt the blaze growing as he tried to control Baird's mind from losing consciousness. The men stood and raised their hands and the fire engulfed Grady. He could hear Baird screaming in agony but not from heat. The fire was freezing cold and Grady watched as Baird's skin turned black from frostbite.

He felt his mind waning as he tried to hold it in reality. He saw glassy crystals form over his eyes and then there was silence. His eyes were fixed on the men, but unable to move. They approached him and mouthed the same words over and over until Grady's vision went black.

Chapter 84

His eyes snapped open and he was back in The Brink.

"NO!"

Grady fumed as he tore into the control room.

"Put me back! I need to figure out how to kill him once and for all!"

The control room blinked and the screen shut off. A small opening appeared in the wall and in it there was a box. Grady took the box and threw it across the room.

"Enough, Waylan! Enough!!"

Grady screamed, maddened by the incessant visions with no indications of how to dismantle Waylan's games.

The opening in the wall seamlessly disappeared and Grady took off for the sliding doors of The Brink furiously. The doors closed before he could exit and Grady turned back to the cavernous hall.

"Goddamnit Waylan! Enough of this!"

The small wooden box righted itself on the floor and floated to the center of the room before being set down on a small empty pedestal. Grady raised an eyebrow and walked to the stand. He took the box into his hands and opened the lid. Inside he found his life-bound artifacts. A small blue agate, an ancient coin, and a seed.

Grady held the trinkets, placing the box back on the pedestal. He turned the coin in his hand and rubbed the smooth river-worn agate between his fingers. His mortality in his hands, Grady sat on the floor of The Brink and stared through them dissociatively.

The control room responds to directions.

The Brink responds in contrast to direction.

"Enough, Waylan. I want to live free of this torment. I want to live my life." Grady bargained in resignation, finally understanding Waylan's game. He'd driven him to madness and taken away any life he'd be able to enjoy. What's more, Waylan Scott presented Grady with the three things he'd never have thought would matter after that fateful night in thirteen forty-nine.

"Just let me live, Baird. Please, just let me live", Grady begged The Brink.

The slightest swish came from behind Grady and he turned his attention to the massive entryway of The Brink. Waylan's loyal sentry stood no more than two feet from Grady.

"Liberation protocol initiated", the android spoke in its typical monotone.

"I'll be seeing you", Waylan's voice emitted from the room, "old friend."

The shot was silent, quick, and point-blank to Grady's head. His body slouched over as his head rested in his own lap. The humanoid guard turned and walked out of The Brink and the doors closed behind him. The lights dimmed as the door of the control room opened and Waylan Scott walked out joining Grady as blood ran onto the snowy white floor.

"Finally, Evescha, I am free of you. Your curse has been broken. Rest in peace, old friend."

Waylan knelt in front of Grady and lifted his head from his lap, gently laying him on his back. He placed the coin and the agate over Grady's eyes, homage to whatever porter of the underworld would see his journey was a safe one. He opened Grady's hand and folded the seed into his palm before crossing his arms over his chest.

"Farewell, this time for good, dear Evescha", Waylan said, almost mournfully as a single tear ran from the corner of his eye.

The Brink dimmed to black, fittingly as though a stage play had just ended and the curtains had come down over the cast. A sliver of light cut through the darkness as Waylan's gargoyle entered the room once again.

"Doctor Scott, the protocol has been executed. Please come with me so we can proceed to the reinstatement protocol."

The android reached a hand out for Waylan but touched nothing but air.

"Lights", it commanded.

As the lights shone brightly in The Brink, the enforcer scanned the area for his creator but there was no one else. Nothing was left in the room other than a small wooden box, a seed, an agate, and a medieval coin in a small pool of blood.

Chapter 85

The deep blue greeted Grady as he floated in the nothingness once more. The ethereal hands of the void carried him just as before.

Când te întorci la mine,

astfel soarta mea va fi anulată

A woman's voice began chanting.

Când te întorci la mine,

astfel soarta mea va fi anulată

Another joined in a building chorus.

Când te întorci la mine,

astfel soarta mea va fi anulată

A third, then a fourth, fifth and sixth.

"*Evescha. My dearest Evescha. Please forgive me for deserting you.*"

"Mother?" Grady's voice reverberated through the ether.

Când te întorci la mine,

astfel soarta mea va fi anulată

Când te întorci la mine,

astfel soarta mea va fi anulată

Când te întorci la mine,

astfel soarta mea va fi anulată

Marioziota gently whispered to Evescha before she pressed her lips to the glowing wound on his forehead.

"Let your fate be undone, my dearest son. Be free of his curse so you may embrace the gift of the mothers."

The hands let go of his body and Grady drifted through the nothingness. He was enveloped in a relaxing cool sensation as he drifted along the lazy river of fate. Abruptly, he felt a violence beneath him as he was surrounded by frigid cold. A panic burst into his chest as he gasped for breath.

Grady's eyes opened as river water rushed over him. Looking up from beneath the water was as though he was looking into a mirror. The man who had killed him two hundred sixty-nine thousand eight hundred twelve days prior loomed over him, his hands around Grady's throat. He panicked as his life flashed before him as he'd always heard would happen when someone died.

The water was clouded with blood as it ran from Fionnghall Alba's mouth. Grady grabbed hold of Alba's wrists and pulled himself from the water just long enough to take a breath, but Alba was too strong and shoved his head under. A maniacal smile formed on his lips as he muttered words that Grady was keenly aware of.

The current stole him from the shore far enough that the rapids formed and he rode the rough waters, his head slamming into the craggy upheavals below the surface. His still body floated to shore and lay lifeless as the shallow wake flapped against him.

Când te întorci la mine,

astfel soarta mea va fi anulată

My mother's voice, as sweet as it ever was. I hear you, my dearest Marioziota, but I cannot see you.

Când te întorci la mine,

astfel soarta mea va fi anulată

Yes, mother, I know the words.

I understand.

It's done.

Please, take me home.

Când te întorci la mine,

astfel soarta mea va fi anulată

The light is so bright. Thank you, mother.

Thank you for escorting me to Gan Eden.

Thank you for helping me end this torturous curse.

Epilogue

Grady's eyes opened and raised an arm to block the sun as it blazed overhead. He looked around and saw nothing but grassy fields and stones. The sounds of babbling water lapping at the shore.

So this is Gan Eden. I often wondered if it would be familiar.

It looks like home.

He went to stand up and his ankle bent oddly underneath him causing him to crash to one knee. As he caught himself, he noticed the blood running from a gash in his arm. Suddenly his head throbbed with immense pain and he fell forward as he retched and vomited a belly full of water into the sand and stone.

Terror caused Grady's skin to go cold as he crawled slowly on his wounded limbs to the water's edge. He leaned over a calm tide pool and a drop of blood fell into the water. He watched as the ripples calmed and the water stilled, a rictus of a smile formed on his face. It was, indeed, his own reflection, but also not quite.

Grady turned his head from side to side trying to negotiate his vision, obviously impaired by a concussion. Blurry at first, then coming into clearer view, he recognized the man in the water staring back at him. Tousled brown hair, soaked with river water. Muddy brown eyes, pupils unable to dilate or contract properly.

An entirely unremarkable man, but a man that Grady knew so well.

A man that Grady had buried centuries ago.

A man whose name had escaped history just as well as Grady Sachs' had.o

Evescha Heller. Good to see you, old friend.

M. von Lindenberg is a prolific no one that lives in a quiet-ish suburban area between two bustling cities. Much like Grady Sachs, there is nothing remarkable about him, yet there is something constantly beneath the surface itching for its time to shine. Author, musician, producer, painter, illustrator: there are lots of words to describe his interests but all of them are hung on the idea that one should never keep their thoughts to themselves.

Life is meant to be a thriller. There are times of mundane nothingness followed by sudden interruptions of highs and lows, fear and victory. This thought keeps M. von Lindenberg up some nights and keeps his mind set on building bridges between fiction and reality.

Note from the author:

Thanks for taking a chance on reading No One's Time. I didn't have "write a book" on my creative bingo card, but I guess it's always been in the ether waiting for the moment to escape. It means the world to me that you've taken the time to (hopefully) enjoy following Grady Sach's through this rollercoaster. Grady's story may not be over, but I guess we'll have to wait and see if he comes knocking on my door for more adventures.